THE FABER BOOK OF
CONTEMPORARY CARIBBEAN
SHORT STORIES

D0480998

in the same series

THE FABER BOOK OF CONTEMPORARY
AUSTRALIAN SHORT STORIES

THE FABER BOOK OF CONTEMPORARY
LATIN AMERICAN SHORT STORIES

ff

The Faber Book of
CONTEMPORARY CARIBBEAN SHORT STORIES

Edited by Mervyn Morris

faber and faber
LONDON · BOSTON

First published in 1990
by Faber and Faber Limited
3 Queen Square London WC1N 3AU

Photoset by Parker Typesetting Service Leicester
Printed in Great Britain by
Richard Clay Bungay Suffolk

All rights reserved

This collection © Mervyn Morris, 1990

This book is sold subject to the condition that it shall not, by way of trade
or otherwise, be lent, resold, hired out or otherwise circulated without the
publisher's prior consent in any form of binding or cover other than that
in which it is published and without a similar condition including
this condition being imposed on the subsequent purchaser.

A CIP record for this book is available from the British Library

ISBN 0–571–15298–8
ISBN 0–571–15299–6 (Pbk)

Contents

To Helen, Christine and Jimmy

Acknowledgements

The editor and publishers would like to thank the following for permission to use the stories in this volume: Macmillan of Canada, a Division of Canada Publishing Corporation, for permission to reprint 'Veins Visible' from *Digging Up the Mountains* by Neil Bissoondath; Erna Brodber for an extract from 'The Spirit Thieves'; Longman Group (UK) Ltd for 'An Honest Thief' by Timothy Callender; Savacou Publications, Kingston, for 'Easter Sunday Morning' by Hazel D. Campbell; Jan Carew for 'Tilson Ezekiel Alias Ti-Zek'; McClelland and Stewart, Toronto, for permission to reprint 'The Man' from *When Women Rule* by Austin Clarke; *Pepperpot* for 'Inez' by Merle Hodge; Abdur-Rahman Slade Hopkinson for 'Marcus Aurelius and the Transatlantic *Baakoo*'; London Magazine Editions for Clyde Hosein's 'I'm a Presbyterian, Mr Kramer' from *The Killing of Nelson John*; Farrar, Straus and Giroux, and Pan Books, for permission to reprint 'My Mother', from *At the Bottom of the River* by Jamaica Kincaid; John Robert Lee for 'The Coming of Org – A Prologue'; Curtis Brown for permission to reprint 'Fleurs' by Earl Lovelace; Ambit Books for permission to reprint 'Mammie's Form at the Post Office' from *Something Unusual* by E. A. Markham; the editors of *Kyk-Over-Al*, published in Guyana, for 'The Duel in Mercy Ward' by Ian McDonald; Earl McKenzie for 'Dry Bones'; Roger McTair for 'Visiting'; Aitken and Stone for 'The Night Watchman's Occurrence Book' © 1967 by V. S. Naipaul; Michael Reckord for 'Dog Food'; Andrew Salkey for 'Anti-Apartness Anancy'; Samuel Selvon for 'Brackley

ACKNOWLEDGEMENTS

and the Bed' reprinted from *Ways of Sunlight*; Longman
Group (UK) Ltd for permission to use Olive Senior's 'Ballad' from *Summer Lightning and Other Stories*; John Stewart
for permission to reprint 'Early Morning' from *Curving
Road*; John Wickham for 'The Fellow Travellers', reprinted
from *Casuarina Row*; Noel Carlyle Woodroffe for 'Legacy'.

Introduction

West Indian literature didn't begin in the 1950s, as reviewers used to imply. It is possible to argue (as Paula Burnett does in the *Penguin Book of Caribbean Verse in English*) that the roots of our literature lie in the eighteenth century and earlier. In *The West Indian Novel and its Background* Kenneth Ramchand takes as his point of departure 1903, with the publication of the first volume in the short-lived All Jamaica Library. Between 1903 and the 1950s a number of books by West Indian authors were published, including at least three important collections of short stories – Eric Walrond's *Tropic Death* (1926), Jean Rhys's *The Left Bank* (1927) and Claude McKay's *Gingertown* (1932).

Yet, because a literature is more than a handful of books, reviewers in the 1950s did well to direct attention to the growing body of West Indian prose fiction. If you look at a year by year bibliography (there is one at the back of the Ramchand) you will see a considerable increase in the flow of books after 1952. Introducing his 1960 anthology, Andrew Salkey noted 'a remarkable upsurge of new writing from the West Indies', fifty-two books in the previous decade.

More than 400 prose fiction books by West Indian authors have been published since 1903. But what matters more than numbers is the general esteem West Indian writing has earned, and the high reputation enjoyed by some of our authors.

In selecting for this anthology, I am happy to have been able to include a few of our well-established writers who were beginning to be known by 1960 – people such as Samuel Selvon, Jan Carew, Andrew Salkey, V. S. Naipaul. The names of several other contributors may also be fairly familiar; among them Austin Clarke and Earl Lovelace, for several books; Erna Brodber, Merle Hodge, Clyde Hosein, Ian McDonald, John Stewart, each for at least one much respected work; Neil Bissoondath, Jamaica Kincaid, Olive Senior, as leading figures among the writers who have more recently emerged. I have avoided stories (and therefore one or two authors) often anthologized. I have given space only to authors alive at the time of my selection. The oldest contributor here was born in 1923, the youngest in 1955. Only three of the stories were published before 1970; at least sixteen first appeared in the 1980s. This is, essentially, a collection of *contemporary* West Indian short stories.

The authors come from Trinidad, Jamaica, Barbados, Guyana, St Lucia, Antigua and Montserrat; but half of them now live and work abroad, in the United Kingdom, the United States or Canada. That is a smaller proportion than would have been likely thirty years ago. More of our writers than formerly are based at home in the Caribbean, though they sometimes travel to read or teach abroad. Few West Indian writers, even overseas, can afford to write full time. The author who stays in the Caribbean usually earns a living at some job other than writing, or must depend on the money earned abroad. Payment in the Caribbean to authors tends to be derisory: as V. S. Naipaul once remarked, it is often assumed in the West Indies that writing is its own reward.

Nearly all the stories here are set in the Caribbean – a Caribbean that is dynamic with tensions of race, class, religion, gender; full of contradictions, as a heritage of European colonialism contends with other cultural forces, such as continuities out of Africa and India. In 'The Spirit Thief' and 'Easter Sunday Morning' we read of battles between Christian and other belief systems. In 'I'm a Presbyterian, Mr Kramer' an Indian in Trinidad, fired by his Christian principles, is up against the corrupting power of the white colonial boss. There are snatches of calypso ('Visiting'); there is a story which centres on stick-fighting ('Fleurs'). Though a few of the stories take place in the town or the city, most of them have rural settings. The collection is dotted with details of folk custom, in town and country alike; there are references to *obeah* ('black magic'), the *baakoo* (a spirit in a bottle), *duppies* (ghosts), to 'superstition'. Some of the stories relate supernatural happenings; some move us towards myth.

Creole appears in some of the stories but need not be a problem for the non-West Indian reader. 'Ballad' is narrated in creole, and the predominant voice on the pages of the 'The Night Watchman's Occurrence Book' is creole. Most of the stories are told in (West Indian) standard English; but a standard English passage will sometimes incorporate a local expression, such as 'facety' (meaning forward or impertinent) in the second paragraph of 'Inez'. There is variety within the Caribbean; each place has its characteristic accent, and each has its own creole. For many readers one of the joys of West Indian literature is the expressive range of its language, shifting along a continuum between creole and standard.

If their language is often distinctively Caribbean, if they project characters and situations which we in the Caribbean identify as ours, these stories also deal with common human concerns: love, friendship, betrayal, social and individual identity, the mother–daughter relationship, manhood, heroism, exile, alienation, injustice, oppression, death.

The two dozen stories in this anthology have given me great pleasure, which I hope readers everywhere will share.

Mervyn Morris
June 1989

Veins Visible

NEIL BISSOONDATH

The illuminated hands of the alarm clock showed 1 a.m. Vernon wondered why it had gone off – he'd set it for 6.30 – and he wondered too why its ring was intermittent and came from a far corner of the bedroom.

The room was dark. The window showed as a dully luminescent square. He could just make out the left edge of the dresser, a slash of icy mirror above it.

The alarm continued ringing. He reached for it, pressed the button. Still it rang, intermittent.

His wife stirred in the bed next to him: 'Vernon, the phone.'

He pulled the sheets back, lowered his feet to the floor, toes searching the rough carpet for his slippers. They weren't there.

The ring, identified now, seemed to grow louder, the pauses shorter, less patient.

He shuffled over to the phone in his bare feet. He thought: Like walking on an unshaved cheek. He felt old. He sensed Jenny sit up in the bed.

'Hello.'

As he listened, his eyes searched the window-pane, seeking to pierce the grey glow. The glass was fogged over; along the bottom a thin sheet of ice had built up; he pressed at it with a fingernail, cleanly detaching a chunk. That part of him that was not engaged on the phone was surprised that the slab of ice seemed to float, that he could move it easily, whole. Then the warmth of his fingertips bored through the ice, touched the glass behind. He

1

realized that the slab was melting and that, while it seemed to float, it was supported only by the liquefied part of itself. A convex pool of water had collected on the window-sill below, like a drop of smoky crystal.

'Where'd they take him?'

His fingers, damp, moved to the film of moisture that gave the glass the opacity of old plastic. In an ever-widening circle, he brushed the moisture aside, sending two runnels of water down the glass, creating a wet port-hole through which he could see a distorted world clothed in white. Fresh snow hid even the streetcar rails, turned the street into an unfolded shroud. The unbroken stretch of red-bricked building on the other side of the street was shuttered, darkened. The restaurants, second-hand book-stores, and used-clothing shops that occupied the street level were dark and, in the yellow thickness of the street lamps, gave no hint of their function. The flats above the businesses were also in darkness except for the dullest ochre in one small window, a night-light, maybe, or that of a cloistered bathroom.

'Where are you now? Who's with the kids?'

A streetcar, its one headlight showing with the diffused yellowness of a flashlight, trundled slowly past, leaving in its wake two thin, black stripes, like a trail. Vernon felt the floor tremble lightly under his bare feet.

'I'll be there as soon as I can.'

Jenny said, 'What is it? It's Hari again, isn't it.'

She turned on the bedside lamp and the reflection of books filled his wet porthole. 'Is he drunk again?'

Vernon didn't answer. He let the phone glide over his ear, down across his cheek; let his arm drop, as if deprived of strength, the receiver, tightly grasped, seeming to radi-ate heat into his hand.

'Did the police pick him up or what?'

The porthole was fogging up once more. Slowly, the books disappeared.

2

'Vern?'

'He's in the hospital.'

'And.'

'An accident. The car ran off the road. The snow.'

'So how is he?'

'Dying.'

She was silent.

There had been no dawn. The sky had gone from ink black to watercolour grey, shutting out day, offering only a restrained approximation of twilight. The snow on the street had been whipped into a brown slush by salt truck and snow tyres, had pooled in the gutters in a brassy sludge. The asphalt looked black and solid, fresh, and the buildings, neon and hand-painted signs now showing at every window, in every doorway, were heavy with the waterlogged density of wood that had travelled the high seas.

The smell of the hospital was still in Vernon's nostrils as he lowered himself from the streetcar, his boots, speckled gaily with paint, sinking into a ridge of slush. To his right, a car squealed to a halt, the driver startled. Vernon, feeling his fragility, acted as if he hadn't noticed; pride seized the scream, of terror, of anger, that had leapt to him.

As he made his way up the stairwell – narrow, walls of dulled ochre, red carpet frayed at the edges, rubbed away in the centre to the original matting – he heard the door to their flat opening, first the squeak of the upper hinge, then the more extended wail of the lower.

Jenny, in her Saturday outfit of jeans and sweater, stood in the doorway. 'I saw you getting off the streetcar.'

He pushed past her, kicked his boots off on to the doormat.

She followed him into the kitchen. 'You were gone a long time.'

'Peter was at the hospital. We were talking.'

3

'What about?'

'Back home. How it was.'

'Of course. What else.'

He slumped into a chair at the small dining table. His eyes were reddened with fatigue; the skin around them, roughened now, no longer buttressed by crescents of fat, looked scaly. In the leaden haze that drifted thickly in through the window above the stove, age proclaimed itself; the light made plain those changes, each subtle in itself, that went unseen from day to day, that revealed themselves only in the stress of the intimate, vulnerable moment.

Jenny thought: He's getting old. And for a moment she panicked, not for herself but for him. Time had been abbreviated; it was as if this night had taken him years away.

'How's Hari?'

'I told you. Dying.'

'What of? What's wrong with him exactly?'

'Everything. He's just breaking down.'

'What are the doctors doing?'

'Nothing.'

'Nothing?'

'There's nothing to do. I saw him. He's flesh. His skin was stripped away. It wasn't neat. You could see his veins.'

'Did you talk to him?'

'You can't talk to meat,' he said with an unexpected vehemence.

She said, 'I feel sorry for him too, you know.'

'Do you?'

The words, of a spare brutality, spoken as if in conversation, took her by surprise; but she acknowledged to herself the fairness of the question. She said, 'It's the changes, Vern, they're too many.' She wanted to add: Look at you. But she said instead, 'Look at me.' And she held her hands out for him to see: the veins, distended, erupting sinuously from the skin; the bones sweeping to the unpainted nails, shorter now and imperfectly shaped; the rings – engagement, wedding, tableaux of a different world, a different time – askew on the finger no longer slender but merely thin.

He looked at her hands, but vaguely, as if part of him had retreated. Then he looked away.

He said, 'We were men of substance.'

She lowered her hands.

He said, '*We* hired people to paint *our* houses.' And he looked at his own hands as if at a curio. He could not recognize them; with the toughened skin, with the speckles of paint trapped in the wrinkles, with the crescents of dirt under the nails, they were those of a stranger. 'Men of substance.'

She said, 'Yes, Vern, substance. But only of a kind.'

He clasped his hands, finger interlacing with finger in deliberate movement.

She said, wearied, 'What's the point, Vern?'

He looked up at her, one eye cocked in accusation.

She said, 'Don't do that.'

He said, 'You don't remember, do you?'

'I do remember, damn you.' She moved agitatedly to the sink, filled the kettle, and – in what still felt like an ancient gesture – lit the stove with a match. The flame leapt around the burner with a sharp, sudden groan, in a contained explosion. 'You can't forget what used to be. I just wish you wouldn't push it. There's no point. You'll end up like Hari.'

'Bullshit.' He said it gently, like an endearment.

She let the kettle clatter on to the flame and turned to face him. 'You talk about substance. Hari: what's substance?'

'He was. We were.' He unclasped his hands and let his face fall into them in an indication of fatigue.

5

'Your substance. Your substance was money, things. It was the Japanese tea ceremony.'

'Bullshit,' he repeated. Yet he wanted to retreat, to plead fatigue. He was tired, but it was not sleep that he sought. The weight that gripped his body seemed to have anaesthetized him, so that while one part of him wanted to run, the other remained indifferent, just as the mind alone revolts at the violence done by a dentist's probes to a frozen mouth. He said, 'The tea ceremony,' he gave a stiff chuckle, 'it was just something outside our experience.'

'It was something outside anybody's experience.' The water boiled. She turned her attention to making coffee: the swish of jar lid, the tinkle of spoon on cup.

The Japanese couple visiting the island had been more exotic than the bare-breasted Nigerian dancers. People spoke of Japs and Nips, recalled the yellow peril and Pearl Harbor – events that had touched the island only peripherally, through the American soldiers stationed there during the war for rest and recreation, what little there had been of it – and it was as if, in the twenty-five years between the end of the war and then, the Japanese economic miracle hadn't occurred, as if the people of the island couldn't connect these visitors, polite to the point of imbecility, with the cars and small trucks that clogged the roads of the island.

The Japanese, small and smiling behind wire-framed glasses, were said to be experts at the tea ceremony. No one in the island knew anything about the tea ceremony: tea was a tea bag, boiling water, milk, sugar. The ritual, in a place without rituals, seized the imagination. The Japanese were invited into the most prestigious homes, lionized, televised. Vernon had provided a cocktail party and a dinner party.

Then, a month after their departure, the unravelling: the island's television station ran a *National Geographic* film of the tea ceremony. It wasn't the same thing. It was vastly

6

different. The truth emerged: the Japanese weren't Japanese at all. They were Korean, they knew nothing about tea, they had taken an impressive bundle of money out of the island with them for 'investment in Japan'. The story had dragged on for weeks and was capped – insult on insult, this – by a picture of the Japanese couple, as they continued to be known, drinking Nescafé in the dining room of the ship that had taken them away.

At first it had seemed like a joke: simple people – simplicity viewed then as a virtue, when they were truly simple, playing at the world until the wider corruption inexorably attracted them – eager to be duped by a greater sophistication. Yet Vernon had always felt that more than a simplicity had been involved, more than an island *naïveté*. A certain stupidity too had played a role, a stupidity easily camouflaged by a flippant self-derision, a self-caricature that turned the stupidity itself into a virtue.

Was this truly, as Jenny insisted, the substance to which he clung? He had always resisted a deeper examination and Hari, like Peter and his other friends, had long rejected the thought that what they had had might have been illusion, a mirage created by sea, sky, sand, and a moneyed circumstance.

And so, slowly, they were being unravelled by a life that demanded effort.

Jenny placed the coffee cup on the table in front of him. She said, 'Are you hungry?'

He shook his head: No.

She said, 'You know, Vern, you're not a weak man. Under the right circumstances.'

He took her words as offered: without irony, without sarcasm, as compliment even. He knew what she meant. He had spent the better part of his life providing, stabilizing, sheltering, practising with a certain gentility, as it seemed now, the art of being a man. But he had inherited his wealth in a place where wealth justified itself

7

only in its very existence, where the acquisition of wealth created its own bars. And this money, inherited, had its own needs, created its own resources, its own talents. When stripped of all that he had taken for granted, all that had come so effortlessly to him, he found the lessons of a lifetime futile. Skills became useless, absurd, and life required a different kind of strength, a strength that could only be grown into, that could not be dredged up from under the collapsed experience of a lifetime.

Vernon had never doubted his ability to survive. But to go beyond survival? To practise once more the art of being a man in the way that he understood it?

Jenny, seated across the table from him, contemplated the coffee in her cup.

He said, 'You're stronger than me. You've always been.' He looked away to the kitchen window; the ice had melted, the steam turned to runnels and streaks. The sky showed like grey canvas. 'When we had to run, you brought your jewellery, you were prepared. Me? I didn't want to believe. How can you accept a total loss? It's easier to turn away. Like me. That's why we live in a dump, that's why I have to paint other people's pretty houses.' He was tired and he spoke the words as they came to him. A bubble formed in his stomach and began an upward movement; his head swirled in slow motion. He gulped at his coffee, stood up and walked over to the sink. The pressure of the bubble eased, his head steadied.

Jenny said, 'You should go to bed.'

'I don't want to.' He turned on the cold water and splashed a palmful on to his face. His flesh felt inert, thickened.

'You remember how Hari used to joke about Noolan?' Jenny's voice cut above the dull thud of tap water hitting the aluminium sink.

'Joke? It was no joke.' His hands clutched into fists, the veins bunched up from under the skin. He thought he saw the blood rushing through them.

He could hear Hari talking. He would move to New-foundland – or Noolan, as Hari would say, tongue burdened by alcohol slurring the name into mythical obscurity – and he would buy a high ladder, he would climb that ladder and sit on the top and gaze over the ocean to the island so he could see the cricket games.

It had been no joke, no one had ever laughed; and it had turned grim the day Hari announced, with a belligerent seriousness, that he had worked out the southerly angle at which he would set the ladder in order to get an unobstructed view of the cricket grounds through a gap in the mountains.

Vernon said, 'Best seat in the house, maan.'

Jenny snorted. 'He couldn't learn to leave that seat. That was his problem. He couldn't get away, not far away enough from what he was running from to see what he was running to.'

Vernon clenched his fists on the counter. The spray of the water still thudding into the sink speckled his arm. 'He wasn't running *to* anything.' He gesticulated with one fist: the stained walls, the peeling door, the window framing grey. 'This?'

She stood up, agitated, moved to the door, leaned against the frame, her arms folded across her ribs, lifting her breasts. 'Yes. This.' An expressionless voice: it struck him as odd, as a reproach.

He opened his mouth to protest; it took extraordinary effort. The sound caught in his throat, bubbled, popped.

The telephone rang in the living room.

Jenny went to answer it, leaving him with a sense of abandonment, of futility. He seemed to face an awesome void.

Still the sound bubbled in his throat. It filled his ears, mingling with the water crashing into the sink to form a roar.

The kitchen – the window, the walls with the cheap, unframed prints, the spare table with metal chairs – tilted upward, losing the horizontal, and it took an effort of lucidity to comprehend that his head was inclining to the left. He could feel the veins and tissue on the right side of his neck tighten, begin to strain. He thought: They must be bulging like cables.

Jenny appeared in the doorway. She spoke, mouthing words he could not hear. Her face tightened and then she was crowding him, reaching around the body he now felt incapable of moving to turn off the tap. The roar lessened, ended. The words no longer bubbled in his throat. His ears felt light, cavernous.

She spoke once more and her words echoed, seeming to come from a great distance. He had to seize on individual sounds to elicit a message from what she was saying.

'It's Peter. He's drunk, he's crying, and he wants to come over.' Her voice was heavy with anger. 'I won't have him here. Not again. No more. He and Hari were always drunk enough.'

'Tell him, tell him . . .' He faltered, straightened his head, the tightened veins relaxed. 'Tell him to go to bed. I don't want to see him. Not now. Not today.' And, expecting guilt, he felt relief, as if freed from a burden he hadn't before recognized.

She said, 'You're tired. Go to bed.'

A vein began to pulse on his temple and, by instinct, she reached out and rubbed it gently with the tips of her fingers.

He was walking on a wide sidewalk. There was sun but no warmth, the air neutral. It was early in the day. People walked by singly, cars could be seen only in the distance.

He walked with a purpose. He was going somewhere but he was glad no one asked his destination. He would not have known what to reply and imagined acute embarrassment at the question.

He looked with a particular uninterest at the stores he passed – record stores, clothes stores, links of fast-food chains – dark interiors offering not mystery or enticement but gloom and the possibility of money ill-spent.

Then, as if it were the most natural thing in the world, he found himself lying on the sidewalk looking up at the sky, ink blue with curls of diaphanous white cloud. That something was not right he was fully aware, but only when he tried to get up did he realize that his torso had been severed diagonally from just under his rib-cage to the small of his back. His hips and legs lay two feet away, beyond reach, like the discarded lower half of a mannequin.

People walked by. He saw the disdainful curve of women's jacked-up ankles, the well-pressed hems of expensive trousers, shoes black and solid. No one took notice of him.

Curious, he examined his lower half. The cut had been clean. There was no blood. The wound appeared to have been coated in a clear plastic and he could see the ends of veins pulsing red against the transparent skin. There was, he knew, no danger.

He wanted to put himself back together again. He knew that all he had to do was get hold of his legs, put them to his torso, and all would be fine. Maybe he would need a little glue, he reasoned, curiously proud of the practicality of the thought, but surely he would be able to keep his parts together until he could get to a hardware store.

He tried to reach for his legs but balance eluded him and he rocked back and forth like a toy rocking-horse, his legs approaching then retreating, approaching then retreating, without ever getting any closer, seeming instead to gain distance so that he became afraid of losing sight of them.

Embarrassment: what a fool he must appear to the passers-by. But surely someone would see he needed help. Surely they understood: didn't this happen to everyone? It had occurred so mildly, so finely, this separation.

A man wearing a grey hat and grey overcoat stopped. He bent down towards Vernon.

It was Hari. Then it was Peter. Then Hari again.

Then it was no one. Just a man.

The man had no arms.

Despair.

It was hot under the covers. He could feel Jenny's body, her warmth, her curves, rising and falling rhythmically next to him. The room was dark, the window luminescent. The left edge of the dresser had the solid angularity of a casket and the slash of mirror above it, white, icy, glowed in the dark. The clock showed a few minutes before one.

His clothes – not his pyjamas, his street clothes, thick and heavy with seams that seared patterns into his skin – enclosed him like a body cast, gripped at him with a glutinous wetness.

He threw back the covers and met the gratifying chill of the air. He eased off the bed, the roughness of the carpet cushioned by his socks, and stood for a minute, uncertain, tasting still the dregs of the despair that had forced him into wakefulness.

The window offered the only light. Changed perspective redefined that corner of the dresser, that sliver of mirror, made them ordinary, graspable. He walked to the window and, in the darkness, it was like gliding: he had no sense of control over his legs, it was as though he were being conveyed.

The glass was fogged over, the moisture thickening the light of the street lamps and lavishing it over the surface like another skin, more substantial than even itself. Vernon rubbed at it with his fingertips and he noticed, with an interest that struck him as a kind of strength, that tonight there was no ice.

His fingers created a wet porthole, the moisture collecting at the edge like a rim.

A light snow was falling. The buildings across the street were shuttered and dark. The street lamp revealed once more a white shroud, the streetcar tracks and slush of the day camouflaged by a fresh, new skin.

The bed creaked behind him. Jenny said, 'Vern?'

He said, 'Yes.'

The telephone rang. He reached for it with deliberation, as if he had been expecting it.

'Hello.'

As he listened he continued to finger the porthole, creating patterns in the water, watching them disappear into the whole, then creating new ones.

'When?'

His hand moved in circles, enlarging the porthole, causing the rim of water to thicken and bulge.

'Now, look here, Peter.'

The rim broke. The water, channelling itself along the bed of the rim, flowed down the window-pane in a single, thick runnel, pooled on the wooden frame, swelled, tumbled over the side, and exploded like a dark stain on the window-sill.

'Screw you, Peter.'

He hung up, still with deliberation, and reached for the porthole, already clouding over.

He said, 'Hari's dead.'

Jenny sighed, got out of bed and went over to him.

He said, 'You know, Peter's dead too.'

She put her arm around his waist. He felt warmth and realized how cold he'd grown. He thought: The whole world, everybody's a refugee, everybody's running from one thing or another.

And then another thought chilled him: But it's happening here too. This country around him was beginning to crack. The angry words, the petty hatreds, the attitude not of living off the land but of raping it. He had seen it before, been through it before, and much more, more that was still to come, until a time when, even from here, the haven now, people would begin to flee.

He saw the earth, as from space, streams of people in continuous motion, circling the sphere in search of the next stop which, they always knew, would prove temporary in the end.

Through the porthole the snow grew heavier, the flakes bloated and ponderous. The street lamp blinked once, twice, then went out. All that remained of the world was Jenny's arm, her warmth, her weight pressing against him. And the vein that pulsed in his temple.

He thought: Where to next, Refugee?

The Spirit Thief

ERNA BRODBER

Things started from early morning. Who except parson had such business with dates? But Miss Gatha *did* have her numbers right. It was the 27th. Sunday, 27 January in fact and that was when silent Mis Gatha started to talk. Anyone who had never seen Miss Agatha Paisley in the spirit before would think is a coconut tree in a private hurricane that was coming down the road. Or somebody else might say is Birnamwood come to Dunsiname. Miss Gatha looking like she had a warning. The long green dress with the tiny red flowers, the head-tie of the same print tied rabbit-ear fashion, the big wooden circles in her ears and the bunch of oleander gripped tight in her hands like they were one and the same. And the swinging and the swaying and the twirling! Miss Gatha now have no ordinary foot walking thump thump and mashing the stones down into the mud. Toes only and the legs and thighs are oars. With her body braced back 45 degrees from the ground, was how Miss Gatha walked that morning through Grove Town. Her ten little black toes, escaping from the long green and red dress, scratched the gravel of the road like a common fowl looking for worms. That was the delicate side of her motion. And then there was the large: still with the back at an angle of 45 degrees to the ground, she would take long steps, beginning with and ending with her heel. It was early and the road was empty because it was a Sunday morning. No one was going to fetch wood or water or going to the field. This was the quiet time. Getting in the mood for the Sunday service.

Miss Gatha had no audience. But Miss Gatha spoke and that was how her private hurricane became a public event.

The spirit led her to the Baptist manse. Seems the warning was for Revd Simpson. So Miss Gatha spoke: 'Nine times three is twenty-seven. Three times three times three.' She recited; she sang; she intoned. In one register, in another; in one octave, then higher. Lyrically, with syncopation, with improvisations far, far out from her original composition. The changes were musical only. The lyrics never changed. 'Nine times three is twenty-seven. Three times three times three.' And then the wheeling, the turning, the bending, the scratching and the moving on the heels. Revd Simpson did not even look outside of his window at Miss Gatha. And though the whole concert was a public event by now, it was with the ears and the head that people saw it. They shooed the children back inside and closed the wooden windows facing the road. Miss Gatha dancing. Miss Gatha talking. Miss Gatha warning. Man would feel. And that would be hard enough. Why watch too? Revd Simpson continued to dress for church. He had to. He was going. But it was going to be a 'Dear Roger' day for him. 'Dear Roger, the scripture moveth me and you in sundry places.' Not a single soul, except perhaps Mass Levi – and he raised his eyebrows to himself – would be in church today. It was Miss Gatha's day. 'Bless her soul,' he said to himself and again to himself, 'There are so many paths . . .'

The spirit moveth too in sundry places. Or perhaps Miss Gatha had called them. For by the time she started her dance back home, visitors had arrived from near and from afar and had occupied her tabernacle. They were men and women. All in dresses. White and red were the colours. Some wore a white dress with a red head-tie. Some a red dress with a white head-tie. Some a white dress with a white head-tie. And others a red dress with a red head-tie. The dress styles varied little but the nature of the head-tie, not at all. All with rabbit ears. All with pencils in the head-tie. All yellow and newly sharpened. Drums rolled, their bum-batti-bum-batti-bum-batti-bum, the next item on the programme of music and recitation, that the Sunday morning offered to Grove Town's people now captives in their own homes. And when the cutting and the clearing was done, and the spirits had recognized each other and Miss Gatha had been let into her tabernacle, singing a hundred times louder than Miss Gatha's had been began. And the groaning. And the dancing of so many feet, stomping on the listener's mind.

Miss Gatha's solo had begun about 8 o'clock in the morning. It had caught Mass Levi in the latrine. He never left it. Nine times three is twenty-seven. Three times three times three. If she didn't change her style so much! If she would only keep one tune, he would be able to follow her and hold her. But that woman was slippery. And trying to catch her was taking away from his concentration and he needed all his energy and particularly today since it was Sunday and it was the 27th, three times three times three indeed. Dealing with her drained him. Now the bum-batti-bum-batti-bum-batti-bum was deafening him. He had to let go of the doll so he could use both his hands to push the sound away from his ears. On came the groaning and the stomping, like a hundred men stepping on his chest to cut off his breath and to force him into an asthmatic attack. He pulled his feet up to his chest to protect himself. A baby in the foetal position. His pants half-way down, his BVD grinning, his bottom in the circle of the latrine seat, his privates hanging down like a wet rat and his doll and his books scattered on the floor of the latrine. That was Mass Levi who could some time ago have tied a thief to a tree and said 'Root'. He had not given up though. He was boxing and kicking off those sounds and those feet thumping his chest, with much determination though with little success.

The tabernacle didn't break for Sunday dinner. The drumming, the singing and the groaning continued straight through to nightfall. Anita had spent all her fifteen years in Grove Town but she had never before sat in on Miss Gatha's performance, though she had heard things. The Holnesses were strangers to the district. They had never seen Miss Gatha operate but they too had heard things. In any case, they had grown up and lived in areas similar to Grove Town so they knew that 'three times three times three' and the singing and the drumming and the groaning that held the district frozen in its grip had meaning. They too closed their doors and windows. Could it be that with the windows closed in the day – for they were always closed at nights – Anita was being oxygen-starved? Eight o'clock had not come in that house without its usual occurrence but thanks to continued prayer, it had been less and less dreadful. Miss Gatha's solo had found that house in prayer and they had given thanks that the thing that usually pulled and pushed the two women in the house was barely felt that morning. Why with things going so well, should Anita now be putting her hands up to her ears, complaining that the noise from the tabernacle was 'suffocating' her? True the whole situation was packed with awe and dread but it was so for everyone in the house this time and nobody else was taking it as hard as Anita, a child who had gone through so much and conquered. And it must have been bad indeed for her, for Teacher Holness just managed to catch her fainting form.

Fainting was one thing. They could fan her and rub her up with smelling salts. And they did. But what to do when the child's face changed to that of an old woman and she began in her stupor to moan and groan like Miss Gatha and her companions at the tabernacle? Where Miss Gatha herself had fallen on the ground; where they had pinned her dress between her legs; where she was thrashing, boxing and kicking and screaming what seemed like 'Let me go'; where her face had changed to that of a beautiful fifteen-year-old and back again to that of a woman of Miss Gatha's sixty odd years and back again and back again and back again until she was silent, her limbs quiet and she was fifteen years old. In the Tabernacle there was no consternation at these changes. There, there was instead joy: 'Amen', 'Thank the Lord', 'Telephone from earth to heaven, telephone.' There, water mother, full in white, lifted the whistle from her belt and with its cord still joined to her waistband, moved it to her lips and blew one long, sharp report. All jumping, singing, drumming and groaning ceased and everyone, including water mother herself, froze. She blew again, said softly 'It is finished' and with that all took what they had and left Miss Gatha's form with its fifteen-year-old face on the ground.

It wasn't strange that Mass Levi should spend the whole day in the privy. He had given up breakfast and, along with it, the company of his wife and young son. He had quite a while now been giving this time to his books, his prayers and the privy. Normally on a Sunday morning though, he would get out and prepare himself for the 11 o'clock service. But even he in his solitary world must hear the singing and the drumming and know that this was a Miss Gatha day and that there would be no church. So it wasn't strange to Miss Iris that he should let 11 o'clock too find him in the privy. He did usually eat Sunday dinner. But since this was not to be a church day, he could have decided to make it a whole day fast. He had had those too. And since he had stopped speaking to anybody or answering their questions, he could be having a whole day fast right there with his books in the privy without letting on to anyone. Miss Iris was not at that time studying what Mass Levi was doing in the latrine: she was far too vexed for that. She was thinking how unreasonable the man had become. How could he sit there all day and expect his wife and son to do their business in a chamber pot or behind a tree somewhere? It wasn't fair.

It was the young girl's scream in the privy that made her consider what was going on with him. She knew that she distinctly heard a scream and wasn't sure but she thought she heard the words, 'Let me go.' She thought too that she had heard scuffling like someone was pulling themself away and like someone had hit someone down. Those loud-mouthed chocolate leaves were in the way. Pulling herself up like a ballet dancer, she tip-toed through them to the side of the latrine and listened. Nothing. But she was quite sure she had heard something. Not even the sound of a man clearing his throat or turning a page now. She listened again and got bold: the man might be sleeping. She would dare. She would peep. But how to get to where the air vent was. The wash tub nearby gave her the answer. She tip-toed through the leaves again, helped it up on her head, tip-toed again, turned the tub upon its face and stepped up. It was the dolly baby that struck her most. What Levi make dolly baby for? Miss Iris couldn't imagine her superior husband asking anyone to make a thing like that for him, so he had to have made it himself. And she didn't even know the man could make image! Then she noticed his position. No normal man could sit in that position and so quiet. No normal man wouldn't by now feel somebody staring at him and shift. Something was definitely wrong. She got bolder.

It was still the doll that caused her most consternation when she eventually opened the privy door. The face on the little thing looked exactly like Euphemia's daughter's face. If it was Calvert who had that doll she could understand. She knew how the boy felt about that child. But the father! Could one have had it and the other one stolen it away? But what would Levi have it for? The question came back: what Levi doing with dolly baby. When she looked closer and saw the knife wounds around the heart and a point at which the knife had gone deeply into the flesh and had gored it, she knew Calvert had nothing to do with that and that this was a very serious matter. She looked at her husband: his fist clenched, his arms crossed at his chest, his knees pulled up, his pants down and his flaccid thing hanging loose, and a whole world of understanding opened up itself to her. He was as dead as a dodo but that was only one thing. The other was a serious, serious thing. She closed the door calmly and made for the manse.

If she were to go to the Reverend's house, Jonathan and Louise might be there. With all this strangeness around they might have decided to stay right there at their workplace. If the Reverend were in church, he would be alone because no service had been kept. She wanted no witnesses to what she had to say and if possible no witnesses to her having come to see him. The church it was to be. Revd Simpson seemed to have been praying. He must have heard the church door open because as she got in through the door, she saw his body rise and turn around. He straightened up and came down the aisle to her with his arms outstretched. He took both her hands, folded them as if for praying, looked into her eyes, gave her no time to make what would have been in any case an incoherent report, just said, 'It is finished. Don't touch the Bible. Take the other books up one at a time in your left hand. Without looking at what is inside, tear the leaves out. Tear each leaf down, then tear it across, then drop it in the pit. Bury the covers – the hard parts of the books – then when you have time, dig them up, pour kerosene oil over them and burn them without reading what is written on them.' He stopped, looked deep into her eyes, inviting collusion: 'Your husband died of a heart attack. Clean him up. I'll be there by the time you've done what I have told you to do.' Then he looked at the shocked face and thought it could do with some answers: 'You are right. He did think he could use the young girl's spirit to get him back his powers. Yes. There are ways and ways of knowing.'

The Revd Simpson then made for the teacher's cottage. 'Miss Gatha can take care of herself,' he said to himself as if it had incorrectly crossed his mind that she couldn't and that he should visit her instead. 'It is finished,' he said to the anxious couple who opened the door to his knock. 'Anita will be all right from now on.' He couldn't just turn around and leave. He was searching for five minutes of pleasantries before he made his way to Miss Iris when he saw the lumpy white figure coming. The words 'Here comes the white hen' came to his head sarcastically. Maydene Brassington had as usual an excuse for coming down to Grove Town. Coachman had not been told that taking Ella down on a Sunday evening was now part of his work. It wouldn't do to issue him with this new directive and expect him to comply within hours. Ella was too new to the situation for her to send her down on her own from Morant Bay. So Maydene had to walk her down and as was common knowledge around, this would be no burden since Revd Brassington's wife did like to take walks at dusk. This was the explanation that she would give to anyone who needed to know why she was in Grove Town. She didn't give it now. No one on that veranda asked, so, as was her wont, Maydene Brassington went straight up to the table and dug her sharp knife into the heart of the matter: 'Miss Gatha says it is finished.'

That morning Mrs Brassington had seen strangers, now one now another purposefully making their way down along the parochial road that led to Grove Town. They were not walking in a group. They proceeded as if none knew the other or his business. But they shared an obvious common bond: they were strange to the area yet asked no questions when they reached the fork in the road. Without hesitation, no glance left nor right, each pressed on. That was strange. Maydene marked that. And more, each one had a drum. It was the drum that interested her most. The features. If there had been just one drum it might have escaped her. But as so many drums passed she was able to remark the features. They looked very much like 'magic drums', 'speaking drums', 'talking drums' – what was their right name? – pictures of which she had seen in a study of African drums in her father's library long, long ago. Then she heard the sounds from Miss Gatha's day. Cook couldn't say if the drums were coming from Grove Town or not, whether there was something special going on there or not that required the presence of those drummers, but the shrug which Maydene knew meant: 'Why don't you stay in your corner, you inquisitive biddy?' told her unequivocally that something was happening. And the sounds continued and she knew that this was an event to which she was called. So off she went wth her alibi.

Only Maydene Brassington would have gone straight to Miss Gatha for answers. Like everybody, she knew that Miss Gatha dealt in drums and in spirits. Unlike everybody else, she seemed not to know that spectating around drums and drummers, spirits and spiritualists was out. She took Ella home and made her way to the tabernacle. There, there was silence. Everyone had gone home and there was nothing to observe save Miss Gatha lying on the floor of her work-house. Like Maydene Brassington, she stepped in. Grove Town would have been surprised to hear Miss Gatha talk to her – hold her eyes and actually tell her: 'Go tell them. It is finished. The spirit thief is gone.' Maydene did not leave at once. 'You will be all right,' she said in what was more a statement than a question but whatever it was, it carried concern. Miss Gatha smiled: 'You know it.' Then she paused and said teasingly, like a man giving his girl her special little name to be used by them only, 'White Hen'. The spirits had finally acknowledged each other. White Hen became incarnate. Maydene was in seventh heaven. It was from that porch that she addressed the Revd Simpson and the couple with him on the veranda of the teacher's cottage.

'This white hen is moving fast,' the Reverend thought to himself when Maydene blurted out her message. He did not know how to play her. He couldn't figure out how far she had reached. 'Miss Gatha has seen fit to recognize her,' he thought to himself, 'but is she just a messenger or something more?' Her 'exit one spirit thief' bowled him for six. 'Classified information. A highly trusted messenger at the very least,' he said to himself at the same time as the thought 'This woman sure is clumsy' bubbled in his head. 'This woman has forced my hand,' he continued. Then he thought again, 'Clumsy or deliberately clumsy?' Whatever . . . he would now have to trump that card. He gave voice, saying to the Holnesses: 'It is not generally known but Mass Levi has passed on. We are calling it a heart attack. It seems he was not such a good man.' They would understand the euphemism. Having spoken, he thought again: 'Yes, knowledge is power. They need that power. They should know.' Then he looked at White Hen. 'Clumsily right,' he said to himself as he nodded in her direction. He smiled and she smiled. She knew he meant: 'Master Willie and Mother Hen have acknowledged you. Why should I resist.'

An Honest Thief

TIMOTHY CALLENDER

Every village has a 'bad man' of its own, and St Victoria Village was no exception. It had Mr Spencer. Mr Spencer was a real 'bad man', and not even Big Joe would venture to cross his path. Besides, everybody knew that Mr Spencer had a gun, and they knew he had used it once or twice too. Mr Spencer didn't ever go out of his way to interfere with anybody, but everybody knew what happened to anybody who was foolish enough to interfere with Mr Spencer. Mr Spencer had a reputation.

Now, at the time I am speaking of, every morning when Mr Spencer got up, he made the sign of the cross, went and cleaned his teeth, and then left the house and went into the open yard to look at his banana tree. He had a lovely banana tree. Its trunk was beautiful and long and graceful, the leaves wide and shiny, and, in the morning, with the dew-drops glinting silvery on them, it seemed like something to worship – at least Mr Spencer thought so.

Mr Spencer's wife used to say to him, 'Eh, but Selwyn, you like you bewitch or something. Every morning as God send I see you out there looking up in that banana tree. What happen? Is you woman or something? Don't tell me you starting to go dotish.'

And Mr Spencer would say, 'Look, woman, mind you own business, eh?' And if she was near him, she would collect a clout around her head too.

So one morning Mrs Spencer got vexed and said: 'You going have to choose between me and that blasted banana tree.'

25

'OK, you kin pack up and go as soon as you please,' Mr Spencer said.

So Mrs Spencer went home to her mother. But, all said and done, Mrs Spencer really loved her husband, so after two days she came back and begged for forgiveness.

Mr Spencer said: 'Good. You have learn your lesson. You know now just where you stand.'

'Yes, Selwyn,' Mrs Spencer said.

'That is a good banana tree,' Mr Spencer said. 'When them bananas ripe, and you eat them, you will be glad I take such good care of the tree.'

'Yes, Selwyn,' she said.

The banana tree thrived under Mr Spencer's care. Its bunch of bananas grew and grew, and became bigger and lovelier every day. Mr Spencer said: 'They kin win first prize at any agricultural exhibition, you know, Ellie.'

'Yes, Selwyn,' she said.

And now, every morning Mr Spencer would jump out of bed the moment he woke and run outside to look at his banana tree. He would feel the bunch of bananas and murmur, 'Yes, they really coming good. I going give them a few more days.' And he would say this every day.

Monday morning he touched them and smiled and said: 'They really coming good. I going give them couple days more.' Tuesday morning he smiled and said, 'A couple days more. They really coming good.' Wednesday morning – and so on, and so on, and so on.

The lovelier the bananas grew, the more Mrs Spencer heard of them, all through the day. Mr Spencer would get up from his breakfast and say: 'I wonder if that tree all right! Ellie, you think so? Look, you better go and give it little water with the hose.' Or, he would wake up in the middle of the night, and rouse his wife and say, 'Hey, but Ellie, I wonder if the night temperature ain't too cold for the tree! Look, you best had warm some water and put it to the roots . . . along with some manure. Go 'long right now!' And Mrs Spencer would have to obey.

One morning Mr Spencer came in from the yard and said as usual, 'Ellie girl, them bananas real lovely now. I think I going pick them in couple days' time.'

'Always "couple days",' she said, peeved. 'Man, why you don't pick them now quick before you lose them or something? You ain't even got no paling round the yard. Suppose somebody come in here one o' these nights and t'ief them?'

'T'ief which?' Mr Spencer said. 'T'ief which? T'ief which?'

The truth was, nobody in the village would have dared to steal Mr Spencer's bananas, for, as I have mentioned, he was a 'bad man'.

Then, one day, another 'bad man' came to live in the village. He was the biggest and toughest man anybody had ever seen. He had long hairy arms and a big square head and a wide mouth and his name was Bulldog.

Everybody said, 'One o' these days Bulldog and Mr Spencer going clash. Two bad men can't live in the same village.' And they told Mr Spencer, 'Bulldog will beat you!'

'Beat who? Beat who? Beat who?' Mr Spencer said. He always repeated everything three times when he was indignant.

And Bulldog said: 'Who this Spencer is? Show him to me.'

So one evening they took Bulldog out by Mr Spencer's, and he came up where Mr Spencer was watering his tree and said: 'You is this Mr Spencer?'

'How that get your business?' Mr Spencer asked.

'Well, this is how. If you is this Spencer man, I kin beat you.' Bulldog always came straight to the point.

'Who say so? Who say so? Who say so?'

'I say so.'

'And may I ask who the hell you is?' Mr Spencer asked. 'Where you come from?'

'You never hear 'bout me?' Bulldog said, surprised. 'Read any newspaper that print since 1950, and you will see that I always getting convicted for wounding with intent. I is a master at wounding with intent. I would wound you with intent as soon as I look at you. You wants to taste my hand?'

Mr Spencer didn't want to, however. He looked Bulldog up and down and said: 'Well, I ain't denying you might stand up to me for a few minutes.' He paused for a moment, and then said: 'But I bet you ain't got a banana tree like mine.'

He had Bulldog there. It was true that Bulldog had a banana tree, and, seen alone, it was a very creditable banana tree. But beside Mr Spencer's it was a little warped relic of a banana tree.

Bulldog said: 'Man, you got me there fir truth.'

'That ain't nothing,' Mr Spencer said. 'Look up there at them bananas.'

Bulldog looked. His eyes and mouth opened wide. He rubbed his eyes. He asked: 'Wait – them is real bananas?'

'Um-hum,' Mr Spencer replied modestly. 'Of course they still a bit young, so if they seem a little small . . .'

'Small!' Bulldog said. 'Man, them is the biggest bananas I ever see in my whole life. Lemme taste one.'

'One o'which? One o'which? One o'which?'

Bulldog didn't like this. 'Look, if you get too pow'ful with me, I bet you loss the whole dam bunch.'

'Me and you going get in the ropes over them same bananas,' Mr Spencer said. 'I kin see that. And now, get out o' my yard before I wound you with intent and with this same very chopper I got here.'

Bulldog left. But he vowed to taste one of Mr Spencer's bananas if it was the last thing he ever did.

Mrs Spencer told her husband: 'Don't go and bring yourself in any trouble with that jail-bird. Give he a banana and settle it.'

'Not for hell,' Mr Spencer said. 'If he want trouble, he come to the right place. Lemme ketch him 'round that banana tree. I waiting for he.'

'C'dear, pick the bananas and eat them all quick 'fore he come back and t'ief them.'

'No,' Mr Spencer said. 'I waiting for he. I waiting. Let him come and touch one – just one, and see what he get.'

A few days passed. Bulldog had tried to forget Mr Spencer's bananas, but he couldn't put them out of his mind. He did everything he could to rid his thoughts of that big beautiful bunch of bananas which had tempted him that day in Mr Spencer's yard.

And then he began to dream about them. He talked about them in his sleep. He began to lose weight. And every day when he passed by Mr Spencer's land, he would see Mr Spencer watering the banana tree, or manuring it, or just looking at it, and the bananas would seem to wink at Bulldog and challenge him to come and touch one of them.

One morning Bulldog woke up and said: 'I can't stand it no longer. I got to have one o' Spencer's bananas today by the hook or by the crook. I will go and ax him right now.' He got up and went to Mr Spencer.

Mr Spencer was in the yard feeling the bananas. He was saying to himself: 'Boy, these looking real good. I going to pick them tomorrow.'

Bulldog stood up at the edge of Mr Spencer's land: he didn't want to offend him by trespassing. He called out: 'Mr Spencer, please, give me one of your bananas.'

Mr Spencer turned round and saw him. He said: 'Look, get out o' my sight before I go and do something ignorant.'

And Bulldog said: 'This is you last chance. If I don't get a banana now, you losing the whole bunch, you hear?'

'But look at ... But look at ... But look at ...' Mr Spencer was so mad he could scarcely talk.

Now Bulldog was a conscientious thief. He had certain

moral scruples. He liked to give his victims a fifty-fifty chance. He said: 'I going t'ief you bananas tonight, Spencer. Don't say I ain't tell you.'

'You's a idiot?' Mr Spencer called back. 'Why you don't come? I got a rifle and I will clap a shot in the seat o' you pants, so help me.'

'Anyhow, I going t'ief you bananas,' Bulldog said. 'I can't resist it no more.'

'Come as soon as you ready, but anything you get you kin tek.'

'That is OK,' Bulldog said. 'I tekking all o' them.'

Mr Spencer pointed to a sign under the banana tree. It read: TRESSPASSERS WILL BE PERSECUTED. 'And for you, persecuting mean shooting.'

Bulldog said nothing more but went home.

A little later in the day, a little boy brought a message on a piece of notepaper to Mr Spencer. It read, 'I will thief your bananas between 6 o'clock tonite and 2 o'clock tomorra morning.' Mr Spencer went inside and cleaned his gun.

Mrs Spencer said, 'But look how two big men going kill theyself over a bunch o' bananas! Why you don't go and pick them bananas *now* and mek sure he can't get them.'

'Woman,' Mr Spencer replied, 'this is a matter of principle. I refuse to tek the easy way out. Bulldog is a blasted robber and he must be stopped, and I, Adolphus Selwyn McKenzie Hezekiah Spencer, is the onliest man to do it. Now, you go and boil some black coffee for me. I will have to drink it and keep awake tonight if I is to stand up for law and order.'

At six o'clock Mr Spencer sat down at his backdoor with his rifle propped up on the step and trained on the banana tree. He kept his eyes fixed there for the slightest sign of movement, and didn't even blink. It was a lovely moonlight night. 'If he think I mekking sport, let him come, let him come, let him come.'

Seven, eight, nine, ten, eleven, twelve o'clock. And no sign of Bulldog. And Mr Spencer hadn't taken his eyes off the banana tree once. In the moonlight the tree stood there lovely and still, and the bananas glistened. Mr Spencer said, 'They real good now. I going pick them tomorrow without fail.'

Mrs Spencer said: 'Look, Selwyn, come lewwe go to bed. The man ain't a fool. He ain't coming.'

'Ain't two o'clock yet,' Mr Spencer said.

And all the time Mrs Spencer kept him supplied with bread and black coffee. He took his food with one hand and disposed of it without ever taking his eyes off the tree. The other hand he kept on the gun, one finger on the trigger. He was determined not to take his eyes off that tree.

One o'clock. No Bulldog.

Half past one. No Bulldog.

Quarter to two. No Bulldog.

Mrs Spencer said: 'The man ain't coming. Lewwe go to bed. Is a quarter to two now.'

'We may as well wait till two and done now,' Mr Spencer said.

Ten to two. No Bulldog.

'Hell! This is a waste o' good time,' Mr Spencer said.

Five to two.

At one minute to two, Mr Spencer looked at his wristwatch to make sure and turned his head and said to his wife, 'But look how this dam vagabond make we waste we good time.'

Then he looked back at the banana tree. He stared. His mouth opened wide. The banana tree stood there empty, and the only indication that it had once proudly displayed its prize bunch of bananas was the little stream of juice that was dribbling down from the bare, broken stem.

Easter Sunday Morning
HAZEL D. CAMPBELL

It wasn't me playing the organ that day, you know. It was like those mechanical pianos that play by themselves. My fingers were moving I know but I wasn't responsible. The organ play louder and louder and keep on playing even when the hymn suppose to stop. I didn't even know what was happening down there because my head stiff straight ahead. Lord, it was frightening! And when the notes just start crashing together I was so scared. And then immediately after that I found myself playing 'Praise God' and the people start singing it same time as if I had already introduced it.

Not even rector don't talk about it yet. It's like everybody still trying to understand what happen.

Some of us would like to pretend that it didn't happen.

You notice how church full up since then.

Yes. It's like it was a sign or something. Like the church renewed. It's real scary.

I never felt so in touch with God since I going to church as on that morning. It was frightening.

I sensed trouble the moment she walked through the door.

I sense trouble through the whole service. We were sitting behind her and she was restless the whole time.

It's when the folk group start singing the Zion songs that she really started getting excited. The moment the drums started she start to twitch.

I don't know. I still think it not quite right to sing them Poco songs and beat drum in church. I don't know. I just not comfortable with it.

I don't know either. Mark you, I like accompanying them. You know it's different and I enjoy it. But I not so sure you're

32

supposed to enjoy yourself in church like that. All that clapping and swaying about almost dancing in church, and the drums, I don't know.

The scariest part was how Mass Luke find the bunch of burn up bush right in the middle of the aisle.

You think she came back?

No. They say nobody has seen her since that.

It was the very first time that they were discussing the incident together. Three weeks had passed and the church was still trying to understand what had happened that Easter morning. It was the one time that an incident with so many eye witnesses didn't have different accounts of what had taken place. Everybody gave almost the same details. There were minor differences only in the estimate of the length of time the incident had taken and the organist had fixed the time almost to a second. It was the length of time it took to play the hymn, 'Oh God unseen yet ever near', twice.

The universal sentiment was that nobody knew exactly what had happened but that it was very frightening.

The April Easter Sunday morning had dawned fresh and calm as the dew-covered trees and bushes and meadow-grass in the village of Walkup Hill. Rainfall in March after a long drought had brought an outpouring of the signs of spring from a grateful earth. Easter morning praises could be heard and seen everywhere. Birds twittered and chirped and sang whole songs as they darted from tree to tree. Every bush and every weed was painted with vibrant colours testifying to its joy at being alive.

Walkup Hill was peaceful, content and holy as the church bells at St Peter Anglican Church began to peal, summoning the faithful also to praise God.

Easter morning service was always extra special at St Peter. For some reason which nobody could remember, that particular church had combined a kind of mini Harvest

Festival with the Easter service so that in addition to the white lilies and other Easter flowers, the church overflowed with the many other gifts of the earth: red otaheite apples, bright yellow oranges and grapefruits; sugar cane, yams and sweet potatoes. Green bananas hugged each other in large bunches, voluptuous ripe plantains tempted the touch. The sights and smells of the Easter celebrations at Walkup Hill Anglican Church injected a special earthy sensuousness into the worship that no other service had.

When the middle-class people who had moved into the area in and around the village had first attended this service, they had thought 'how quaint'. But they had liked it, so that the only change now was that the baskets were prettier and more artistically arranged by the Decoration Committee and everybody was pleased.

It was like this with many things in Walkup Hill these days, a mixture of old customs and new ways. For the village had been changing from backwoods on the outskirts of the city to a middle-class suburb.

It had started with one man, a lawyer, who had his roots in Walkup Hill and who had built his home right beside one of the many streams which tumbled through the village on their way to the thirsty flatland below. His friends had envied him the peaceful nature of his home far from the city crowds and noises, and since it didn't take more than three-quarters of an hour to reach the city, the villagers found themselves being besieged by requests for land. One enterprising developer had even turned what appeared to be a rocky hillside into a very charming housing scheme.

Now, in the mornings, the narrow road winding out of the village was busy with fancy motorcars and villagers with their donkeys often getting in each other's way as old-timers and newcomers learned to tolerate each other's ways. In truth most of the villagers didn't really mind the change. For one thing the newcomers didn't plant food so the tiny market did good business most of the week and some villagers who used to go to the big market in the nearest town at the foot of the hill now found that they could sell their foodstuff right there in Walkup Hill.

Several village daughters found employment in the new homes. The village shop expanded to take care of the increased demand for goods, and with the cash for the land they had sold, old-timers fixed up their houses or bought more animals and tools and Walkup Hill assumed an air of prosperity which other villages further away envied.

The newcomers also took over leadership of community organizations and since they had money to contribute or were good at fund-raising, these also prospered – like the new Community Hall and the improved cricket pitch, the toilets in the market, and most of all the churches.

Walkup Hill had two churches. Three really – the Methodist Church, St Peter (the Anglican Church) and the Church of the Holy Redeemer of the Resurrection. The last named, a revivalist church, usually had the largest weekly attendance although most of the villagers would tell an outsider that they were either Anglican or Methodist meaning that they had been christened in one or the other.

By coincidence it seemed that many of the newcomers were Anglican and they quickly took over St Peter.

Attendance used to be so small, the church had been looked after mainly by a deacon, a parish rector visiting once a month or less to administer communion and over-see church matters. But in no time at all this changed and it was established that the congregation was large enough and contributing enough to have its own parson. A rectory was built, facilities at the church upgraded, a few additions made and St Peter instead of sitting forlornly on the peak of a hill as it had been wont to do, now stood, its old stone walls softly proud of the new attention and a sparkling new cross on its roof testifying that it was taking over the leadership of the spiritual community in Walkup Hill.

Some of the old-timers who had kept things together through the years of its backwater existence were a little put out by the new leadership which tended to ignore them, not out of malice, but simply because they were anxious to get on with their jobs and were impatient with the slower, more cautious manner in which the old-timers lived their lives.

Anyway, St Peter became the pride of Walkup Hill and many villagers who had ceased attending now resumed their membership to the detriment, in particular, of the Church of the Holy Redeemer of the Resurrection.

One such was Mother White. She had come back to St Peter, she told somebody, because it seemed that the church had got new power, power which she coveted.

Mother White was not an ordinary villager. She could see things and do things – so people said. They didn't actually call her an obeah woman, but it was said that she had strange powers to cure people of strange illnesses. Illnesses which ordinary doctors could not even diagnose. She could take off evil spirits, and a bush bath by Mother White could cure the most serious disease.

But strangely she didn't always practise her calling. Very often she was an ordinary citizen like anybody else. But sometimes . . .

Once there was a girl given up for dead. She came from another village and her people brought her to Mother White as a last resort. Her case was so hard that Mother White had left her lying in the thatch-covered room where she gave baths and had disappeared for a whole half day searching for the bushes which she needed.

She returned almost exhausted with a tale that the spirit riding the girl had followed her and had tried to prevent her getting the right bushes.

As she told it: 'Everytime I put out mi hand fi pull up the right bush, wha you think come up? Stink weed! A looking guinea hen, a find horse whip! A looking rosemary, a find lovebush! This is a hard case.'

She had kept the half-dead girl for two days giving her baths and potions and the whole thing had ended with a drum ceremony to pin the evil spirit so that it wouldn't follow the girl home.

Since the girl lived far away, the villagers never heard if she had recovered but nobody doubted Mother White's powers.

Until her own son began to act funny.

It was said that he had given a girl in a nearby village a baby and had promised to marry her but during the time that she was sexually unavailable he had taken up with another girl. The baby's mother had 'put something on him' in revenge.

The villagers looked on curiously to see how quickly Mother White would cure her son. But nothing happened. Ceremony after ceremony was held, but, if anything, the boy got worse. One day he ran amok with a machete and was taken away to the asylum in the city.

Had Mother White lost her powers?

It was during this time that she returned to St Peter where she had been a confirmed member a long time before.

The first Sunday morning she appeared in church the newcomers, many of whom had never heard of her, were quite startled.

She was dressed in bleached calico with two or three layers of thickly gathered long skirts. Her head was tied with calico under her hat. When she entered the main doorway she did a kind of curtsy then walked up the aisle to the altar where she made the sign of the cross and spun around three times, her many skirts billowing around her. Then she walked down the aisle stopping at the pew which caught her fancy.

This she did every Sunday morning and at communion

time she would be among the first at the rail, where after receiving the sacrament, she would walk straight out of the church and go home without talking to anyone.

After many Sundays witnessing this behaviour the church relaxed since it seemed that she was harmless. Some of the younger members even began to giggle at her performance. Some of the old-timers, however, were apprehensive. Later, they would say that they knew something was wrong from the beginning, but since nobody listened to them any longer . . .

It was a child who first awakened the church to the fact that Mother White was up to no good.

One Sunday morning, on their way home after service, the Wynter family passed Mother White walking her stiff, swift walk through the village centre on her way to her home hidden away in the bushes.

One of the Wynter children suddenly asked, 'Why that old lady don't like the communion, Mama?'

'Of course she takes communion, every Sunday,' the mother answered.

'But she don't drink it,' the child insisted.

'What you mean?'

'Last week I was outside – you member I went to the toilet? – and she came out of church and spit out the communion in a bottle that hide in her skirt.'

Wynter mother and father looked at each other puzzled, then the mother said quickly, 'I'm sure it wasn't that. And, by the way, don't I tell you not to linger when you have to go outside?'

In that way she shifted the conversation from the child's interest in the strange woman. But later she discussed the situation with her husband who thought that there had to be a simple explanation for what the child had seen.

'Why would anyone want to spit out the communion?' he asked. It didn't make sense.

His wife however was sufficiently puzzled to mention it

to some other church members the following week, and she asked the same question – 'Why would anybody want to keep the wine? It has its place only in church!'

Two old-timers were in the group and didn't contribute to the conversation. However, during the week, the church later learned, a group went to the rectory to tell the parson about their suspicion that Mother White was using the church and the communion for evil purposes. That could be the only reason why she was not swallowing the communion wine but saving it.

The parson, brought up in the city, had a modern scientific mind and was inclined to dismiss the story.

'True, the woman is strange, but each of us has our little ways,' he told them. 'It's just that Mother White is a little more eccentric than most.'

Still they insisted that he should at least observe her so that they could be satisfied that everything was all right. Great harm would come to the church, they predicted, if she was really using the communion for devilish purposes.

When the parson asked what she could possibly do with the communion, they told him in some detail what they knew of her history.

The following Sunday he was away, so communion service was not held. But sure enough, the next communion Sunday, Mother White turned up, went through her usual act and those watching saw how, as she stepped outside the church, she stopped, took a bottle from her pocket and spat out what had to be the communion wine into it. She also wrapped what appeared to be the wafer in a piece of paper, put both in her pocket and walked quickly away.

Parson was surprised and a little worried when he heard this report. He had no choice but to put the matter before the church's Advisory Committee. So he called a special meeting and together with the witnesses they discussed the situation. Nobody had ever heard of such a thing before. They were appalled and a little bewildered and afraid, because the old-timers were talking about obeah and devil dealings and they were not quite sure how to handle Mother White.

It was decided that the parson should seek advice from the bishop but meanwhile they would withhold the communion from Mother White.

As the parson summed it up, 'We can't prevent her from coming to church but we can withhold the communion since we have witnesses that she is not receiving it in the holy tradition of the Church.'

'Suppose she makes a fuss?' somebody asked.

'That would only prove that she was up to no good,' another replied.

It happened that the next communion service was held on Easter Sunday morning.

The church was packed, as usual, on Easter Sunday. Many who hardly attended church during the year made a special effort to be there at Easter and at Christmas. Indeed one of the parson's favourite jokes was to wish some of his audience Happy Easter at Christmas and Merry Christmas at Easter.

So St Peter was full. Old-timers and newcomers dressed up, feeling peaceful and content with the world as they walked in quietly and took their seats.

Easter lilies filled the brass urns at the altar. Brightly coloured fruits and other offerings wooed the congregation into a feeling of worship and praise, for the Decoration Committee had spent a busy Saturday and had outdone themselves with the flower and harvest arrangements. They were both celebrating the resurrection of their Lord and reaffirming his goodness in providing mankind with so many gifts from the earth.

The organist entered and began the soft prelude. The congregation sat in expectation of the grand march up the aisle of the altar boy with the cross followed by the rector and choir. This was one of the few occasions when St Peter followed a formal pattern, for their services tended to be more informal than in many other Anglican churches.

Suddenly there was a rustle at the main door and a harsh voice crying 'Holy is God! Holy is the Lord!'

Everybody turned around and there was Mother White at the entrance.

Her calico skirts looked whiter and stiffer than usual. Beneath tie-head and hat her wizened features glistened from the oils with which she had rubbed her face.

In her hands she held a bunch of dried bush which looked as if it had been slightly scorched by fire. She also had a single dried mandora coconut, large, smoothed like a calabash and shining as if it too had been rubbed with oils. She walked slowly up the aisle and those sitting near could smell white rum and strange oils as she passed.

At the altar rail she plunked her bunch of burnt bush into the midst of the beautiful white Easter lilies, rested the coconut on the ground, made the sign of the cross, spun around three times and then returned down the aisle.

At the end of the aisle near the doorway she spun around three times again, then, counting off seven rows from the door, she indicated to those in the crowded pew on the left side that that was where she intended to sit.

Two people got up and gave her the aisle seat while others shifted uncomfortably. Somehow her presence had introduced a new influence into the church. Many could sense it and it made them uneasy. The smell of alcohol and strange oils were an unwelcome addition to the already heady odours in the church.

One woman, outraged at the ugly bush in the midst of the lilies, plucked it out and went to a side door and threw it angrily outside. Somebody else spirited away the coconut.

Somehow, after all that, the holy procession up to the altar seemed something of an anti-climax.

It was to be an unusual service that morning for the Advisory Committee had decided to get a group of folk singers as part of the entertainment during the service. Many of them felt that the church could do with a little modernizing of the pattern of its service. Some churches, they argued, were even including dance as part of the worship. The Freedom Singers were seated in the front pews and the two drummers were already stationed near the organist waiting to offer their praises in the folk tradition.

Things went calmly enough for the first part of the service. They sang the usual Easter songs of praise and joy for the resurrection of Christ, and the choir did a special number. It was when the drummers for the Freedom Singers struck up that the first obvious signs of trouble began.

The Singers started with 'Me alone, me alone ina de wilderness'.

Those near to Mother White reported that she began to twitch and shake as soon as the drumming started. So much so that two more people left the pew. When they started to sing 'Moses struck the rock', she got up and began to wheel and turn in the aisle.

A few visitors thought that this was part of the entertainment and were delighted. But the parson, who was a red man, turned redder, and many in the congregation began to frown. Mother White was going too far.

Still nobody made a move to try to quiet her or lead her outside as had been done on occasion with certain stray persons who had tried to disrupt the service. And after the drumming ceased she returned to her seat where after a few more twitches she kept quiet and the parson with a feeling of great apprehension began his sermon.

Jesus Christ by his resurrection had enabled Christians everywhere to overcome Evil and the Power of Darkness – was the main message.

Much later when they were still trying to analyse it, the congregation would agree that it was from this point that the battle began. Imperceptibly. Nothing spectacular. Just a heightening of tension in the church; a strangely powerful ring in the parson's voice affirming the power of Christ in a way they had never heard him do before; and quite unexpectedly storm clouds shielding the sunlight so that someone got up and turned on all the lights in the church.

Then came the invitation to communion.

'My brothers and sisters in Christ, draw near and receive His Body which He gave for you, and His Blood which He shed for you. Remember that He died for you and feed on Him in your hearts by faith with thanksgiving.'

Mother White was among the first to move out of the pews to go to the rail to receive the communion.

Organist and congregation prepared to sing 'Let us break bread together on our knees' as usual, but the parson surprised them by giving instructions for the hymn,

> O God, unseen yet ever near,
> Thy Presence may we feel;
> And thus inspired by holy fear,
> Before thine altar kneel.

He recited the words as the faithful took their place waiting to receive the body and blood of Christ.

Mother White was second at the rail and when he came to her, the words 'The Body of Christ given for you' just would not come out, so he shook his head and whispered, 'Mother White, I cannot in all good conscience offer you this sacrament.'

There was a pause as Mother White looked in her upturned hands where there was no expected wafer. She looked up at the parson puzzled but he was moving on to the person beside her.

The first most of the congregation knew about what was

43

happening was when she sprang up and began to stamp her feet and shout:

'I want me communion. I come fi mi communion and I must get it. You have fi gi me.'

For a second there was a shocked silence in the church, the singing petered out and the bewildered congregation wondered what was happening.

The parson repeated loudly so that all could hear, 'Mother White, I cannot in good conscience offer you this sacrament.'

As if on cue, those who had been in the aisle waiting their turn quickly retreated to their seats as if clearing the battle-ground as Mother White began to shout and stamp in earnest.

As if on cue too, the congregation took up back the hymn and without knowing why, began to sing louder and louder. The louder she screamed and shouted, the louder the organ played and the louder the congregation sang. When they reached the last verse,

> Thus may we all thy word obey
> For we, O God, are thine;
> And go rejoicing on our way
> Renewed with strength divine

they sang with a fervour and belief that most of them had never before felt in their faith.

Meanwhile the parson stood motionless at the altar, the Host still in his hands, his head bowed in prayer.

But still Mother White shouted and when the hymn ended the congregation started it all over again without even a pause. The organ pealed out as it had never done before and the congregation sang as they had never sung before. Small children hugged their parents in fright as Mother White began to foam at the mouth. She spun around not three times but seven times one way and seven times the other. She rolled rapidly on the floor down the aisle and returned as rapidly. She stood up and her body, washed with sweat, shook and trembled. At one point it seemed that her head alone was spinning leaving her body motionless.

And still the congregation sang.

Suddenly, when it seemed that they could get no louder, when it seemed that their very souls were being lifted out of their bodies, the organ made a loud crash of discordant notes frightening everybody, and in the silence which ensued Mother White shook herself violently once more and then quite calmly and peacefully took up her hat which had fallen on the floor and walked out of the door.

And without any directive, organ, parson and congregation burst into the hymn

> Praise God from whom all blessings flow;
> Praise Him all creatures here below;
> Praise Him above ye heavenly host;
> Praise Father, Son and Holy Ghost.
> Amen.

At Amen, without another word, as if still on cue, without waiting for the established dismissal everybody quietly and quickly left the church and went home.

No lingering to greet each other and exchange talk and comments on the service as usual, for the emotional experience they had just undergone was too much for discussion yet.

Even the parson, who usually stayed until all had departed, left St Peter that morning without a word to any of his flock.

And as they hurried away the rain clouds dispersed and the bright April morning Easter sun streamed down on them once more, warming them and lighting up the cross on the roof of the church triumphant.

Tilson Ezekiel Alias Ti-Zek

JAN CAREW

He'd been drinking *dharu* all day long with Ramkissoon, a cattle rustler from the Maichony savannahs, and Ram had the smell of fear coming off him like the stench from a ramgoat. There was a quality of heaviness about Ram as if he was born with weights on his spirit. He talked heavily and walked heavily and ate and drank heavily. By sundown, when the sky had long streaks of fire and smoke stretching from end to end of the horizon, Ram was drunk and repeating the same story he'd been telling since morning.

'Boy, Ti-Zek, was cat-piss-and-pepper!' Ram's eyes were so red they looked as if he'd pasted hibiscus petals over the eyeballs.

Ti-Zek, reclining on a bed of banana leaves, said derisively, 'All-you too blasted stupid! Three grown men going to thief cattle in broad daylight from Singh ranch? All-you must've had too much bad-rum in all-you damn head. That was suicide, pardner! Don't tell me you didn't know was Buddy ranch! Government call in the guns an' yet Buddy got more guns than you got thirst for drink, and what's more he can use them. That man can hit a twenty-five-cent piece at fifty yard.'

'Buddy is a *douglah* like you, Ti-Zek,' Ram mumbled.

'Whatever kind of blood he got in him is bad blood, an it mix with poison. That bitch more bad than a snake in the grass.'

'Ti-Zek, tell me something, how come you get that rass name?'

'If I tell you, you won't believe me.'

'Try me.'

'Why you never ask me this question before? I done know you gone on fifteen years, and now all of a sudden you burst the question over me head.'

'Never wanted to know before.'

'Mi mother wanted me to have a name that nobody else had. So she christen me Tilson Ezekiel.'

'And who cut it down to Ti-Zek?'

'Me self nuh!'

Ram changed the subject, and said reflectively, 'Buddy resemble you, you know, Ti-Zek. Sometimes me can't tell who is who.'

'You jumping from one thing to the other like a grass-hopper in a bush fire, Ram. One or two rass drink in you head an' you can't talk sense, nomore!' Ti-Zek sucked his teeth contemptuously. 'If I know Buddy, he let you get away an' he shoot them other two Unablers you had with you for sport.'

'When the bullet hit Charlie, he spin like a leaf in the wind. Charlie turn a leaf spinning in the wind. Charlie boy, rustling was not for you, old man! Should've stick to pragging. Prags, boy, prags! The whole country livin' by prags.' Ram leant his leonine head to one side and rolled his inflamed eyes.

'And how Jag go, Ram?' Ti-Zek asked, although he already knew.

Ram pretended to be too drunk to understand the question. He didn't want to talk about Jag's death or the way he himself had escaped swimming across the Maichony river, while scores of alligators basked on the muddy banks eyeing him malevolently. Scores? Well, perhaps there were only a few, but they looked like scores.

'Jag was a rass,' he muttered. 'A real rass.'

Day cleaned with a suggestion from Ram that they do a job on the estate together. And having made the suggestion, alcoholic fumes rose in Ram's brain like incense. He kept thinking in this state of euphoria that he should go to Arjune, the Sadu, for a good-luck charm to tide him over his current spell of bad luck but Ti-Zek drove the thoughts from his mind with a burst of harsh banter.

'Do a job with you, Ram? Don't mek sport. You' brain an' you' frame too slow to keep up with me, pardner. And besides I like to work alone, all alone with my own sour self.'

'I broke, man, an' desperate, an' me chile mother facing starvation.'

'Which chile mother, Ram? I thought you lost count of the woman them who mother pickny for you.'

'You gotto help me, Zek.'

Against his better judgement Ti-Zek decided to join Ram in shifting a couple hundred coconuts from Boodoo's estate.

It was noon time. Low clouds were sifting the sunlight. The wind had vanished from the foreshore and was skulking somewhere deep in the forests. A pair of bluesakees were playing mating games in a low thicket of black sage and ants bush. They darted from one clump of bushes to the other and their wings were the colour of bluebells.

Ti-Zek and Ram had picked the dry coconuts and were peeling them on wooden spikes they had driven into the ground. They worked quickly. The job had to be done before the Rangers resumed their patrols after breakfast.

But Roberts, a bitter old man and the bane of raiders, had been tipped off by the rum-shop owner who had heard Ram mumbling his secrets aloud between sleeping and waking. Roberts should have retired a long time ago, but a passion for hunting men kept him alive and on the job. For him, retiring to a quiet life would have been worse than death.

The first shot caught Ram in the back of the head, and falling forward, his own wooden spike pierced his throat.

Ti-Zek ran bird-speed zig-zagging so that Roberts couldn't take proper aim. Two buckshot pellets caught him in the right leg, one close to the Achilles tendon and the other in the big outer muscle of the thigh. Roberts made a gesture of pursuit but soon gave up, cursing himself for his age and decrepitude. He left Ram's body on the spike and went for help. He knew that Ti-Zek was bold and vengeful.

'That Ti-Zek like a Manipuri tiger,' he said to himself as he walked away. 'You frighten him and he will take a roundabout trail and come right back to strike at whatever make him run away.' Ti-Zek, as Roberts had suspected, ran a wide circle and returned to the spot where Ram had fallen. He himself was bleeding but had traced his wounds to their sources and was satisfied that they were only superficial ones.

'Jesus Christ, Ram had bad luck! Mantop was hunting him down for the whole of last month. Peculiar how Mantop does play games with some people before he snatch them, and I swear he was playing a tiger and bush rabbit game with ole Ram. Two times in three months Mantop make a pass at Ram. During September rains a boat engine explode on the Mahaica river and toss him twenty foot in the air. He had bad back for months after that. Then Buddy shoot them two Unablers who was rustling cattle with him, and now, the third time, old man Roberts, half blind and decrepit, erase his name from the register of the living.'

Ti-Zek watched Roberts hurry away noisily with his double-barrelled shotgun cradled against his chest.

They say that Roberts can palaver with the dead, that he can gaff with jumbies on moonlight nights when he's alone in shadowy and silent coconut groves.

Ti-Zek didn't mind ghosts. What frightened him was the thought of being caught in a web of prison and desolation by one of those unfree spirits forever hunting him down.

He suppressed a feeling of revulsion, removed Ram's

body from the spike that held it fast, laid it on the ground and covered it with banana leaves. Above him the sky was the colour of a buck-crab's back – a hard metallic blue – and carrion crows were already circling, floating on air currents and tracing patterns as though invisible and deft hands were using them to write a secret calligraphy.

Ti-Zek, crouching in the shadows, waited around as long as he dared. He didn't want the carrion crows to rob Ram of his eyes, because Ram was the kind of man who always needed to see where he was going.

Long before he had stumbled into this unexpected and sudden exit of death, Ram had declared, 'Pardner, me don't want to go to Heaven. Them say the big *chibat* does feed you on milk and honey there. That will only be a lotta work for me, man, milking cow and goat, carrying them out to the pasture, sitting up all night to protect them from vampire bat. And who goin' keep the bee hive, and gather the honey, and have bee stinging them and shutting up they eye? No, pardner, give me hell anytime! With all them friends and enemies down there, me will only have to work a two hour shift a day stoking fire.'

'So go well, Ram, I will miss gaffing with you. Remember that story you tell me 'bout this big *chibat* who, when his first son born, decide that the boy-chile should have the most reliable company in the world to grow up with? How this big *chibat* search and search and wrack he brain till he come up with the bright idea that the most reliable companion on this earth was Mantop? So he search out Mantop and say, "Mantop, I want you to stand godfather for me one-boy.' And Mantop say, "All right, but there will come a time when I will have to come for him like everybody else." And the boy father say, "Well, that's you and he story. All-you two will have to settle that when the time come." So Mantop become godfather for the boy, and the boy become the village doctor. Now, as a doctor, he see Mantop the Reaper come for old and young, weak and strong, rich and poor, and he keep thinking, "All right, so Mantop is me' godfather. The two of us close as sweat to skin. I wonder if he will come for me the way he does come for everybody else?" So the doctor ask him, "Mantop, why you don't make me you' pardner for all time?" "Can't do that," Mantop say. "Is only room for one of us in this job." So the doctor go away, and from that time he start to learn all of Mantop tricks: how to enter a house anytime of day or night. An' Mantop, seeing how smart this doctor trying to get, decide to come for him before his time was up. The night Mantop come, the doctor get a real fright and he brain start to work overtime. When the quaking inside him abate, and he could find he tongue and give voice again he say, "Godfather, give me two more days to settle up me affairs, then you can come!" And Mantop agree. But as soon as Mantop leave the doctor get busy, and seal up every crease and crack and crevice in the house, board and bar the windows, and all he lef' open was one key-hole and he put a bottle to that key-hole and wait. Mantop come again jus' like he say, and when he see that he godson seal up everywhere he get vex like hell, an he call out, "Godson, open up this minute!" But the doc didn't answer. Well, wasn't long before Mantop find the key-hole and slip in and land right inside the bottle, and the doc jump up and seal him in, and although he cry out to make stone weep, the doc take the bottle and bury it in he back garden. Well, with Mantop gone, the doc act like he own land and sky, and he make mirth with anyone who try to stand in his way. He rob people of they land; he take 'way they wife and daughter; he properly parade himself and take advantage. But he didn't know that with Mantop gone, Time stop and wait till he come back so nothing new was happening day in and day out. The doc was jus' stumbling round and round, walking the same trail in circles; till he get fatigue. And one day, when he couldn't think of nothing better to do, he start planting vegetables in the back garden, and forking up the ground and he break the bottle that had Mantop locked up inside it. Mantop didn't wait then; he strike at once and carry the doc away.

'Well, old man Roberts give you a quick passage to the Beyond, pardner, so you an' you' friends will do shift-work stoking fire below. Go 'long you merry way, boy! I gotto go bird-speed. I can hear them coming. At least I save your eyes, Ram, so you can see where you going. And these two buck-shot in me leg biting me. I will send message to Sister Rhona an' ask she to come and fix it. She got a healing hand, and she will boil up some bush and in no time the wound will heal.'

They came with dogs. Ti-Zek made a detour to the main canal and swam as quietly as an alligator for half a mile to ensure that the dogs would lose his scent.

Old man Roberts said, 'Eh, eh, somebody move the body.'

'Is that damn thief-man Ti-Zek,' a young ranger with muscles up to his ears said. 'I wish you caught him instead.'

'Is fifty odd years I work on this estate, boy, and in all that time there never was a thief like Ti-Zek.' Old Roberts spoke as though he had a profound respect for Ti-Zek, and this surprised the younger rangers.

The muscle-bound one said, 'Me will get him sometime, man.'

But Roberts cautioned him, 'Don't bite off more than you can chew, boy; learn the ranger work, and study Ti-Zek like a book, read every sign he lef' behind him, and if you suspect he around, every blade of grass that move might not be the wind moving it; it might be Ti-Zek waiting to ambush you. I wish I had Ti-Zek as a ranger. This estate wouldn't lose a single coconut.'

They made a stretcher out of plaited coconut branches and carried Ram's body to the threshing floor of a rice mill that had long been abandoned to rust and moss and rats

52

and sleepy serpents. Narine walked slowly down the pathway from his house leaning heavily on a gnarled letterwood stick. He approached the corpse and prodded it with his stick, and staring ahead of him his eyes became calm and contemplative.

Here was a thief shot in the act of robbing him of the rightful fruits of the land he had inherited from his ancestors! He wished that the soul of this lost one, this spawn of Kali the Destroyer, could migrate for an eternity from the body of one wild beast to another. He stood there for such a long time that the others around him became restless and uncomfortable. Ram's brains, pouring out from the back of his head, looked like fallen petals of a yellow hibiscus, and this viscous pulp almost touched the toes of Narine's shoes.

Roberts cleared his throat loudly, and looking up from his daydream Narine ordered one of the young Rangers to go and fetch the police, 'Boy, make sure you find Inspector Gordon. Tell him that Uncle say he must come right away.'

'I will find him,' the Ranger said. 'I not coming back with nobody else.'

The Inspector was a big man who walked as softly as an ocelot. He had a thick neck and the veins on it stood out like lianas; but even when he was as hearty as a red howler monkey in the mating season, one was conscious of his small eyes, and how cautious they were, and how sly and cunning they could be, and how absolutely they belied his apparent joviality. Standing beside Narine with the sun behind him, the Inspector looked like a dark boulder shielding a blade of grass.

'Gordon, I too glad to see you, man, too glad.' Narine extended a hand that was veined and gracile and trembling like a leaf in a gentle wind.

The Inspector took the small and vulnerable hand in his immense one, and declared, in a voice that sounded like the roll of drums, 'Came as soon as the boy came and told me you had some trouble here, Uncle. I was on my way to settle a disturbance in Baggotstown. Is human-beast we have to deal with these days, Uncle.'

The Inspector exchanged a few pleasantries with Roberts whose deceased wife had been a distant relative of his, and then he took out his notebook and began to question him officially. Roberts gave a rambling description of what had transpired and the Inspector, again and again, brought him back to the main point. Narine listened so impassively that the flies crawling on the face of the corpse and those on his own face seemed to be crossing the same surfaces of dead flesh.

The young muscular Ranger was anxious to give his version of what had happened. He felt that he could do a much better job than Roberts, but a look from the old landowner was enough to let him know that the choices were his silence or his job.

'It's clear as rain water that Ram and Ti-Zek was working together, Inspector. Them two was always close as sweat to skin, and . . .' Roberts would have continued.

But the Inspector interrupted him, 'Leave Ti-Zek out of this, Roberts!'

'Leave him out, Inspector?' Roberts looked up, and his big veined eyes sunk in wrinkled flesh were wide open with bewilderment.

The Inspector smiled and explained patiently, 'Come, come, Roberts, old man, a black man and an Indian joining forces to rob a notable landowner? No, sir, that's politics. My job is to uphold the law, to deal with crime. So here is what the official story will be, and this will be the whole truth and nothing but the truth et cetera: Ram was caught red-handed stealing coconuts at 10.30 in the morning of April fifth. You and two young Rangers called on him to surrender, and you surrounded him. You called on him to give himself up peacefully three times. He took a few steps forward, as though he was going to comply, and then he

54

picked up a cutlass and rushed at Ranger Telford. You shot him. With a story like that everybody comes out looking good and there's no untidiness about the affair.'

The Inspector's eyes made four with each of the Rangers in turn and they nodded their agreement and lowered their heads.

'Come to the house and have a drink, Gordon,' Narine said. 'Is a long time since you come this way, man.'

'Glad to, Uncle,' the Inspector said. And when they were out of earshot of the others, he added in a low voice, 'There's a nice little piece of property in Georgetown that I have my eyes on, Uncle, and I'll need a mortgage.'

'After all, is co-operation and self-help these days, Gordon.'

'So what you want us to do with the body, Inspector?' Roberts called out.

'I'll notify the hospital as soon as I get to a telephone. They'll send an ambulance. Look out for the ants and the wild dogs and the carrion crows. Don't want to spoil things for the autopsy, you know.'

Roberts watched the two walking up the pathway to the big house with its green gables and the darkness inside which often made Narine keep the lights on in the day-time, and he kept repeating under his breath: 'The wild dogs and the carrion crows and the ants!' And he said to himself, 'This is a place with vultures and creatures and things to back-up the vultures. Wild dogs and carrion crows and ants and cannibal fish.'

'You said something, skipper?' the young Ranger asked.

And Roberts told him that he could go home to his wife and children since they all had a hard day. 'I will keep vigil over the body,' he said. 'Never know when that ambulance will turn up.'

Darkness swallowed the sunset with a single gulp and stars scattered themselves across the skies like flocks of gilded ricebirds surprised by a scarecrow. The moon nudged its way above canopies of coconut palms and moonlight and smoke from Roberts' pipe drove away the mosquitoes singing around his grizzled head. Navy-blue shadows squatted under the trees like tethered beasts. The old man, with his shotgun across his knees, listened to rainfrogs crying out to the moon and who-you birds conversing with ghosts; and every now and then he swayed and nodded drowsily, murmuring strange orisons between sleeping and waking. Around midnight, he heard the chicken in his backyard coop, behind the ricemill, stirring restlessly. He stood up and shook himself and stamped the ground to banish the stiffness from his joints. Palm fronds, stirring fitfully in the wind, made rusty whispers echo in dark groves where owls and mice played secret games. As if the wind and moonlight had filled him with the breath of life again, Ram stood up, shook himself like a wet dog and began walking away. Roberts, when he recovered from the shock and amazement and fear that had overcome him, called out and fired a warning shot; but Ram, looking back and covering the hole in his throat with his right hand, disappeared in the shadows.

Roberts felt himself floating down a river in his canoe until he struck a submerged log and the canoe capsized. He found himself swimming endlessly in opaque depths. When the ambulance arrived, the body had vanished and Roberts was in a coma. He never regained consciousness.

For months afterwards, the villagers kept telling stories of how this or that one had seen Ram and Roberts walking side by side, and how the two had always smiled a cunning, secretive smile, and how Ram was forever covering the hole in his throat with his hand.

Sepersaud Narine died in his sleep six months later. His body, frail and floating in a sea of wild flowers, lay in state in the cool dark living room of the big house. A cluster of pandits chanted prayers to the gods and their messengers in the Hindu pantheon who would take the soul of the deceased back into an eternal web of transmigrations.

The cremation ceremony took place on the foreshore in mid-afternoon when the tide was low and the wind was whispering requiems in the verging courida groves. The pandit intoned and the distant sea and the wind and the mourners responded. Flames from the scented wallaba pyre bent the body in two. It looked as though the corpse was sitting up, defying the fire and at the last moment trying to cheat death. But those who attended the funeral swore that they saw a hand reach into the flames, push the body backwards and hold it down until it disintegrated.

Narine's heirs, as he had stipulated in his will, recovered his ashes, and placed them in a marble urn in the centre of his seventy-square-mile estate. The urn was surrounded by coconut palms, ants bush, black sage and yellow cassia flowers.

The night after the urn was installed Ti-Zek drove a wooden spike close to it and carried out a ritual of stripping hundreds of coconuts so that the husks obliterated the fading wreaths piled on the ground. As Ti-Zek worked, the moonlight striped the ground with shadows and who-you birds cried out malevolently to one another. He shelled the coconuts on the spike rhythmically and interspersed his actions with words: 'Uncle, is how much land a man does need after all? You had so much that from your housetop to the end of the sky a man couldn't see all that was yours, and now all you can claim is enough earth to cover your blasted ashes. You had to leave all that land, and the money in the bank and the bad-mindedness to crush other people lives in you weak trembling hand. When Mantop come for you, in you' sleep, you couldn't offer him deeds to the land or cash in the bank, 'cause he is a dealer in life and death. So, Uncle, I working close to the miserable ashes they put in a stone jug, an' you can't do nothing 'bout it, an' you' Rangers them afraid of the moonlight and the jumbies and all them people who die on this estate with the taste of bile in they mouth and blood in they eye and emptiness in they heart 'cause they hurt so much they couldn't feel pain nomore. So I taking these coconut for all them mute folk who life you squeeze like *simitu* on a vine when you suck out the sap and throw away the skin, them people who grey-hair they life and toil like slave to make oil from you' coconuts-them. Is only Ram and me get away from you; both of we free like the wind is free or a harpy eagle does be in the wide, wide sky, out of your reach. So let you' ashes eat all the land it can eat and never rest in peace!'

The who-you birds called out more insistently, and the estate workers, listening inside their cruel huts, shivered and shut out the moonlight and the shadows and the rusty murmurings of wild palms.

The muscular young Ranger who had succeeded Roberts stumbled upon Ti-Zek's handiwork on his foreday morning patrol, and making sure that his only witnesses were singing birds, he laughed until he cried.

The Man

AUSTIN CLARKE

The man passes the five open doors on two floors that shut
as he passes, moving slowly in the dark, humid rooming-
house. Slowly, pausing every few feet, almost on every
other step, he climbs like a man at the end of a double shift
in a noisy factory, burdened down also by the weight of
time spent on his feet, and by the more obvious weight of
his clothes on his fat body, clothes that were seldom
cleaned and changed. Heavy with the smell of his body
and the weight of paper which he carries with him, in all
nine pockets of trousers and jacket and one in his shirt, he
climbs, leaving behind an acrid smell of his presence in the
already odorous house.

When he first moved into this house, to live in the
third-floor room, the landlady was a young wife. She is
widowed now, and past sixty. The man smells like the
oldness of the house. It is a smell like that which comes off
fishermen when they come home from the rum shop after
returning from the deep sea. And sometimes, especially in
the evening, when the man comes home, the smell stings
you and makes you turn your head, as your nostrils
receive a tingling sensation.

The man ascends the stairs. Old cooking rises and you
think you can touch it on walls that have four coats of paint
on them, put there by four different previous owners of
the house. Or in four moods of decoration. The man
pauses again. He inhales. He puts his hands on his hips.
Makes a noise of regained strength and determination.
And climbs again.

The man is dressed in a suit. The jacket is from a time when shoulders were worn wide and tailored broad. His shoulders are padded high, as his pockets are padded wide by the letters and the pieces of paper with notes on them, and clippings from the *Globe and Mail*, and envelopes with scribbling on them: addresses and telephone numbers. And the printed words he carries in his ten pockets make him look stuffed and overweight and important, and also like a man older than he really is. His hips are like those of a woman who has not always followed her diet to reduce. He meticulously puts on the same suit every day, as he has done for years. He is a man of some order and orderliness. His shirt was once white. He wears only shirts that were white when they were bought. He buys them second-hand from the bins of the Goodwill store on Jarvis Street and wears them until they turn grey. He changes them only when they are too soiled to be worn another day; and then he buys another one from the same large picked-over bins of the Goodwill store.

He washes his trousers in a yellow plastic pail only if a stain is too conspicuous, and presses them under his mattress; and he puts them on before they are completely dry. He walks most of the day, and at eight each night he sits at his stiff, wooden, sturdy-legged table writing letters to men and women all over the world who have distinguished themselves in politics, in government and in universities.

He lives as a bat. Secret and self-assured and self-contained as an island, high above the others in the rooming house; cut off from people, sitting and writing his important personal letters, or reading, or listening to classical music on the radio and the news on shortwave until three or four in the morning. And when morning comes, at eight o'clock he hits the streets, walking in the same two square miles from his home, rummaging through libraries for British and American newspapers, for new words and ideas for letters; then along Bloor Street, Jarvis Street, College Street, and he completes the perimeter at Bathurst Street. His room is the centre of gravity from which he is spilled out at eight each morning in all temperatures and weather, and from which he wanders no farther than these two square miles.

The man used to work as a mover with Maislin Transport in Montreal. Most of the workers came from Quebec and spoke French better than they spoke English. And one day he and a young man dressed in jeans and a red-and-black chequered shirt, resembling a man ready for the woods of lumberjacks and tall trees, were lifting a refrigerator that had two doors; and the man said 'Left'. He misunderstood the man's English and began to turn left through the small apartment door. He turned old suddenly. His back went out, as the saying goes. And he developed 'goadies', a swelling of the testicles so large that they can never be hidden beneath the most restraining jockstrap. That was the end of his moving career.

This former animal of a man, who could lift the heaviest stove if only he was given the correct word, was now a shadow of his former muscle and sinews, with sore back and calloused hands, moving slowly through a literary life, with the assistance of a private pension from Maislin Transport. He has become a different kind of animal now, prowling during the daytime through shelves of books in stores and in libraries, and visiting acquaintances as if they were friends whenever he smelled a drink or a meal; and attending public functions.

His pension cheque came every month at the same time, written in too much French for the rude bank teller, who said each time he presented it, even after two years, 'Do you have some *identification*?'

He used to be sociable. He would nod his head to strangers, flick his eyes on the legs of women and at the faces of

61

foreign-language men on College Street, all the way west of Spadina Avenue. He would even stop to ask for a light, and once or twice for a cigarette, and become confused in phrase-book phrases of easy, conversational Greek, Portuguese and Italian.

Until one evening. He was walking on a shaded street in Forest Hill Village when a policeman looked through the window of his yellow cruiser, stopped him in his wandering tracks and said, 'What the hell're you doing up here, *boy*?' He had been walking and stopping, unsure along this street, looking at every mansion which seemed larger than the one before, when he heard the brutal voice. 'Git in! Git your black ass in here!'

The policeman threw open the rear door of the cruiser. The man looked behind him, expecting to see a delinquent teenager who had earned the policeman's raw hostility. The man was stunned. There was no other person on the street. But somehow he made the effort to walk to the cruiser. The door was slammed behind him. The policeman talked on a stuttering radio and used figures and numbers instead of words, and the man became alarmed at the policeman's mathematical illiteracy. And then the cruiser sped off, scorching the peace of Forest Hill, burning rubber on its shaded quiet streets.

The cruiser stopped somewhere in the suburbs. He thought he saw Don Mills on a sign post. It stopped here, with the same temperamental disposition as it had stopped the first time in Forest Hill Village. The policeman made no further conversation of numerals and figures with the radio. He merely said, *'Git!'* The man was put out three miles from any street or intersection that he knew.

It was soon after this that he became violent. He made three pillows into the form of a man. He found a second-hand tunic and a pair of trousers that had a red stripe in them, and a hat that had a yellow band instead of a red one, and he dressed up the pillows and transformed them into a dummy of a policeman. And each morning at seven when he woke up, and late at night before he went to bed, after he washed out his mouth with salt water, he kicked the 'policeman' twice – once in the flat feathery section where a man's testicles would be, and again at the back of the pillow in the dummy's ass. His hatred did not disappear with the blows. But soon he forgot about the effigy and the policeman.

Today he had been roaming the streets, like every day, tearing pieces of information from the *Globe and Mail* he took from a secretary's basket at the CBC, from *Saturday Night* and *Canadian Forum* magazines. And the moment he reached his attic room, he would begin to compose letters to great men and women around the world, inspired by the bits of information he had gathered.

And now, as he climbs, the doors of the roomers on each floor close as he passes, like an evil wind. But they close too late, for his scent and the wind of his presence have already touched them.

With each separation and denial, he is left alone in the dim light to which he is accustomed, and in the dust on the stairs; and he guides his hand along the shining banister, the same sheen as the wallpaper, stained with the smells and specks of cooking. He walks slowly because the linoleum on the stairs is shiny too, and dangerous and tricky under the feet.

Now, on his last flight to his room for the night, his strength seems to leave his body, and he pauses and rests his hands, one on the banister and the other on his right hip.

The cheque from Montreal will arrive tomorrow.

He feels the bulkiness of the paper in his pockets, and the weight of his poverty in this country he never grew to love. There was more love in Barbados. On many a hot afternoon, he used to watch his grandfather rest his calloused hand on his hip as he stood in a field of endless potatoes, a field so large and quiet and cruel that he thought he was alone in the measureless sea of green waves, and not on a plantation. Alone perhaps now too, in the village, in the country, because of his unending work of bending his back to pull up the roots, and returning home when everyone else is long in bed.

And now he, the grandson, not really concerned with that stained ancestry, not really comparing himself with his grandfather, stands for a breath-catching moment on this landing in this house in which he is a stranger. He regards his room as the country. It is strange and familiar. It is foreign, yet it is home. It is dirty. And at the first signs of summer and warmth, he would go down on his hands and knees in what would have been an unmanly act and scrub the small space outside his door, and the four or five steps he had to climb to reach it. He would drop soap into the water, and still the space around the door remained dirty. The house had passed that stage when it could be cleaned. It had grown old like a human body. And not even ambition and cleanliness could purify it of this scent. It could be cleaned only by burning. But he had become accustomed to the dirt, as he was accustomed to the thought of burning. In the same way, he had become accustomed to the small room which bulged, like his ten pockets, with the possessions of his strange literary life.

He is strong again. Enough to climb the last three or four steps and take out his keys on the shining ring of silver, after putting down the plastic bag of four items he had bought through the express check-out of Dominion around the corner, and then the collection of newspapers – two morning and two afternoon and two evening editions. He flips each key over, and it makes a dim somersault, until he reaches the last key on the ring which he knows has to be the key he's looking for.

Under the naked light bulb he had opened and shut, locked and unlocked this same blue-painted door when it was painted green and red and black, so many times that he thought he was becoming colour-blind. But he could have picked out the key even if he was blind; for it was the only key in the bunch which had the shape of the fleur de lys at its head. He went through all the keys on the ring in a kind of elimination process. It was his own private joke. A ritual for taking up time.

He spent time as if he thought it would not end: walking along College Street and Spadina Avanue when he was not thinking of letters to be written; looking at the clusters of men and women from different countries at the corner of Bathurst and Bloor; at the men passing their eyes slowly over the breasts and backsides of the women; at the women shopping at Dominion and the open-air stalls, or amongst the fibres of cheap materials and dresses, not quite pure silk, not one hundred per cent cotton, which they tore as they searched for and tore from each other's hands to get at cheaper prices than those advertised at Honest Ed's bargain store. And he would watch how these women expressed satisfaction with their purchases in their halting new English.

And now in the last few months, along those streets he had walked and known, all of a sudden the names on stores and the signs on posts appeared in the hieroglyphics of Chinese. Or Japanese? He no longer felt safe, tumbling in the warmth and shouts of a washing machine in a public laundromat in this technicoloured new world of strangers.

He had loved those warm months and those warm people before their names and homes were written in signs. They were real until someone turned them into Chinese characters which he could not read. And he spent the warm months of summer writing letters to the leaders of the world, in the hope of getting back a reply, no matter how short or impersonal, with their signatures, which he intended to sell to the highest bidder.

He came from a colony, a country and a culture where

the written word spelled freedom. An island where the firm touch of the pen on paper meant freedom. Where the pen gripped firmly in the hand was sturdier than a soldier holding a gun, and which meant liberation. And the appearance of words on paper, the meaning and transformation they gave to the paper, and the way they rendered the paper priceless, meant that he could now escape permanently from the profuse sweat and the sharp smell of perspiration on the old khaki trousers and the thick-smelling flannel worn next to the skin. This sweat was the uniform, and had been the profession of poor black grandfathers. Now pen and paper mean the sudden and unaccountable and miraculous disappearance from a colonial tradition where young bodies graduated from the play and games and beaches of children into the dark, steamy and bee-droning caverns and caves of warehouses in which sat white men in white drill suits and white cork hats, their white skin turning red from too much rum and too much sun, and from their too-deep appetites for food and local women. For years before this graduation, he could find himself placed like a lamp post, permanent and blissful in one job, in one spot, in one position, until perhaps a storm came, or a fierce hurricane, and felled him like the chattels of houses and spewed him into the gutter.

So he learned the power of the *word*. And kept close to it. When others filled the streets and danced in a Caribana festival and wore colours hot as summer in a new spring of life, this man remained in his isolation; and he cut himself off from those frivolous, ordinary pleasures of life that had surrounded his streets for years, just as the immigrants surrounded the open-air Kensington Market. He thought and lived and expressed himself in this hermitage of solitary joy, writing letters to President de Gaulle, President Carter, Willy Brandt (whose name he never learned to spell), to Mao Tse Tung, Dr Martin Luther King and Prime Minister Indira Gandhi.

The few acquaintances he called friends and met for drinks on the eighteenth-floor bar of the Park Plaza Hotel, and those he visited and talked with and drank with in their homes, all thought he was mad. And perhaps he was mad. Perhaps his obsession with the word had sent him off.

The persons to whom he wrote were all unknown to him. He did not care for their politics or their talent. But he made a fortune out of time spent in addressing them. It was an international intrusion on their serious lives: 'Dear Prime Minister, I saw your name and picture in the *Toronto Globe and Mail* this morning. I must say I was most impressed by some of the things you have said. You are one of the most indispensable personages in this western world. This western world would come to its end of influence were it not for you. You and you alone can save it and save us. Long may you have this power. Yours very sincerely, William Jefferson.'

'Look what I pulled off!' he told Alonzo. He held the glass of cold beer bought for him on the account of friendship, and a smile came to his face. The smile was the smile of literary success. He had just promised Alonzo that he would defray all his loans with the sale of his private correspondence. A smile came to Alonzo's face. It was the smile of accepted social indebtedness. 'The university would just *love* to get its hands on this!' *This* was the reply from the Prime Minister: a plain white postcard on which was written, 'Thank you very much, Mr Jefferson, for your thoughtfulness.'

He would charge the university one hundred dollars for the reply from Prime Minister Gandhi. Perhaps he could sell them his entire correspondence! Why not? Even publish them in *The Private Correspondence of William Jefferson with the Great Men and Great Women of the Twentieth Century*.

Alonzo did not know whether to continue smiling or laugh right out. He could not decide if his friend was slightly off his head. He needed more proof. The letter from Mrs Gandhi, which he did not show, could supply the proof. But it was a man's private business, a man's private correspondence; and not even the postman who delivered it had the right to see it. If this correspondence went on, Alonzo thought, who knows, perhaps one day he may be drinking beer and associating with a man of great fame, a famous man of letters, hounded by universities to get a glimpse of this correspondence . . .

While the man is trying to unlock his door, the urge overtakes him. The key-hole had not answered the key. And the urge to pee swells over his body like a high wave. This urge would overcome him almost always when a porcelain oval hole was not immediately available. It would take him into its grip and turn his entire body into a cramping, stuttering muscle-bound fist. Always on the wrong side of the street, too.

He was on Bloor Street once, in that stretch of shops and stores and restaurants where women wear furs and carry merchandise in shopping bags with Creeds and Holt Renfrew and Birks proclaimed on them, where the restaurants look like country clubs and the shops like chapels and banks, where he could not get the nerve to enter the stained-glass door with heraldry on it, jerk a tense glance in *that* direction and receive the direction to *there* or get a sign to show him the complicated carpeted route to 'wash rooms' printed on a brass plate. Not dressed the way he was. Not without giving some explanation. Not without alarming the waitresses dressed more like nurses and the waiters who looked like fashion models.

Once he dashed into Holt Renfrew. It was the last desperate haven. The water was heavy on his nerves, on his bladder. His eyes were red and watery. He barely had strength to speak his wish. Experience with this urge had cautioned him, as he stood before the glass case of ladies' silk underwear, that to open his mouth at that moment, when the association of this urge with ladies' panties was in full view, meant a relaxation of his grip on the water inside him. Then it would pour out on to the carpeted floor of Persian silence, perhaps even dribble on to the feet of the young clerk whose legs he could see beneath the thinness of her almost transparent dress.

The young woman saw his stiffness and posture, and with a smile and a wave, showed him the nearest haven. It had 'Employees Only' inscribed on the shining brass. When he was finished, he could not move immediately. The loss of weight and water was like the loss of energy. 'Have a good day, sir!' Her smile was brighter then.

He was still outside his room. The key was still in the hole. He did not have the strength to go down two flights of stairs to the second-floor bathroom beside the room of the woman who lived on welfare.

To have to go down now, with this weight making his head heavier, did something with his hand and the key turned.

He was safe inside his room. Relieved and safe. He did it in the pail. He keeps this pail in a corner, under the table on which is a two-ringed hot plate. In times of urgency, he uses it, and in times of laziness and late at night. He adds soap flakes to the steaming liquid to hide its smell and composition, and when he carries the plastic pail down, the woman on welfare cannot smell or detect his business. He relishes his privacy.

Sometimes he has no flakes of soap, so he drops a pair of soiled underwear into the urine and walks with it, pretending there is no smell; and if the coast is clear, he bolts the lock on the bathroom door and does his business and laundry like a man hiding from his superstition.

He had heard that a famous Indian politician used to drink his own pee. And it overcame him.

He is safe inside his room. He breathes more easily now.

He is home. His room relaxes him. It is like a library of a man obsessed with books and eccentric about the majesty of books.

Red building blocks which he stole two at a time are placed in fours at each end of the white-painted three-ply shelves. And the shelves end, as a scaffold should, at the end of available space, the ceiling. The same construction occupies all four walls. There are books of all sizes, all topics, all tastes.

The space between the bottom shelf and the floor is crammed with newspapers which are now yellow. There are magazines with the backs missing through frequent use. Each new magazine goes into the space which can get no larger. Statements of great political and international significance, the photograph of a man or a woman to be written to, are torn out from their sources and pinned to the three-ply shelves with common pins; and there are framed photographs of writers whom this man regards as the great writers of the world. No one else has heard of them.

He has collected relics of his daily passage throughout the city, in the same two square miles, not going beyond this perimeter. He has never again ventured into that part of the suburbs where the policeman had picked him up. Among his relics are jars and bottles, and one beautiful piece of pottery that looks as if it had been unearthed in an archaeological digging somewhere in the distant world. It is brown and has a mark like antiquity around its swelling girth; and where it stands on an old trunk that could have belonged to a sea captain, or to an immigrant from Europe or the West Indies, large enough to transport memories and possessions from a poorer life to this new country, this little brown jug gives age and seriousness to the other useless but priceless pieces in his room.

In all the jars and bottles, and in this brown 'antique' jug, are dried branches of trees, flowers, sprigs and brambles. Dead beyond recognition.

The man collects dead things. Leaves and brambles and flowers and twigs. And he must like this death in things because there is nothing that lives in his room. Nothing but the man himself. He does not see them as dead things, or as meaning death.

He has five clocks. They are all miraculously set at the same, precise time, with not a second's difference. Every morning, using the time on the CBC radio as his standard and barometer, he checks and re-checks each of his five clocks; and when this is done, he sits on his old-fashioned, large and comfortable couch, upholstered in green velvet that now has patches like sores in the coat of a dog, with knobs of dull mahogany at the ends where the fingers touch, or rest, or agitate (if he is writing or thinking about a letter to an important personage in the world). He would sit here, now that he has set his time, and listen to the ticking, secure ordering of the meaning of time; pretending he is back home in the island that consumes time, where all the clocks ticked at various dispositions and carried different times. Canada has taught him one important discipline. And he has learned about time. He has learned always to be *in* time.

Paper bags are stuffed between books, folded in their original creases and placed there, anxious for when they can be used a second time. A cupboard in the room is used as a clothes closet, a pantry and a storeroom. It contains more paper bags of all sizes, of all origins, from all super-markets; but most are from Dominion. They are tied and made snug and tidy by elastic bands whose first use he has obviously forgotten. On the bottom shelf of the cupboard are plastic bags imprinted with barely visible names of stores and shops, folded in a new improvised crease and placed into a large brown paper bag.

All this time, he is walking the four short lengths of floor bordered by his books, stopping in front of one shelf, running his fingers absentmindedly over the titles of books. The linoleum floor is punctuated by the nails in his shoes that walk up and down, late into the night of thoughtfulness, of worrying about a correct address or a correct salutation. Now he stands beside a large wooden table made by immigrants or early settlers on farms, in the style of large sturdy legs the size and shape of their own husky peasant form. This table does not move. It cannot move. On it he has storeroomed his food and his drinks, his 'eatables and drinkables', and it functions as his pantry of dishes and pots and pans. At one end of the table is the gas hot plate, the only implement for cooking that is allowed in this illegally small living space.

On the hot plate is a shining aluminium saucepan battered around its girth by temper, hunger and burned rice.

He uncovers the saucepan. The food is old. Its age, two or three days, has thickened its smell, and makes it look like wet cement. The swollen black-eyed peas sit permanently among hunks of pig tails. He is hungry all of a sudden. These two urges, peeing and eating, come upon him without notice and with no regard to the last time he has eaten or peed. So he digs a 'pot spoon' into the heart of the thick drying cement of food and uproots the swollen hunks of pig tails whose oily taste brings water and nostalgia to his eyes, and he half shuts his eyes to eat the first mouthful.

He replaces the lid. He puts the 'pot spoon' between the saucepan rim and the lid, and pats the battered side of the saucepan the way a trainer would pat a horse that has just won on a long-shot bet.

He takes off his jacket. It is two sizes too large. Then he takes off his red woollen sweater, and another one of cotton, and long-sleeved; and then a third, grey, long-sleeved, round-necked and marked 'Property of the Athletic Department, University of Toronto'.

He is a man of words, and the printed claim of ownership on his third pullover never ceases to amaze and impress him.

Stripped now of his clothes, he is left in a pair of grey long-johns. And it is in these that he walks about the wordy room, ruminating as he struggles late into the night to compose the correct arrangement of words that would bring him replies from the pens of the great. Sometimes his own words do not flow as easily as he would wish. And this literary constipation aborts the urge to pee. At such times he runs to his Javex box, where he keeps all the replies he has ever received. He reads them now, praying for an easier movement of words from the bowels of his brain.

'Dear Mr Jefferson, Thank you for your letter.'

That was all from one great personage. But it was good enough. It was a reply. And an official one at that. A rubber stamp of the signature tells you of the disinterest or the thick appointment book of the sender, that perhaps the sender does not understand the archival significance of the letter he has received from Mr William Jefferson.

'This is to acknowledge receipt of your letter.'

Another reply from a great personage. Even the stamp, print and address are reproductions of the original. But the man believes that some value lies even in this impersonal reply.

'Dear Mr Jefferson, We are very glad to know that, as a Barbadian, you have introduced us to the archives of the University of Toronto, which is considering maintaining a Barbados collection. We wish you every success in your significant venture.'

This is his most valuable letter. It is signed by someone who lives! A human hand has signed it. But he cannot untangle the name from its spidery script. He does not know who has replied to him. For typed beneath the script is only the person's official position: Secretary.

He understands more than any other living person the archival importance of these letters. And he treasures them within a vast imagination of large expectations, in this large brown box which contained Javex for bleaching clothes before it fell into his possession.

He has been nervous all week. And this nervousness erupted in strong urges to pee, strong and strange even for his weak bladder. The nervousness was linked to the price of his collection. This afternoon he had spoken to someone at the university. Over the telephone the voice told him, 'Of course! Of course, Mr Jefferson. We'll be interested in seeing your collection.' It was a polite reply, like the written ones in his Javex box. But as a man obsessed by his relics, who attaches great significance to their esoteric value, he inflates that significance. He is also a man who would read an offer to purchase in a polite reply from the university. He is a man who hears more words than those that are spoken.

He starts to count his fortune. This letter to him from a living Prime Minister would be the basis of his fortune. His friend Alonzo would get a free round of beer at the Park Plaza roof bar. He would pay his rent six months in advance. He would have more time to spend on his private correspondence with the great men and women of the world.

He holds the Prime Minister's letter in his hand and examines the almost invisible water marks on which it is typed. He studies the quality of the official stationery made in Britain and used by the West Indies, and compares it to that of Canada and the United States. He decides that the British and West Indies know more about prestigious stationery. He continues to feel the paper between big thumb and two adjoining fingers, rubbing and rubbing and feeling a kind of orgasm coming on; and in this trance, he reads another letter.

'Dear Mr Jefferson, Thank you for your kind and thoughtful letter. Yours, Prime Minister's Office.'

Above this line, 'Margaret Thatcher' is stamped in fading ink. Still, it is a mark on history; 'a first' from a poor woman whom history had singled out to be great.

When he is in his creative mood, he moves like a man afraid to cause commotion in a room in which he is a guest, like a man moving amongst bric-à-brac, priceless mementos of glass and china and silver locked in a glass cabinet. He moves about his room soundlessly, preparing his writing materials and deepening his mood for writing.

His stationery is personalized. 'William Jefferson, Esquire' is printed in bold letters at the top of the blue page. And below that, his address. He writes with a fountain pen. And when he fills it from the bottle of black ink, he always smiles when the pen makes its sucking noise. This sucking noise takes him back years to another room in another country when he formed his first letters. And he likes the bottle that contains the ink. It has a white label, with a squeezed circle like an alert eye; and through this eye, through the middle of this eye, is an arrow which pierces it. 'Parker super Quink ink. Permanent black.' It suggests strength and longevity. It is like his life: determined and traditional, poised outside the mainstream but fixed in habit and custom. Whenever he uses this fountain pen, his index finger and the finger next to that, and his thumb, bear the verdict and the evidence of this permanent blackness. This *noire*. He sometimes wishes that he could use the language of Frenchmen who slip words and the sounds of those words over their tongues like raw oysters going down the throat!

'What a remarkable use of the tongue the French have! That back of the throat sensation!' he told Alonzo one afternoon, but in such a way as if he were speaking to the entire room in the Park Plaza Hotel bar.

Noire.

Many years ago, in 1955, the minute his feet touched French soil at Dorval in Quebec, the first greeting he heard was *'Noire!'* The sound held him in its grip, and changed his view of ordinary things, and made him fastidious and proper and suspicious. The only word he retained was *noire*. It was not a new word to him. For years even before that greeting, and in Barbados on a Sunday afternoon after the heavy midday meal, he used to sit at the back door looking out on to the cackling of hens, one of which he had eaten earlier, inhaling with the freshness of stomach and glorious weather the strong smell of Nugget shoe polish as he lathered it on his shoes and on his father's shoes and his mother's shoes and his grandfather's shoes. So he had already dipped his hands into *noire* long before Canada.

He had known *noire* for years. But no one had addressed him as *noire*.

He likes the *noire* of the ink he uses, as he liked the *noire* in the Nugget which gave his shoes longer life and made them immortal and left its proud, industrious and indelible stain on his fingers.

Tomorrow the University of Toronto is coming to buy his papers. He runs his hands over his letters in the Javex box, hundreds of them, and thinks of money and certified cheques. He empties all his pockets and puts the papers on the table. He picks up each piece like a man picking flesh from a carcass of bones. Who should he write to tonight?

The silent books around him, their words encased in covers, do not offer advice. But he knows what they would answer. He finds it difficult to concentrate. Tomorrow is too near. The money from his papers, cash or certified cheque, is too close at hand. He spends time spending it in his mind. And the things contained in tomorrow, like the things contained in his Javex box, have at last delivered him, just as his articulate use of pen confirmed the value of the word and delivered him from the raving crowds of new immigrants. He has gained peace and a respectable distance from those aggressive men and women because of his use of the word.

'Should I write to the President of Yale University?'

The books, thick in their shelves around him, and few of

which he has read from cover to cover, all these books remain uncommunicative and have no words of advice.

'Should I write to President Reagan?'

His five electric clocks continue to keep constant time, and in their regulated determination, refuse to disclose a tick of assistance.

'The Prime Minister of Barbados?'

Barbados is no longer home. Home, he had told Alonzo ten years ago, 'is where I pee and eat and write.'

He gets up and turns on the flame of the hot plate under the saucepan. 'While the grass is growing, the horse is starving,' he tells the saucepan. He smiles at his own wisdom. The heat makes the saucepan crackle. 'While the grass is growing . . .' The thin saucepan makes a smothered crackling sound. The hot plate seems to be melting the coagulated black-eyed peas and rice and pig tails. The hot plate is crackling as if it is intent upon melting the cheap alloy of the saucepan and turning the meal into soft hot lead, and then spreading its flame over the letters on the table, and then the table itself, and then the room. He lowers the flame.

'Fire cleans everything,' he tells the hot plate. The saucepan stops laughing with the heat. His meal has settled down to being re-cooked.

But he is soon smelling things. The nostalgia of food and the perspiration from his mother's forehead as she cooked the food, and the strong, rich smell of pork. He smells also the lasting wetness of flannel shirts worn in the fields back on the small island.

He gets accustomed to these smells. And he thinks again of new correspondence since all these on the table before him would be gone by tomorrow, sold, archived among other literary riches. A hand-rubbing enthusiasm and contentment brings a smile to his face.

'I'll write the Prime Minister of Barbados!'

The smell comes up again. With the help of the smell, he

is back on the small island, witnessing spires of blue smoke pouring out from each castle of patched tin and rotting wood where his village stood. He can hear the waves and the turbulent sea, so much like the turbulence of water he boiled in the same thin-skin saucepan to make tea. As he thinks back, his eyes pass over used tea bags spread in disarray, an action caught in the midst of an important letter when he would sometimes drop a used tea bag into the yellow plastic pail.

'Dear Prime Minister . . .'

He reaches over to the hot plate and raises the flame. He sees it change from yellow to blue, and smiles. 'The horse is starving . . .'

'Certain important universities have asked me to act as a liaison to encourage you to submit your . . .'

The fragile aluminium saucepan is losing its battle in the heat of warming the food. But it is the smell. The smell takes his mind off the letter, and off the great sums of money, cash and certified cheques. He is a boy again, running home from school, colliding with palings and dogs and the rising smells of boiled pork reddened in tomatoes and bubbling over rice like the thick tar which the road workers poured over a raw road under construction.

He can taste his country now. Clearly. And see the face of the Prime Minister, greedy to make a name for himself in a foreign institution of higher learning, and obtain foreign currency for his foreign account.

'. . . I have lived a solitary life, apart from the demonstrations and protests of the mainstream of immigrants. I have become a different man. A man of letters. I am more concerned with cultural things, radio, books and libraries, than with reports . . .'

Something is wrong with his pen. The flow is clogged and constricted, just like when he's caught with his pants up in a sudden urge to pee, and having forced it inwards, cannot get it outwards. And he gets up and heads downstairs. Just as he's moving away from his door, still on the first three or four steps going down, he turns back. 'My pen is my penis,' he tells the door.

He picks up the yellow plastic pail. He throws a shirt and underwear into the brown stagnant water. It looks like stale beer. Before he goes through the door again, he picks up the unfinished letter to the Prime Minister of Barbados, and in his long-johns, armed with pail and paper, he creeps out.

The stairs are still dim. And he smiles. He moves down slowly, hoping that when he reaches the second floor the woman on welfare who occupies the toilet longer than any other tenant would not be there.

The saucepan has now begun to boil, although there are more solids than liquids within its thin frame. Popcorn comes into his mind. He doesn't even eat popcorn! He doesn't even go to the movies! The saucepan is turning red at the bottom. If he was in his room, he could not tell where the saucepan's bottom began and where the ring of the hot plate ended.

He thinks of roast corn as he reaches the closed door of the only bathroom in the house. He stands. He listens. He smells. He inhales. And he exhales. He puts his hand on the door and pushes gently, and the door opens with a small creak. He stands motionless, alarmed to see that the bathroom is indeed empty. Where is the woman on welfare?

. . . at night, back home, in the crop season when the sugar canes are cut and harvested, they burn the corn over coals . . .

Right then, above his head, the saucepan explodes. He doesn't hear it. The black-eyed peas and rice burst out, pelting the cover before it, and the table top is splattered like careless punctuations marks. It falls on his fine blue stationery.

The explosion comes just as he holds the yellow pail at a

tilt, over the growling toilet bowl. In the same hand as the pail is the unfinished letter. The urine is flowing into the bowl and he stands thinking, when he sees the first clouds of smoke crawling down the stairs, past the open bathroom door.

The smoke becomes heavier and makes tears come into his eyes. He is crying and passing his hands in front of his face, trying to clear a passage from the second floor, through the thickening smoke rising like high waves. Up and up he goes, no faster than when he entered the house that afternoon, struggling through the smoke until he reaches the steps in front of his door. And as he gets there, it seems as if all the books, all the letters, all the bags of plastic and paper shout at once in an even greater explosion.

Before he can get downstairs to call for help from the woman on welfare, he thinks he hears all five of his clocks alarming. And then, in the way a man who has been struck by a deadening blow waits for the second one to land, he stands, expecting the five clocks to do something else. It is then that he hears one clock striking the hour. He counts aloud until he reaches eight, and then he refuses to count any longer.

Inez

MERLE HODGE

Mrs Henry was ready to call the police. The children and the dogs had to get breakfast, she and Henry had to have their coffee, and the confounded girl was ten minutes late. And she had warned her, two years ago when she started, that if she ever came late, every minute would be deducted from her wages. This was the first time but it would also be the last.

And to think that the facety girl had, just the day before, put God out of her thoughts and asked for an advance on her week's pay. In the middle of the week!

'Only five dollars, ma'am.'

'Five dollars! But that is half your pay – you can't get half your pay in the middle of the week!'

When the clock struck eight, Mrs Henry was seized with panic. Suppose she had been fool enough to give her the five dollars! She had no idea where the girl lived, she knew nothing about her, she would just have disappeared like that with her five dollars.

Mrs Henry now wanted to phone Matilda's Corner Police Station and report an attempted robbery.

The roll call revealed twelve absences. Praise be, sighed the teacher, God forgive my thoughts. But see my trial if all fifty-five of them turn up here one morning. And thank you, Jesus, Carlton didn't find his way to school today again (forgive me, Lord). He must be in the Plaza begging five cents, or his mother must be catch him up there yesterday and break his foot (I not wishing it on him, Lord).

But where is Maxine?

Maxine was very rarely absent, or late. She always arrived shining clean, her hair neat, her uniform well ironed, although it had long lost its colour. Maxine with a wisdom beyond her years. She was bright, bright, and would learn rapidly, if there was more time to teach her.

Yesterday Maxine had inquired of the teacher whether there was any way she could turn into a boy.

It was because the Baby-Father had said to her mother that the Last One still didn't look much like him, so he wasn't bringing one cent more, she could get his father to support him, and furthermore he wasn't bringing a cent more for Audrey either, though he wouldn't say it wasn't his pickney, but God strike him dead if he was going raise any gal-pickney, for gal-pickney grow into woman, and woman is a curse, don't the Bible say so? All woman bad like Satan.

So Maxine wanted to turn into a boy as soon as possible.

Afterwards, Miss Williams had gone into the Principal's office and looked into the records, just to make sure. But she was not mistaken, Maxine's date of birth made her seven years at her last birthday.

Where was Maxine today? The teacher felt a vague uneasiness. Then her heart sank, oh God! Suppose . . .

Maxine had related to her how the Baby-Father had tried to box her mother (Maxine wasn't too sure why), and how when she picked up the kitchen knife he left, swearing he would bring the police for her.

The father of Maxine, Donovan and Junie had posted his guard at the gate, as usual, for it was the last day of the month. But the boy had not yet raised the alarm. Almost two hours and his spar Nelson was still on standby, ready to take over his domino hand for him when he would have to make a hasty exit.

There had been one false alarm. Out of the corner of his

eye he had seen the little boy coming into the yard and had sprung up from the bench – dominoes flying left and right – reached round the side of the house and dived into Wally's room. But David had only come in to use the toilet.

Malcolm was beginning to relax – maybe the miserable woman wasn't coming this month to hold out her hand. How was a man supposed to feed himself and *three* pickney out of what he got at the end of the month? He had told her to give the children to the Government, and that was final. Let the Government feed them, they had money to buy thousand-dollar suit from England for the Governor-General, so they must can feed the pickney them.

Presently David came back into the yard, reported that the Baby-Mother was still nowhere in sight, and collected his ten cents.

It was dark now, she never came this late. Nice, thought Malcolm. She must be decide to rest me. She must be decide to carry the pickney them go give the Government.

Cho, she no just haffe box-down one of them, break them hand, for police to come charge her for ill-treatment and carry-way the whole of them?

The landlord arrived, punctual as doom. The tenants paid, or tendered their excuses, and Mr James was waiting for Inez. It was seven o'clock and none of the tenants had any idea where she was. The room was empty, and not a single one of her children was to be seen either. The yard neighbour who kept an eye on them in the daytime had not seen them all day.

Inez owed three months' rent. The door of the room was not locked. Mr James opened it and stood, dejected, looking in. He shook his head wrily. It was a detestable business, what he was going to have to do. For if he didn't, his wife would come down and personally carry out the operation, and then it would be even more unpleasant.

Mrs James had no use for sluttish women who spent their lives breeding bastard children and then expected you to feel sorry for them when they couldn't pay their debts. She was always willing to teach them a lesson.

He was all for selling the damn properties so he would never have to walk into a tenement yard again, stepping over dusty, snotty children to confront the stone-faced hostility of their parents. He would gladly sell all the properties. But over her dead body.

Now once again they were going to have to evict, seize . . . seize what? The Klim tin sitting smoky and awry in the dead coals? The low, lumpy bed wth the deep well in the middle?

He wished with all his might that Inez could come through the gate this very minute, bringing even part of the rent; then he could give her some more time – Mrs James might not object to that. Otherwise . . . it was a scene which he had never got used to; each time made him years older. A shouting swearing woman, her children screaming, crashing of kitchen utensils, crowd gathering, police . . .

The nurse on her way out noticed the same silent knot of children still sitting on the bench. The waiting room was nearly empty now, most of the day's crowd had been seen to, there were not many numbers left.

She stepped back and went over to them. The younger ones drew closer round the girl who sat clutching a paper bag and an empty rum bottle.

'Where is your mother?'

'She soon come, ma'am,' said the girl, without conviction.

'You have a number? One of you sick?'

'No, ma'am.'

'Then what you doing here?'

The children stared, mute. Maxine lowered her eyes.

'Don' know, ma'am,' she whispered.

The nurses fed them, bought them ice-cream, put the two youngest ones to sleep on an examining table.

When the police came, Nurse Johnson asked one of the officers what they were going to do. He threw her a glance of part weariness and part scorn as though she had asked a naïve and unnecessary question.

'Look for the mother, ma'am,' he explained in a long-suffering voice, 'and charge her with abandonment.'

The dogs had been barking at the edge of the gully for a full hour, an ominous, nerve-racking sound, for it echoed down the gully and from the caves on the other side.

But now there seemed to be another noise that chilled your spine – a long scream or a baby crying; and now it was all the dogs in the neighbourhood barking, shrieking at the edge of the gully.

Mrs Campbell pulled in her children, locked the doors and the windows, and sent the maid down to the gully to look.

The maid flew back holding her head and screaming. Before she reached the house, Mrs Campbell was on the phone to the police.

She lay on the bottom of the gully, face downwards. The Last One lay cosy in the crook of her dead arm, but he was crying now because his bottle had rolled away from him, his bottle of corn meal and water.

Marcus Aurelius and the Transatlantic *Baakoo*
ABDUR-RAHMAN SLADE HOPKINSON

I'll always remember him as a spoiler. Let me try to tell you what he spoiled.

It was a Saturday afternoon. The sun was hot, the sun was singing; and the light went bouncing off the white sand of the beach and off the limestone houses and the houses with plaster walls that were painted in a pale cream. On its way in from the deep to the beach, the sea played an ascending colour scale. Far out, it was a deep blue that was almost black, then it was cobalt blue, then that lovely blue-blue-green, then a sparkling green-blue-green, then green, and then it pushed itself up the beach in a long, loose, tumbling curl of white foam. The sea breeze sliced the foam from the tops of the waves; and the foam flew through the air, a salt, horizontal drizzle, and it sprayed the trunks of the casuarina trees behind our house.

Monty, Pomp and Fish-Head were bobbing up and down in the sea, and pelting each other with a hard, red rubber ball. We called that game 'cork-sticking', and it could be played on land or in the water. I put aside the water-colour I had been working on. I wanted to be out there with them. I owed Fish-Head one, for clouting me that morning on my ear with the ball when I wasn't even expecting anything. 'Heh heh heh!' laughed Fish-Head. 'You get a bitch-lick, though!' But Mummy told me to stay inside and help her get ready for the guest. That man really spoiled things.

He arrived at about half past one, from the airport, in a

taxi. A halo of gloom slipped out of the taxi with him and accompanied him up our front step and into our living room, and hung over his head as he collapsed on the sofa. The halo was invisible, as people say, but I could see it. Mummy taught me to see the halo that everybody carries over his head. She used to say, 'Boy-ee, always look out for a gloomy halo. Be careful of gloomy people.'

'Why, Mummy?' I would ask her.

'Because they are ungrateful. The good Lord gives us so many gifts.'

The taxi driver brought the two suitcases up the front step, plunked them down in the doorway, collected his fare from the man, and left eagerly, as if he was running away from something. Maybe he too had seen the halo. I carried the suitcases through the house and out through the kitchen door and into the cottage. Then I came back and asked Mummy if it was all right for me to go and play now.

'Stay a bit,' she said. 'Please. This is Mr Marcus Aurelius Roopsingh.'

'Call me Marcus Aurelius, ma'am,' he said, and hung his head.

Spoiler. He sank into the sofa with the great weight of his tiredness and gloom. He was a tall man with narrow shoulders and a heavy belly that sloped away from him, so that he could rest his hands on it, even when he was standing up. He had a tiny mouth; and its left corner twitched constantly, and at the same time his head would give a tiny jerk, as if he were bothered by a fly. Two thin fringes of straight grey hair fell away from the parting, which he placed a little off-centre to the left. And over his head hung this huge, black, invisible halo of gloom. I was already seeing a cartoon drawing of him forming in my head.

'Would you like to have lunch now, Mr Roopsingh?' Mummy asked him.

'Marcus Aurelius, ma'am,' he said. 'I'm so tired. No, thank you. So tired.'

'Go take a nap, then,' said Mummy. 'You're our first guest for the season. It's very quiet in the cottage. You can have lunch later. Then Boy-ee here can take you down to the beach; maybe you two can go for a swim.' She stared at me out of the corner of her eye, and that meant, 'I hope you heard what I said.'

'Can't swim,' groaned Mr Roopsingh. 'Sink! Can only bathe. Can only wash.'

'Then Boy-ee will swim,' said Mummy, 'and you will wash. Now, you must go and rest.'

Mr Roopsingh rose shakily, mouth twitching, head jerking. I led him down the long corridor and through the pantry and the kitchen and out through the kitchen door. In his correspondence with Mummy he had said that he wanted 'rest' above all, and Mummy had prepared the cottage in the backyard for him.

Mummy would not let me go and join the boys, even after Mr Roopsingh had gone to rest. 'I may need you,' she said. 'That man is a little strange, don't you see?'

I went and sat on the back veranda, in a rocking chair. Way down the beach, I could see Monty, Pomp and Fish-Head still in the sea, taking turns at slinging the ball at each other, flat over the water. The ball would ricochet off the water, often scoring a direct hit on the head or chest of one of the boys.

I put two fingers between my lips and whistled at them. From the backyard a hoarse, tormented voice cried, 'O me Gad! Wha' is dah?' I ran to the end of the veranda, from where I could see the cottage. Mr Roopsingh stood at the bedroom window in store-new, bright orange pyjama pants, but naked from the waist up. His chest was heaving, and he turned his head jerkily from left to right, from right to left, like a startled owl.

'Wha' whistlin' so?' he gasped.

'It's only me,' I said. 'Just calling to my friends down the beach.'

It was mid-afternoon before he came over to the main house for his lunch. I was getting angrier and angrier. I had sworn to myself that I would get that Fish-Head before the sun went down. But Mummy insisted that I had to wait and see if Mr Roopsingh wanted me to take him for a sea bath.

Mummy and I sat with him while he doodled with the fork in his plate of stewed red-fish, and boiled breadfruit and yam.

'You look upset, Mr Roopsingh,' said Mummy, adding, 'if you don't mind my saying so.'

'If I only tell you,' answered Mr Roopsingh. He spoke correctly most of the time; but when he got really excited, his speech would go broad and flat, and would let go some of its grammar. 'I need rest bad-bad. You-all got *baakoo* on this island?'

'*Baakoo*?' asked Mummy innocently, her glasses hanging low on her nose.

'Let me tell you,' said Mr Roopsingh. 'Back in Guyana. My neighbour, Mr Granger. Everybody-in-town say that how Mr Granger got this spirit, a *baakoo*, how he does keep it corked down tight in a green bottle that he got buried in the yard under the sour-sop tree. This *baakoo* pass down from father to son to grandson. It look like a little-little man, 'bout five inches tall, with a old, old face: that is, if it let you see it; but most of the time it stay invisible. And you best don't let it get out of that bottle! If it only get out – trouble!'

'What kind of trouble, Mr Roopsingh?' I asked.

'Let me tell you,' he answered. 'One afternoon I see this green bottle on my front step, and something about it tell me it was the *baakoo* bottle. I was 'fraid to touch it, but I was more 'fraid to leave it there. I know Granger must-be put it on my front step for it to take a liking to me, so he could-a get rid of it. I pick up the bottle careful, and I go to the fence and I call Granger and I tell him to take back his bottle, as I had no use for it. I don't mind telling you: I was trembling, like a leaf in a storm. Granger shake he bald head and say is not he bottle. I was trembling so bad that I drop the bottle, and it fall on a stone and break. Lord, Lord!'

The left corner of his tiny mouth was twitching. A few drops of gravy dribbled from his lip.

'What happened?' asked Mummy, trying hard not to smile.

'Ever since that afternoon – no peace! Stones pelting me house like war going on; and when I look outside, not a soul. Dishes tumbling down in the kitchen and breaking – and I know that nobody in the kitchen 'cause I does live by meself. Sometimes the electric bulb in my bedroom just start swinging. One morning I go in the kitchen and on the stove I see a pot of pepperpot that I certainly didn't cook. And as I looking at it, the pot tip itself over and spill everything on the floor. Sometimes at night I does hear one set of howling under my bed, like a dog when it see a ghost.'

His whole body shook, as if he had ague. 'I couldn't take it no more, Mrs Haynes! I lock up that house, and I come to Barbados for a rest. My nerves gone. Gone!'

He pushed his half-finished meal away from him. His head fell forward, and his chin rested on his chest. His halo got really dark. Mummy looked at me and made a small, crisp gesture with her head.

'All right, Mr Roopsingh,' I said to him. 'Let me take you for a sea bath.'

Our house stood on top of a rocky bluff. A short flight of steps, cut into the rock, led down to the stretch of beach below. A few minutes later I was helping Mr Roopsingh down the steps. I went down them ahead of him, and led him by the hand. His long, wide bathing trunks flapped around his belly and his knees.

Glancing down the beach, I saw quite a few people on the sand and in the water. But Monty, Pomp and Fish-Head had gone.

We walked a little way down the beach, and then I led him into the water. He entered it fearfully, on tiptoe. When the water reached as far as his knees, he squatted.

I had a vivid picture of myself catching Fish-Head in the sea, so that he could not run away (and if he submerged, I would wait until he came up for air), a picture of me slinging that hard, red rubber ball so that it skidded off the water, ducks-and-drakes style, and clomped Fish-Head on the side of his fish-head. But that would have to wait until the next day. Mr Marcus Aurelius Roopsingh had ruined my afternoon. Spoiler!

He was speaking to me. 'Guess what,' he said.

'What, Mr Roopsingh?'

'Tonight I am going to sleep well. I know it. For the first time in months. Guess why.'

'Why, Mr Roopsingh?'

'One thing about *baakoo*: it can't cross sea water. I safe in Barbados.'

The midnight sky was filled with the light of the full moon, which hung over our house with its ring of light like a double halo. The cottage where Mr Roopsingh slept looked pale grey in the moonlight; and it was framed by the tall, feathery casuarina trees, that were black against the light-filled sky. And the perfume of those flowers, the lady-of-the-night, drifted through the air; their scent was so beautiful, I was sure it could drive a person mad. Dear God! It was a tender, blessed moment: as if the world were showing me a great secret.

I crouched in the yard, near the back door of the cottage, a small pile of stones at my feet. I drank the moonlight; I sucked in the perfume of the lady-of-the-night; I was light-headed.

Reaching past my throat with my voice, right into the pit of my stomach, I fetched up such a howl that I frightened myself. And at the same time, using both hands, one after the other, I slung two stones over the cottage so that they fell on the galvanized iron roof from a good height. They made a terrible clatter as they struck the roof, rolled down its slope and fell to the ground. The peace and beauty of the night were shattered. Again I howled, again I lobbed two stones on to the roof, aiming for the spot above Mr Roopsingh's bedroom.

A window was flung open, and Mr Roopsingh stood at the window in the moonlight, in his orange pyjama trousers, naked from the waist up. He could not see me behind the clump of lady-of-the-night.

'The *baakoo*!' he screamed. 'The *baakoo*! The thing follow me. Mercy!'

I could not stop myself.

I howled, I lobbed stones. He leaned his upper body through the window and screamed.

Stone after stone. Stone after stone.

The kitchen door of the main house opened. Mummy called out, 'What in heaven's name is the matter with you, Mr Roopsingh?'

Slinging with my right arm, then immediately after with my left, I tossed the last two stones from my pile on top of the cottage.

'You see how the thing follow me?' screamed Mr Roopsingh. 'You see how this thing cross the Atlantic?' He was in utter terror.

I slithered away from the bush, crept low as a snake past the kitchen of the cottage, and behind the row of casuarina trees, and so by a long roundabout way till I stood below my own open bedroom window. I pulled myself up and over the window-sill, and crept into bed. The smell of the lady-of-the-night flooded into my room. I lay there, wondering whether Mummy would come to check on me in a few minutes, or whether she would wait until morning and challenge me then. Mummy could see right through my head – any time.

I could still hear Mr Roopsingh screaming.

I'm a Presbyterian, Mr Kramer
CLYDE HOSEIN

Leaving behind the fields of waving cane, Reginald Cor-
nelius Hassan came to the hogplums that lined the road at
the bend. He wheeled the Raleigh into the ditch, took the
notebook from his plastic lunch bag on the handlebar and
sat in the shade to read the tabulations pencilled in his
small handwriting.

He rolled down his sock and rubbed the ankle he had
broken years before when he had slipped in a soap pan
while measuring encrustments of lye and nigre.

The pain eased and he set off again, riding now through
coconut groves. The hot, moist salt blew through the
leaves, continuing the murmur of the sea. Soon the bay lay
on his left. Gulls and frigate birds cried as they circled
above fishermen who were pulling in their seine.

The road turned away from the shore and he was cycling
under golden laburnum.

'I'm a Presbyterian, Mr Kramer, and I'll have you know I
won't stand for this iniquity,' he said.

He passed the fields of experimental Bourbon cane, the
white bungalows with their tall hibiscus hedges, the Club
at the edge of Humboldt Park, and stopped at the
watchman's gatehouse at the picket fence. He breathed the
smells of tallow and copra and when he walked into the lab
it was fragrant with cedarwood oil and lavender that
spiced the lingering scents of acids.

He moved to his cubbyhole in the corner from which he
could see, across the courtyard, the accounts department
at the rear of the main building and beside it, like a doll's

house among the Honduras pines, the converted cottage, Kramer's office.

'Mr Hassan, Mr Hassan!' Betty hurried in with the gas-chromatographic analyses of the new rape oil. 'He telephoned already and asked me to come.'

'You're talking about a margarine expert, you know, from Head Office. They don't make joke about the quality of men they send from London, England.' Hassan's mind caught in the report before him. He reached out and took up the ringing phone.

'Hassan, my office is in a mess again. I need one of the girls to tidy up a bit. Ask Betty to come over.'

'Yes, Mr Kramer, I'll tell her,' said Hassan. He studied her wide hazel eyes. 'Yes, right away. She's right here, sir.' He put down the receiver.

Another young woman in a red-monogrammed Caribbean Oil lab coat came in. 'The soap chip reports, Mr Hassan,' Irma said.

'Mr Kramer wants you to come over and do a little tidying for him, Betty,' Hassan said.

The women looked at each other.

'I'm a bench chemist, Mr Hassan,' said Betty. 'I don't have to clean up Mr Kramer's office.'

Irma said, 'Mr Hassan, you don't know that man. I'm going to do my work, *oui*.'

They went back to their tasks. He turned to say something to them and saw the other lab assistants huddled in the spectroscope room.

'You women have nothing to do?' As they dispersed, his mind went back to Ayesha's words and her bruises when she had left the lab the month before. He contemplated the panelled door of the shimmering white office. He imagined Rudolf Kramer behind that door at his mahogany desk, surrounded by photographs of his war exploits, waiting for Betty.

'Nonsense!' he called out. 'This man infiltrated the

95

German lines. The High Command was so thankful for the information he got that they decorated him.' As if matching his mood, the sun went behind a cloud. He saw Nandram Lalsingh peering through the window in the accounts department. Hassan said, 'You girls have an imagination, you hear.'

The phone rang.

'Yes, Mr Kramer, I told her,' he said in a lower voice. 'Very well, sir, I'll tell her again, sir.'

He exploded. 'Betty, you go over to that man's office right away. I don't want him calling me again.'

Softly, Betty began to cry. She groped between the benches and sat on the stool beside him. 'Mr Hassan, I'm not feeling well this morning, and this man Kramer is such a ruffian and a brute.' She covered her face with her hands. 'I can't have sex with him this morning.'

His face went null. He watched the jack spaniards bristle upon their nest waxed to an eave lath. Lalsingh moved nearer to the window.

'And worst of all, Mr Hassan,' Betty went on, 'he gives us only five dollars for it.'

Sunlight rippled upon the fields, swept over the factory and across the courtyard, where Mr Hewett and his uniformed chauffeur were walking towards the main office. Betty shut her eyes and touched her throat. 'Ask Irma! Ask Ruth! Ask Devaki!'

Hassan watched Kramer lock his office and stand among the pines, in which cicadas called for rain. 'Don't cry, don't cry,' Hassan said as gently as he could. Kramer got into his Jaguar and sped towards the Club.

All morning Hassan expected Kramer's temper tantrum. At last he said, 'Why should I allow a man of no moral rectitude whatever to distress me?'

At twelve the women went to the commissariat. In his cubbyhole, Hassan brooded as he ate his corned beef and rice. He remembered Mr W. S. Fisher, Kramer's predecessor, the pioneer of Green Palm soaps and founder of the cricket team. *There* was a gentleman.

Advancing from the stairs, a flurry of white and blond hair and beard, red and wild-eyed, Kramer said, 'When I give an order I expect it to be carried out.' He strode between the benches as if he would smash the tallow test apparatuses. 'Carried out at once!' He slapped his palm on the bench, sending the lunch bag skating by the enamel carrier from which Hassan ate.

Hassan leapt from his stool and stepped back. 'I did what you asked, if you mean that message for Betty.'

'You damned well know what I mean! As soon as she comes from lunch, send her down!'

Hassan said, 'I'm a Presbyterian, Mr Kramer, and I won't stand for this iniquity.' The sound of his voice seemed inadequate and, even as he prepared to speak again, he wondered if he should.

Kramer, who had begun to walk away, turned. 'What did you say?'

'I said you can't come here with your ungodly ways and take advantage of these women. I'm a Presbyterian and we have our duty to perform, I'll have you know.'

'Little man, know your place,' Kramer said. 'Don't look for trouble.'

When Betty came back from lunch, Hassan told her, 'Mr Kramer said it's either you come to his office or be fired.' She packed her bag and went home for good.

He was cycling towards a flaming sky that sprayed amber light upon the sea, the coconut palms, and the fishermen in their wayside stalls. Crushed canes that had spilled from tractor-trailers and black cylinders of dried laburnum pods broke the cycle's hum: retribution, retribution, retribution. He had seen nothing but trouble since the day he had answered back. Weeks of Kramer's importunate demands had taxed his thoughts, his time and his hands.

And today, a sign of danger. Mr Hewett behind his desk, thin-haired, damp-eyed, speaking as to a son. 'You've done a good job here, Hassan, I'm well aware of that, but this report by Mr Kramer is just not good enough. That whole batch of soap could have been ruined.'

Now the sky darkened as Hassan neared the town. On the main road that he remembered as a track between crumbling workers' barracks, he suspended his reflections in order to steer between parked taxis and bullock carts filled with grass.

He could hardly eat. He went to his back garden and sat on his hunkers under the cocoa-orange tree. His wife came to the bay sapling and called but he did not answer. His sons and other barefoot boys were playing 'Stick 'em up' in the light of the full moon. 'Carefree,' he said after their wild shouts. Kramer again weighed upon him: 'Such a lying, vain, ungodly man,' he said. 'Accusing *me* of producing an unstable soap.'

He could not sleep. He rose and paced the dining room in which, at the frosted casement window, his little bed was set. His mother had died on it and it had stayed there where her body had been laid out. 'Such a lying, vain, ungodly man,' he said again and went out to the gallery, still in his merino and cotton sliders, and watched the clouded sun bring a grey dawn.

Two hundred and seventeen: he counted the pedal strokes to the hogplums. Like the semp that flew up from the carpet of quailed fruit, his mind soared to thoughts of his margarine research: he was trying to extract an essential oil from local botanicals that would replace butyric acid; work would suppress worry.

The factory whistle went at seven when Hassan, on his perch under the fluorescent lamps, tackled the production reports on the glyceryl esters and, when the women came running out of the rain, he had the charts ready for Kramer.

'Like you sleep here last night, Mr Hassan?' Devaki

asked. He smiled at her joke and assigned their tasks.

His thoughts were clear, his mind sharp. He spared no effort – instructing, encouraging, cross-checking as they worked. Then he turned his attention to the essential oil research, keeping Kramer's smile in front of him as he tested, observed, and wrote in his notebook. He broke off and was listening to the rain beat upon the roof, when he saw Kramer step from the Jaguar and open his umbrella. Hassan followed him to his office.

Kramer had unlocked the door and was pulling open the burgundy drapes. Hassan stood on the steps.

'What do you want, Hassan?'

Hassan ignored the menace in the tone. 'It's about cleaning your office, Mr Kramer.'

'Well, what about it?' Kramer lit the pipe and turned steel eyes upon Hassan.

The back of his shirt soaked, Hassan took a step inside. 'Sir, I am a man of peace. If your office needs cleaning, let me do it.'

Through the door he could see into the back room: the chenille spread flung on the bed, pistols hanging from a wooden plaque, a framed document.

'Come, let me show you something,' Kramer said. He seemed to gnash his teeth as he beckoned Hassan to the photographs on the wall behind his desk. 'Who is this man?'

'It looks like you, sir.'

'Very perspicacious, yes indeed, for a man on a yellow-dog contract wanting to do housekeeping. 1943, in Belgium. I killed a man with my bare hands the night that picture was taken.' Kramer locked his hands together. He seized Hassan's arm and led him closer to the wall.

'In those three years after I was dropped behind German lines I was a miner,' he tapped a photograph in the last row, 'and, here, a boxer.' He smiled at Hassan and then shouted in German or Dutch.

'And this is Canada – Camp X, an Allied installation, where men of a dying breed made this world safe for people like you. And who is this?'

'Winston Churchill, sir; a fine man,' Hassan said, seeing in Kramer's eyes evidence of capture, torture, imprisonment. 'A great man, and you shook his hand. What a privilege, sir!'

'And this my uncle, your chairman, the very ruthless Baron Stephan Dieter von Humboldt.' Kramer picked up his wet umbrella and whacked the desk. 'So, you see, I can do no wrong.' He swept his arm over the scattered files and magazines towards the rest room. 'No, Hassan, this is woman's work.'

Hassan's shoulders sagged; he walked back to the lab in the pelting rain. 'Reggie boy, dog eat your supper, *crapaud* smoke your pipe and dust take your ashes.'

He smiled at Irma, Devaki and Ruth who had turned together to read his face. When he got to his stool he saw the eyes at the accounts department window.

'Lalsingh,' he shouted, 'don't you have anything better to do! You, you spy!'

The next day, just before lunch, Lalsingh came into the lab. 'Ai, Reggie man, somebody troubling you or what?' He carried his tea in a rum bottle. 'I getting pressure too; don't think it's you alone. Bring your bag and come, man.'

They walked along the side of the factory and through the gully of Bermuda grass to Humboldt Park. They crossed the green field and the still-damp cricket pitch and sat on the rain-washed roller in front of the grandstand.

'These people don't care for us,' Lalsingh said. Hassan was reminded of a rat, thin whiskers espaliered against the curve of lip and cheek. He dipped his spoon into the saltfish and potatoes and examined the ground that was corkscrewed with earthworms' castings.

'A man like you,' Lalsingh said, 'with an external degree and everything; a man working hard, hard, day and night.

And what do you get my friend? A kick in the arse. Every damn day, kicks.'

'I like work,' Hassan said.

'We should help one another.'

'The wrath of the Lord shall be upon him,' Hassan said.

He spent the whole afternoon in the production meeting over which Kramer presided.

It was twilight when the meeting ended. Kramer, the production managers, the engineer, and the operations co-ordinator went to their cars and drove away towards the Club. Shrieking birds filled the royal blue sky.

Hassan locked up and went to the Raleigh that leaned against a corner of the lab. He lit the Silver King kerosene lamp.

The watchman came out of the gatehouse and held up his arm. Hassan pressed the brake lever and put his foot to the ground.

Before he could protest, the man lifted the lunch bag from the handlebar.

'What's wrong?' asked Hassan.

The man unzipped the bag and held it open. 'Ai, ai, ai, what is this here, man?'

Hassan flinched from the man's breath. 'I don't know how that got in there.' Between his enamel carrier and his notebook were two bars of soap.

The watchman laughed, 'Go ahead,' he said. He re-zipped the bag. 'Go ahead, man.'

Hassan pumped the pedals as hard as he could. When he passed the lighted bungalows he stopped and flung the soap far into a field.

As soon as he got home he went to the toolroom under his house. He took the cutlass and split the pitch-pine block into tablets like bars of soap.

Whenever a car stopped, he looked out at the road, expecting to see the police. Stars pinpricked the velvet sky.

*

'You're late, Mr Hassan,' the morning-shift watchman said and laughed.

Hassan put his lunch bag on the bench and saw Irma coming out of Kramer's office. Devaki said, 'Mr Hewett just ring. He ask me to tell you to come and see him as soon as you arrive.'

'All right,' he said and took down a clipboard but he could not focus on the words and figures. He looked for Lalsingh at the window. The phone rang.

Hewett asked, 'Didn't you get my message, Hassan?'

The women looked up as Hassan walked to the door and out into the hard light.

Hewett riffled some papers. Irma, sitting between Kramer and Lalsingh, hung her head.

'Well, Hassan,' Hewett began, 'there's another serious charge against you. Sit down, please.'

Hassan drew the Windsor chair to the edge of the carpet. 'Sir,' he said, 'I am a loyal employee of Caribbean Oil. For twenty-five years I've run my blood to water here, as you know. I'm a Presbyterian, sir, and I did not steal that soap. I don't know who put those bars in my bag. I'm not a thief, sir.'

'What's this?' Hewett sat forward, putting his elbows on the desk. 'I'm talking about Mr Kramer's complaint. He tells me that you've been going around telling staff – and God knows who else – that he's been having some, ah, sexual relationship with the girls from the laboratory.'

Hassan stared at Lalsingh; his heart beat faster and faster.

'It's true, sir. Ask the girls. Ask Irma!'

'Well, Irma?' Hewett turned to her.

'Sir, Mr Kramer never asked me to do anything like that.' She spoke to the floor.

Kramer drew a thumb and finger along a pleat of the drapes that hung behind him. 'Bill, if I may,' he said, 'I would suggest that this man be confronted with the exact words he has been using to defame my character.'

Lalsingh began to speak.

The pictures that swirled in Hassan's head brought their own words that smothered Lalsingh's voice and made it sound far away in the blurred room.

An image came to him of his grandfather, Pappy, he had called him, lined up with the other men and women outside the sugar factory, waiting the whole day for their pay.

'Lachmi Narain Hassan,' the driver of the gang of labourers called.

'Sah,' replied the old man. He stretched out his hand but the shilling dropped into the mud.

The picture of the bent old man, his weak eyes fixed to the ground, faded and Hassan saw that he was alone with Hewett who said, 'And what do you have to say for yourself?'

Hassan could not reply.

'Well then, Hassan, I'm very sorry but, in view of your silence and the evidence, I have to ask you to resign immediately or be dismissed.'

Hassan went to the lab and sat looking at the jack spaniards' nest and at the women busy at work as he composed the lines on a foolscap sheet.

He folded the letter and began to empty his drawer. He put his notebooks in the lunch bag and was filling a small box with his personal papers and toiletries when the watchman came to the doorway and said, 'Mr Kramer sent me to help you.'

'Tell Mr Kramer I don't need help.' Hassan picked up his bag and held the box in the crook of his arm.

'Good riddance,' he said on the stairs as he left the man behind.

He took the letter to the office and handed it and his keys to the accountant. The cheque was already prepared.

In the hall, he glanced at it: three months' salary. His mind grew darker.

He wheeled the Raleigh along the drive and through the gateway. 'Look out! Look out!' the tractor-trailer driver shouted and Hassan pulled the bike to the grass verge.

'A man from London, England,' he said, ignoring the driver's curses. 'A man who shook Churchill's hand.'

He felt the pressure in his thighs as he leaned into the wind and then he was flying under golden laburnum towards the dazzle of sand and sea.

•

My Mother

JAMAICA KINCAID

Immediately on wishing my mother dead and seeing the pain it caused her, I was sorry and cried so many tears that all the earth around me was drenched. Standing before my mother, I begged her forgiveness, and I begged so earnestly that she took pity on me, kissing my face and placing my head on her bosom to rest. Placing her arms around me, she drew my head closer and closer to her bosom, until finally I suffocated. I lay on her bosom, breathless, for a time uncountable, until one day, for a reason she has kept to herself, she shook me out and stood me under a tree and I started to breathe again. I cast a sharp glance at her and said to myself, 'So.' Instantly I grew my own bosoms, small mounds at first, leaving a small, soft place between them, where, if ever necessary, I could rest my own head. Between my mother and me now were the tears I had cried, and I gathered up some stones and banked them in so that they formed a small pond. The water in the pond was thick and black and poisonous, so that only unnamable invertebrates could live in it. My mother and I now watched each other carefully, always making sure to shower the other with words and deeds of love and affection.

I was sitting on my mother's bed trying to get a good look at myself. It was a large bed and it stood in the middle of a large, completely dark room. The room was completely dark because all the windows had been boarded up and all the crevices stuffed with black cloth. My mother lit some candles and the room burst into a pink-like, yellow-like glow. Looming over us, much larger than ourselves, were our shadows. We sat mesmerized because our shadows had made a place between themselves, as if they were making room for someone else. Nothing filled up the space between them, and the shadow of my mother sighed. The shadow of my mother danced around the room to a tune that my own shadow sang, and then they stopped. All along, our shadows had grown thick and thin, long and short, had fallen at every angle, as if they were controlled by the light of day. Suddenly my mother got up and blew out the candles and our shadows vanished. I continued to sit on the bed, trying to get a good look at myself.

My mother removed her clothes and covered thoroughly her skin with a thick gold-coloured oil, which had recently been rendered in a hot pan from the livers of reptiles with pouched throats. She grew plates of metal-coloured scales on her back, and light, when it collided with this surface, would shatter and collapse into tiny points. Her teeth now arranged themselves into rows that reached all the way back to her long white throat. She uncoiled her hair from her head and then removed her hair altogether. Taking her head into her large palms, she flattened it so that her eyes, which were by now ablaze, sat on top of her head and spun like two revolving balls. Then, making two lines on the soles of each foot, she divided her feet into crossroads. Silently, she had instructed me to follow her example, and now I too travelled along on my white underbelly, my tongue darting and flickering in the hot air. 'Look,' said my mother.

My mother and I were standing on the sea-bed side by side, my arms laced loosely around her waist, my head resting securely on her shoulder, as if I needed the support. To make sure she believed in my frailness I sighed occasionally – long soft sighs, the kind of sigh she had long ago taught me could evoke sympathy. In fact, how I really felt was invincible. I was no longer a child but I was not yet a woman. My skin had just blackened and cracked and fallen away and my new impregnable carapace had taken full hold. My nose had flattened; my hair curled in and stood out straight from my head simultaneously; my many rows of teeth in their retractable trays were in place. My mother and I wordlessly made an arrangement – I sent out my beautiful sighs, she received them; I leaned ever more heavily on her for support, she offered her shoulder, which shortly grew to the size of a thick plank. A long time passed, at the end of which I had hoped to see my mother permanently cemented to the sea-bed. My mother reached out to pass a hand over my head, a pacifying gesture, but I laughed and, with great agility, stepped aside. I let out a horrible roar, then a self-pitying whine. I had grown big, but my mother was bigger, and that would always be so. We walked to the Garden of Fruits and there ate to our hearts' satisfaction. We departed through the south-westerly gate, leaving as always, in our trail, small colonies of worms.

With my mother, I crossed, unwillingly, the valley. We saw a lamb grazing and when it heard our footsteps it paused and looked up at us. The lamb looked cross and miserable. I said to my mother, 'The lamb is cross and miserable. So would I be, too, if I had to live in a climate not suited to my nature.' My mother and I now entered the cave. It was the dark and cold cave. I felt something growing under my feet and I bent down to eat it. I stayed that way for years, bent over eating whatever I found growing under my feet. Eventually, I grew a special lens that would allow me to see in the darkest of darkness; eventually, I grew a special coat that kept me warm in the coldest of coldness. One day I saw my mother sitting on a rock. She said, 'What a strange expression you have on your face. So cross, so miserable, as if you were living in a climate not suited to your nature.' Laughing, she vanished. I dug a deep, deep hole. I built a beautiful house, a floorless house, over the deep, deep hole. I put in lattice windows, most favoured of windows by my mother, so perfect for looking out at people passing by without her being observed. I painted the house itself yellow, the windows green, colours I knew would please her. Standing just outside the door, I asked her to inspect the house. I said, 'Take a look. Tell me if it's to your satisfaction.' Laughing out of the corner of a mouth I could not see, she stepped inside. I stood just outside the door, listening carefully, hoping to hear her land with a thud at the bottom of the deep, deep hole. Instead, she walked up and down in every direction, even pounding her heel on the air. Coming outside to greet me, she said, 'It is an excellent house. I would be honoured to live in it,' and then vanished. I filled up the hole and burnt the house to the ground.

My mother has grown to an enormous height. I have grown to an enormous height also, but my mother's height is three times mine. Sometimes I cannot see from her breasts on up, so lost is she in the atmosphere. One day, seeing her sitting on the seashore, her hand reaching out in the deep to caress the belly of a striped fish as he swam through a place where two seas met, I glowed red with anger. For a while then I lived alone on the island where there were eight full moons and I adorned the face of each moon with expressions I had seen on my mother's face. All the expressions favoured me. I soon grew tired of living in this way and returned to my mother's side. I remained, though glowing red with anger, and my mother and I built houses on opposite banks of the dead pond. The dead pond lay between us; in it, only small invertebrates with poisonous lances lived. My mother behaved towards them as if she had suddenly found herself in the same room with relatives we had long since risen above. I cherished their presence and gave them names. Still I missed my mother's close company and cried constantly for her, but at the end of each day when I saw her return to her house, incredible and great deeds in her wake, each of them singing loudly her praises, I glowed and glowed again, red with anger. Eventually, I wore myself out and sank into a deep, deep sleep, the only dreamless sleep I have ever had.

One day my mother packed my things in a grip and, taking me by the hand, walked me to the jetty, placed me on board a boat, in care of the captain. My mother, while caressing my chin and cheeks, said some words of comfort to me because we had never been apart before. She kissed me on the forehead and turned and walked away. I cried so much my chest heaved up and down, my whole body shook at the sight of her back turned toward me, as if I had never seen her back turned toward me before. I started to make plans to get off the boat, but when I saw that the boat was encased in a large green bottle, as if it were about to decorate a mantelpiece, I fell asleep, until I reached my destination, the new island. When the boat stopped, I got off and I saw a woman with feet exactly like mine, especially around the arch of the instep. Even though the face was completely different from what I was used to, I recognized this woman as my mother. We greeted each other at first with great caution and politeness, but as we walked along, our steps became one, and as we talked, our voices became one voice, and we were in complete union in every other way. What peace came over me then, for I could not see where she left off and I began, or where I left off and she began.

My mother and I walk through the rooms of her house. Every crack in the floor holds a significant event: here, an apparently healthy young man suddenly dropped dead; here a young woman defied her father and, while riding her bicycle to the forbidden lovers' meeting place, fell down a precipice, remaining a cripple for the rest of a very long life. My mother and I find this a beautiful house. The rooms are large and empty, opening on to each other, waiting for people and things to fill them up. Our white muslin skirts billow up around our ankles, our hair hangs straight down our backs as our arms hang straight at our sides. I fit perfectly in the crook of my mother's arm, on the curve of her back, in the hollow of her stomach. We eat from the same bowl, drink from the same cup; when we sleep, our heads rest on the same pillow. As we walk through the rooms, we merge and separate, merge and separate; soon we shall enter the final stage of our evolution.

The fishermen are coming in from sea; their catch is bountiful, my mother has seen to that. As the waves plop, plop against each other, the fishermen are happy that the sea is calm. My mother points out the fishermen to me, their contentment is a source of my contentment. I am sitting in my mother's enormous lap. Sometimes I sit on a mat she has made for me from her hair. The lime trees are weighed down with limes – I have already perfumed myself with their blossoms. A humming-bird has nested on my stomach, a sign of my fertileness. My mother and I live in a bower made from flowers whose petals are imperishable. There is the silvery blue of the sea, criss-crossed with sharp darts of light, there is the warm rain falling on the clumps of castor bush, there is the small lamb bounding across the pasture, there is the soft ground welcoming the soles of my pink feet. It is in this way my mother and I have lived for a long time now.

The Coming of Org – A Prologue
JOHN ROBERT LEE

for Roderick Walcott

After midnight mass Papa's yard would be bright with
lanterns and flambeaus and warmed by the blazing fire
over which a huge pot of meat was stewing. The women
with their many coloured madras worn like crowns would
be busy loading the table in the middle of the front room of
the house with bottles of sorrel and ginger beer and rum
and whisky. At this time of year, no self-respecting family
was without plenty for neighbours and visitors. As for the
children, they would be out of bed and in the way of
everyone. The musicians would be settling themselves in a
corner of the house; then, in their own good time, the
chantwelle and the musicians would begin to sing the songs
of the Christmas season and of the flower societies and
soon the people would begin to call out 'Vive la Rose!'
because they belonged to the society of la Rose and they
had always been loyal to the Roses. They would respond
to the chantwelle's sung challenges to the rival society of la
Marguerite with fervour and with joyous shouts of
triumph. Vive la Rose! And they would dance the old
dances until they were hungry. And later they would all
gather around the wooden steps that led down into the
yard and everyone would grow quieter as the violon wailed
sweetly and sadly. And as they gazed into the leaping
flames of the wood fire, deep within them the music would
make their hearts soft and yearning for what they couldn't
say. Then Mama would call to Papa who sat among the
musicians with the shac-shac on his lap: 'Eh bien, Papa,
when you was youth, you had hear your grand papa talk

about when Ti Jean had leave the home of his mother and go and look for his brothers and had to swim the big sea?' and everyone would call to Papa, 'Oui, oui, Papa, quittez l'histoire dit,' let the story tell, and they would sit even nearer together. Papa would say, with a wide grin and a tremendous flourish of the long shac-shac: 'Eh bien, Messieurs mesdames, e dit kreek' and they would shout happily into the night, 'Krak!' and for the next few hours before daybreak the old contes and songs, the stories and histories of these ancient scattered people would fill the small dirt yard. Ti Jean and his adversaries, Compere Lapin and his tricks, the real history of the village and its long dead characters, familiar spirits of good and evil, they all would move among the shadows that lurked outside the edges of the protecting firelight. The children, now afraid to go to sleep, would move closer the skirts of their mothers and sisters as *boloms* and *soucouyants* and cloven-footed old men of dark forests shrieked and screeched and howled outside the hibiscus and croton hedges that encircled the yard.

At another festival once, they had heard a stranger, a wandering drum-maker, tell of one he called Org. He had spoken suddenly from his dark corner and when the people expressed ignorance, no one had heard speak of Org, he had gone on to talk intensely and in a low sharp-edged voice of this mysterious person: it was certain that everyone had to meet him some day.

'Ah, Org, c'est Basil,' someone said confidently.

'Non, is not Basil, is not la mort. But a man can die when he meet Org. Man, woman or child can see Org. Mais no one else see him but you. When a man meet Org, that man can die or he can disappear. Org does make a man change. Some get better. Some get worse. Non! Org not God or the Saviour or the Devil! But Org can appear a beast, Org can be creature, or Org can be human being.'

'M'sieu, ou ka parler bêtise! Is stupidness you talking!'

'Listen!' The stranger ignored the interruption. 'Org can live around a man all his life. Org can be part of your living. You, all your life, see this other person. A person as far as you knowing, with a life, a family, a job, *toute bagai*, everything. But one day, you will discover that is only you ever know this person. One day you will know, you will not guess, you will know this is Org. Appearing in front of you. And you will never be the same!'

The people were silent. The night was full of the snapping fire, the cracking wood, the smell of stewed meat, the insistent cacophany of all the insect sounds and the far off barking, barking, ceaseless barking of someone's dog. The people wanted to be nearer to each other, but Org stood between them.

Finally a voice said, a little too loudly: 'M'sieu Tambou, Mister drum-maker, peut-être c'est ou qui c'est Org-là. Maybe it is you who is Org?'

The people laughed. Several comments were heard. Papa called the stranger to come and get some rum and some more meat. The short, fat red-skin man came forward into the light, fixing his hat on to his head and looking slyly at everyone, with his large protruding eyes. Then everyone wanted something to eat or drink and soon they were beginning to leave for their nearby homes as the dark night slowly began to turn purple and dawn lit the tops of the humped hills.

They never saw that stranger again, but the new spirit of Org had arisen out of their hearts to take his place among the other heroes of this dispersion. Who he was, no one could say exactly, but the mystery of him made young and old a little more thoughtful in their lives.

Each man who heard the story of Org knew it was truth. A great private question was answered that had brooded unasked in his spirit. He began to look for the coming of Org. He understood better now the strangeness that had come upon many of them for many generations. God, the

Saviour, the Devil and Death were known and respected. But Org? Who really was he? An answer out of a dark abyss at the bottom of which growled and snarled the unknown statement of their deepest troublings. So familiar and yet so mysterious. Mysterious as he was, or perhaps because his mystery was his power, he established a firm rule over the festival fires and the moonlit yards and the wakes for their dead.

Tison closed the door of the apartment quietly. He stood on the third storey veranda looking up at the stars. Over the roofs opposite he could see the lights of ships and small yachts in the harbour. He watched the lighthouse beam flash regularly into the distant clouds. It was about one o'clock. Except for the occasional car or distant barking dog, it was quiet. Below, the street was deserted.

Tison felt good. Marcia was snoring softly when he slipped out. A short note to say he loved her, a kiss on the closed eyes. Yes, that was the way to treat woman. Treat them good. Love them good. With little gifts, little notes, little surprises, a man kept a woman under control. Yes. It was an art. He felt proud that he had taught himself well.

He wasn't ready yet to go to the small comfortable house he rented just outside the town. It was still early. He would go up to the ghetto yard a couple streets away where there would be people and reggae music and good herb. And maybe that Rasta daughter he had been keeping his eyes on would be there. He felt in the mood for that kind of company. Tonight he felt sharp and in control. Yes, Tison felt good.

He moved quickly now, happily, down the several flights of stairs and into the street. In the cool night, he tucked himself warmly into his tight dark-blue denim jeans and jacket, pulled his closed-neck sweater up around his throat, drew his red beret close over his hair, trying for the Ché Guevara effect. His high heels loud against the pavement gave him a feeling of power. His long slim legs made large strides past the small doll-like houses and the late-night bars. He tucked his hands deep into his pockets and glanced often at his smooth dark baby-faced handsomeness in the glass windows of the uptown stores.

The yard was off a narrow alleyway and as he turned into the alley from the main road he was hailed by the youths who lounged along its length. He was popular here. He played the music they liked on his afternoon radio programmes. The smell of herb was everywhere and several youths approached him with their small flat tins, offering the best of Colombian or Jamaican or local weed. He walked jauntily on toward the yard, humming the music of Bob Marley's latest album that played very loudly from a nearby house. He moved with the certain ease of a popular man, smiling at everyone and greeting many by name.

He turned to the right off the alleyway now, went through a high wooden gate between two houses and passed into the large enclosed yard. Several groups and individuals were scattered around. From a huge stereo speaker reggae dub music throbbed. Tison bought some joints from his favourite pusher, then settled near one of the groups to smoke and listen to their conversation. It was a mixed group of Rastamen and others and talk ranged from police brutality to the quality of the herb to the latest reggae tunes. Tison felt warm with sympathy for their causes. He enjoyed being here with them. He enjoyed their admiration.

He pulled deeply on his second joint and began to look around for the young Rasta girl. His feeling of well-being and self-satisfaction was increasing and he began to think that he would seek out the girl, buy enough herb and invite her up to his house.

He saw her sitting by herself on a small bench, her back against the high concrete wall that encircled the yard. Her eyes were closed, hands folded in her lap.

'Hail, daughter,' he said, settling near her, smiling.

She opened her eyes and turned slowly to look at him.

'Hail, man, Meester Dee Jay. Iree?' She smiled slowly and he thought how truly black and beautiful she was. Dimples were deep in her cheeks.

'Yes-I,' he drawled, offering one of the joints, lighting it with his small lighter.

'Thanks-I.' She did everything slowly and deliberately. A wave of tender emotion swept over him. She was nice.

She sucked on the joint appreciatively. 'Some good local in the yard tonight,' looking at the joint, holding in the smoke, and then, wreathed in smoke, 'Praise Jah.'

'Praise Jah, daughter,' leaning back against the wall, climbing with the herb to move in glowing, warm fantasies and visions, with her beautiful at the centre. He glanced through the sweet smoke at her face, strong, dark and beautiful under her red, gold and green tam, and began to think of how he could speak the invitation to his house. From where he sat, he could see her strong thighs and firm good legs thrust out from the bench and he wanted very much to stroke their black strong beauty.

She passed her joint to him and he could see her young firm breasts move freely under her bodice.

Tison began to talk about how he didn't like this Babylon city and in fact did she know that he was from the country he only came here to get the white man schooling and because he didn't like the shitstem that was why he lived outside the shitty, where it was like the country. Yes, he was roots. He described his fruit trees and told her about the ital vegetables growing in the kitchen garden of his landlady and how quiet and cool it was up there and how he enjoyed living by himself where he could smoke and meditate and read his Bible in private without anybody to disturb him. She must come and visit his yard sometime.

'Yes-I,' she agreed, she must do that sometime. Yes-I,

some herb, some ital, some music, that was all the I needed to praise Jah and live in inity and peace and love. Yes-I. Praise Jah.

She rolled some herb of her own and as they smoked again, him feeling most irey now, and speaking with great enthusiasm and joy, he said, as if suddenly inspired, Look, it was still early, why didn't they take a walk and go up to his house now, it wasn't far, he had his stereo, some tapes with his best patois programmes, plus Bob's latest LP, also he had ital food, they could cook a jot, and they could get some more herb, he had the dunza, so if she wanted, they could go up now.

She turned to him. Slow. She looked directly into his eyes, red now and heavy-lidded from the herb. He suddenly felt uncomfortable and terribly exposed. At the same time, he became very aware of a group of bare-headed Rastamen standing silently near them. And when she laughed, her teeth white in her dark face, he was certain she was mocking him.

'Another time, Meester Dee Jay man, not dis night.' Too quickly, he stammered something about it being all right, it was 'cool, cool, don't dig nutten'. And when one of the young Rastamen, hair long and thick around his head and shoulders came up to speak to her, ignoring him completely, he began to feel threatened. When she moved off with the Rastaman, not saying anything to him again, Tison felt as if the whole yard knew what had happened between him and the girl.

He sat by himself for a while, everything now falling rapidly into confusion, the heavy bass of the nearby music now unbearably loud and him whirling in his head feeling hurt, rejected, vexed with himself. He didn't want to smoke again, but he tried to keep a cool front and dragged on the joint in his slow, superior manner.

Tison left the yard when he felt enough time had passed. As he went by a group outside the gate, they laughed, and he was sure they were laughing at him. The alleyway was deserted now, except for the pushers watching everyone carefully who entered or left the yard. No one hailed him now. He put his head down and walked quickly towards the main road.

All his well-being was gone. The happy high had left him and he began to feel more and more afraid. It was the nameless fear of a bad trip. He recognized it. It seemed now as if everything he heard and saw was against him. Snippets of conversation seemed to be aimed at him. Signs all seemed to carry a message especially for him. Words leaped up from scraps of newspaper at his feet. Judgement was all around.

A cold sweat broke out over his body. His heart began to miss beats. The scene with the girl gnawed at his mind and was at the centre of his confused emotions. He tried achingly to find his way back to the earlier calm. Should he go back to Marcia's? He stopped on the sidewalk, feeling a great indecision. No, he only wanted to get home now. His home was safe and he could sleep off this bad high.

Tison took the road on the outskirts of town that would lead him directly home. It was a dark road, with street lamps at long intervals, not used much at this time of night. He was the only person on it now. But it was the shortest way home. He began to move quickly. He tried to focus his mind on something definite: he tried to go over his conversation with the girl, rationalizing that it wasn't as much of a rejection as he had at first imagined, that no one had really heard them and furthermore he was only inviting her to listen to some programmes. He saw her legs again, thrust out from the bench, smooth, firm and dark. He walked more briskly. Her laughter and her abrupt departure left him empty within, hurt and ashamed.

His mind felt like a deep hole into which everything was falling and he couldn't fix anything at all. He couldn't concentrate on anything. The irrational fear beat its way inside his stomach.

Tison was now about half-way up the road. At the approaching bend that turned on a small bridge it was the darkest part. After this it was well lit all the way to his house. He wanted to be inside it, the door shut behind him. He hurried toward the bridge, anxious to be past it. He fought off the paranoia that filled his head with frightening thoughts and made him stumble. A couple times he looked back to make sure no one was following him.

He let out a sharp, involuntary squeal when he heard the sudden noise out of the darkness ahead. He felt his hair crawl across his scalp. His heart lurched painfully and he stopped.

Demonic creatures of all shapes raced through his mind. The long-shut doors of childhood memory were flung open and all the ghosts of dark nights beyond fire-lit yards rushed out, screaming and cackling.

The sound came again, more loudly, more different from anything he had ever heard. Tison began to whimper in his throat for God. He knew he was utterly terrified. Part of his mind realized he was near the bridge, over the edge of which was a deep ravine. He broke wind. He groaned and trembled in the chill of his sweat. The girl's face and mocking laughter flashed clear before his eyes. The dreadlocks who had gone off with her was waiting with a cutlass near the bridge! That must be it! Why wasn't he more careful, he regretted with all his heart. And old women with the bodies of beasts and peeling skins chattered through his tortured consciousness.

Despairingly, he turned around to run fast. But suddenly a hand with claws that scratched his neck hard, took hold of the back of his collar and dragged him down. He knew he was screaming. He could not hear himself. He felt his body pressed against the edge of the stone bridge and then he was lifted and slammed a number of times on it until he lay terror-shocked and still. His head was over the ravine far below and he could hear the water of the small stream flowing through it. His face was cold. His teeth chattered uncontrollably. His face was wet with tears.

The hand with the claws pulled at him again, and somewhere behind it the terrifying noise had increased. He slumped over to lie on his back, his face to the stars and to the moonlight just now edging over the tall, dark, creaking bamboo trees.

Tison saw everything from a long way off now, far through the pain and the fears and the herb that still whirled around in his head and his stomach, far through the voices and absurd scenes clear in his eyes and the jingles from his radio shows.

In the whitening night he now saw over him (with a far, baffling incomprehension) one of the town's well-known derelicts, Fanto, naked as night, eyes wide and unseeing, spittle foaming at the mouth, straddling him, Tison, popular patois DJ; Fanto, slobbering and muttering incoherently, tearing at his throat with both hands, and from far away but still too close, with a strange and absolute clarity, Tison observed: in Fanto's face a horrible fullness of mad lust, fixed, no more man: beast, crazed, depraved utterly; he heard the mocking laughter of the girl again and saw her smooth black legs and he felt Fanto's tongue obscenely slaking his mouth; and he saw Marcia's face, eager, mouth open, eyes shut, labouring; and his whole soul and mind and body revolted and drew themselves together inside of him for one almighty puke but he could not move; and he felt Fanto tighten his legs around him all the time chattering through his dribbling, toothless mouth; and he saw the dimpled backside of Joan the pilot's wife and heard the giggling of Margaret the High School student and his mouth and nose and eyes and ears were filled with the stench and stink and slobbering and panting and wheezing of Fanto; and Tison remembered himself. And he screamed down through his soul for the horror of himself and when Fanto stretched frantically along his body and began to flail on him with his head and arms and legs and belly, Tison left it all far away and tried to die but he couldn't and he realized, at last, that he had met his Org.

Papa sat looking through the window into the yard, while Mama busied herself with breakfast. Papa watched his son pause over the fork he was pressing down with his foot into the small kitchen garden, and look up to the great mountain La Sorcière whose top was covered with mist today. The young man's locks were almost down to his shoulders now and as Mama stopped for a moment by her husband to look out at her son, she sighed again as she had so many times in the past months.

'But why the boy have to do that to himself, eh Papa, tell me. We sacrifice to give him a good schooling in town, he get a good job in town, everybody know him, and he leaving it to turn Rasta and come back here to say he diggin' garden.'

She sucked her teeth hard in annoyance.

'Eh, Papa. And you wouldn't speak to him. Make him stop that stupidness. Everybody saying he mad, is something they do him, a intelligent boy like that.'

Papa poured himself some water from the clay goblet. He drank deeply before he spoke.

'Mama, I tell you already. The boy not mad. Leave the boy.'

He looked out to where his son was turning the earth again.

'Is so it is when a man knowing himself. Not all reach man the same way.'

He leaned on the window and looked up to the top of the mountain.

'Some never reach. Some never reach.'

Mama sucked her teeth again and returned to the kitchen muttering. One of the children ran into the house crying and Papa lifted her up.

'OK, doodoo, what happen, eh?'

'Papa, Papa, brother say that if I don't go away from him and the others, he will call Org for me. I just want to play with them. But I 'fraid of Org, Papa.'

'Hush, doodoo, hush. Org won't take you. Hush.'

Papa looked out to where his son had just pushed the fork firmly into the ground and had flung his green shirt over his shoulder. He came to the window and told Papa that he was going up to the hills.

Papa watched him stride away on his long legs.

The child called out, 'Rasta, you not 'fraid Org take you when you go in the hills?' The young man did not turn around.

Papa said: 'Hush, child, hush.' Papa thought: My son meet Org already. Maybe now he going to meet God.

He held the child in his arms as Mama came out with a saucepan in her hand to stand by him and they watched their son move slowly down the path, go through the gate in the hibiscus hedge, the flowers bright red in the early light, and move toward the hills.

Fleurs

EARL LOVELACE

In the middle of the morning the stickfight drums began calling out to stickmen all over Cascadoux, in a grand terrible voice, so that in the Roman Catholic church acolytes at the mass found themselves moving in step with its deeper rhythm, and the drowsing old men awakened suddenly, startled by a voice they couldn't quite pin down and for the rest of the mass continued to gaze vaguely about the church as if to locate whoever it was that was calling their names.

After mass the fellows who usually spent Sunday mornings underneath the almond tree, playing rummy or shooting dice, were gone; and except for Piko crumpled drunkenly on the ground in front Loy's closed rum shop and Traveller pacing near the bus stop, his battered suitcase stuffed with old clothes and ancient newspapers, bound with tattered neckties and pieces of string, the Junction was deserted, as villagers returned from church. Walking behind her last two children, Fleurs' wife could feel her dress rustle and she felt the drums throbbing male and insistent inside her, quickening her heartbeat, making her feel a lofty dizziness and a victorious female surrender that made her remember the first time Fleurs took her in his arms and she looked up and saw how tall he was. For a moment her mind went back to that time and that tall Fleurs years ago, and she slowed down to hold the memory better; but, then, seeing her two children moving further and further from her, she quickened her step, deciding that it was better to leave that time behind her.

When she got home she saw Fleurs sitting on the back step, sharpening his cutlass, noting in the same eye-sweep the heaps of grass and weeds about the yard, and she chuckled, saying to the children, 'I wonder what *vaps* hit your father that make him decide to choose today to cutlass the grass?', when suddenly it hit her: What Fleurs doing home, when down at Nathan shop drums was beating? 'Fleurs?' But seeing the way his back was set and feeling the weight of the silence surrounding him, she stifled her question, thinking softly to herself, I better stay out his way this morning, making for the front instead of going through the back door as she had intended, calling out, 'Fleurs, we come back!', the grunt of his reply satisfying her that her assessment of his mood was correct.

He went on sharpening his cutlass, grating the three-cornered file smoothly along the edge of the blade, watching the blade's edge gleam with every sharpening, eroding stroke, watching the grated metal fall off in tiny flecks. He was thinking of the sharpening of the cutlass and how every stroke of the file that sharpened it eroded it, made it thinner. Usually when his cutlass was worn down from sharpening he would turn it into a knife. You could sharpen a cutlass down to a needle, down to nothing, he thought, plucking the edge of the blade with his thumb to test it for sharpness.

Satisfied with its sharpness, he moved into the yard; and, bending before the uncut grass, he drew back his arm and swept his lifted cutlass through the grass, his hand going around and around in long swinging arcs, the cutlass scything through the grass, the cut grass, swept up in the swing of the cutlass, flying around his head, making in the morning sunlight a dissolving halo of green cascading grass.

From down the hill he heard a shout and a greater blaze of drumming and he breathed in and out self-consciously to keep himself calm. Bango reach, he thought, pausing.

Bango, champion stickfighter, obeah man who nobody could defeat. Yes, is Bango who reach, hearing the deepened hush after the great shout and a new blaze of drumming, feeling a chill in his bones and a great wave, like fear, flow through him, through his belly and his knees and his ankles, and in his mind seeing Bango, with his black hat and his grey jacket, the grey of the feathers of a chicken hawk, and with that bird's blood-red eyes, stepping towards the *gayelle* with the shuffling gait of a dancer or a thief, his head moving from side to side and his two hands upraised, triumphant, as he gave his wide gold teeth grin and the crowd parted for him and the three women he always brought to the stickfights with him.

Behind him, shaking a *shac-shac* and holding aloft his 'bad' stick, the one mounted with the Amerindian spirit would be the usual one, the priestess, black, smooth, her red head-tie setting off her round face with its piercing eyes and high cheek bones. He tried to picture the other two. Last year, following her, with his other stick and a bottle of rum, was an Indian girl with a cricket cap on, delicate, loose, with the scent of violation and surrender about her, walking with a jaunty gladness as if she was proud to be counted as one of Bango's women; then, a tall one, a *travaseau*, a mix-up one, brown, smooth, slatternly, with careless languorous movements and a face without shame, one eye black and blue where Bango had recently cuffed her; this one, looking, as she swept long loose and sullen to the front of the *gayelle*, into every stickman's eyes, as if she had come to seek a hero and was parading herself as the prize. But the stickmen were afraid to look at her lest she stir them to the craziness it was to tackle Bango.

They wouldn't miss me yet, he thought. They would be watching Bango, with his women taking off his jacket and his Shango priestess woman spinning around and making a libation with the white rum before giving him the bottle to take a drink. Now with the rum in his belly he and his women would begin his chant and he would go into the ring with his own terrible leaping dance, slow and fast and tall, and out of his terrible blood-red eyes he would take all in, in the full ocean of his gaze, feeling their weight, their lightness, seeing the envy in their eyes, their fear, searching for the something that was missing among them. Let him look, Fleurs thought.

Fleurs' wife heard the noise from her kitchen, and she looked out and saw the grass flying to the sound of Fleurs' cutlassing, and she rattled the pots and pans, making a noise, hoping for his attention; but he didn't look in her direction. She had changed into home clothes and she called loudly to one of the children, so that Fleurs would hear, 'Go and ask your father if he want something to eat.'

The child came back saying, 'Pa don't want nothing.'

Still loudly, for Fleurs to hear, she said, 'What happen to your father? When I don't cook he does quarrel, when I cook he not eating.'

She went outside then, appeared before him with her moon face and her head tied with an old cotton dress, about her a kind of softness, the newness which she had come with from mass: 'What happen? You don't want nothing to eat? Whole morning you ain't eat nothing, you know!'

He looked at her sideways, 'Watch yourself there,' making a step backwards, flicking his cutlass expertly at the grass, 'I ain't hungry.'

She stood her ground, 'Fleurs, why you don't go and fight Bango? That is what you want to do, not so? Why you don't go?'

He glanced at her through the corners of his eyes, 'I want to fight Bango?'

'And that is what you do every year for the fifteen years I know you.'

'Well, I finish now. I done. Everybody in Cascadoux make friends with Bango, what I fighting Bango for? Ain't you yourself say that?'

'I say that?'

'Yes. You say that.' He paused, looking at her and seeing the hurt in her eyes. 'But is true. Is just that you say it. It don't matter who say it. Is true. All the stickmen make friends with Bango.'

'How I could say everybody make friends with Bango? Mr Joseph ain't make friends with Bango.'

'Mr Joseph is a old man. Mr Joseph can't fight Bango. He could talk, yes; but Mr Joseph can't fight Bango.'

'I didn't mean it so. I didn't mean that it don't have nobody at all. It still have fellars who does fight Bango. Ancil and Calloway and Johnny and the one they call Beast: they does fight Bango.'

'Ancil and Calloway and Johnny and Beast? Bango does fart on them.'

'What you getting vex for?'

'A set of impressionists, that is what they is: just giving a impression. They don't really want to fight. They want to make style. They want to look pretty.'

'And that is not what I saying, Fleurs? Is not the same thing I saying: they creating an impression and you killing yourself in the ring.'

'And you want me to go?' He began to cutlass again.

'Anyhow,' she said, 'they will send and call you. They will send Phipps to call you.'

'Phipps? Let Phipps come.'

'They will send Phipps to call you, Fleurs. And Phipps will come and call you and you will go.'

'I will go?'

She tried to put a smile on her face, 'You will go, Fleurs. Phipps will come up the hill with his big fat self, blowing, shouting loud loud, "Hold the dogs before they bite me. With this sugar in my blood, I can't take a dog bite, you know." He will say, "Fleurs, man, what the hell happen with you? Man, what the arse you think you doing? You don't hear the drums? You don't know that you is the onliest man in Cascadoux to fight Bango?'' He will come and make a big joke with you and give you a lotta talk and you will scratch your head and all your vexation will leave you, and you will go. You will go!'

'I will go?'

'Is fifteen years you doing it, Fleurs. People don't stop doing what they doing so long just so.'

'I will say, "Phipps, you see me here. I is a man with five children, and they have to eat. And I have a wife and she have to eat, and my yard. Look how tall the grass grow up in my yard. And is fifteen years I fighting Bango. Fifteen years for what? All the other stickmen make friends with Bango. What I fighting Bango for?"'

'"For the village," he will tell you. "For Cascadoux. For pride."'

'You know,' he said softly, 'in a way I wish I coulda make friends with Bango. I would make friends with Bango, not because I 'fraid Bango but because Bango is . . . Bango is true . . .'

'What you mean Bango is true? You don't know about all the wickedness Bango do, people land he take, people wife . . .'

'Because Bango is true to Bango. Because with all his tricks and his wickedness and his boasting and all the things I don't like him for, when you in the ring with Bango, you know he coming to kill you and you have to really battle.'

'And that is why you have to fight him, Phipps will tell you.'

'Not this time, though. No.'

'No?'

Later, from the kitchen, Fleurs' wife heard above the sound of Fleurs' cutlassing a new blaze of drumming, and she felt a strange anxiety, a kind of fear as when Fleurs was fighting. She had her ears cocked, listening for the dogs to bark, expecting Phipps or one of them to come and call

Fleurs. When Phipps came she would give him a good piece of her mind. The onliest time they prepared to come up this hill is when they want Fleurs to do something for them. Let him come.

She heard the drumbeat and the noise and shouting as she went about her chores; but she didn't hear the dogs bark. After a while she didn't hear the sound of Fleurs' cutlass. She figured that he was on the back steps giving the blade a new edge; but when she looked outside she saw him at the place underneath the spouting where they caught water. He was at the barrel bathing. The children were playing cricket over in the little abandoned place where their neighbours had once lived.

Fleurs came into the kitchen. He had changed his clothes and she saw that he had his stick with him. With great effort she held her question. He looked a little sad, but fresher, and the terrible silence of earlier in the morning did not surround him.

With her ears straining for the bark of the dogs, she spoke. 'So where you going?'

'I going to meet Bango.'

'Yes,' she said, 'is better you make friends with him. At least he will respect you.'

He smiled, 'I not going to make friends with Bango.'

'Lord!' she said, with a kind of prideful anger. 'I don't know what Cascadoux would do without you.'

'Is not for Cascadoux I doing this for,' he said.

'Is not for Cascadoux?' She was looking into his eyes and seeing in them the truth, the earnestness, the fire and softness that had made her decide fifteen years ago that he was the man she wanted to struggle with and struggle for. She touched his arm, 'You know whole day you ain't eat nothing.'

He relaxed a little then. 'You know I don't like to eat on this day.'

She went to the door with him. The children had

stopped their game to watch him too. And she watched him walk down the hill, a little taller than he had been earlier in the morning, but not quite as tall as that time long ago.

She still kinda hoped Phipps or somebody would come before he disappeared down the hill. She really wished one of them would come. Phipps and them was a set of dogs. She oh God really wished Phipps would come. But, how many things she wished for in her life ever happen?

When Fleurs reached the stickfight *gayelle* he saw the crowd gathered and he felt the excitement: but he didn't quicken his step. In front the rum shop in the open where everybody could see him Calloway stood with his face set up in beast. Three different coloured handkerchiefs were tied around his forehead, a set of black and red beads were around his neck, and he had tied a red cloth in the middle of his stick. He was running the stick through his fingers. He looked powerful. Fleurs didn't see Johnny or Beast; but across the road was Ancil with his brightly coloured shirt open and all his chest outside. Standing next to him, holding one of his hands, was his woman, Mary, old enough for people to take her for his mother and to take the baby-faced smooth-skinned Ancil for her son. He glanced at Ancil. Ancil clean-faced and featured like a woman, with delicate hands and long fingernails with which he marked the cards gambling. Mary, with a pair of rimless spectacles on, a dress that showed off her bottom, the pride of her body, and stockings.

Ancil was standing half turned from her, watching at her with his head drawn back. Seeing Fleurs, he called out, 'Fleurs, tell this woman to let go my hand, please.'

'No,' Mary said. 'No. You not going in there. I not letting you go in no stickfighting.'

'You see my troubles,' said Ancil, not moving his head, a quiet smile on his face, trying to look cool.

Bango was parading in the ring. Fleurs didn't say anything. He went straight through the crowd to the inside of the *gayelle*. No shout went up at his entry. Nobody didn't even notice that Fleurs was only now coming in; but, when he put his foot into the ring, the golden grin on Bango's face widened and the muscles on Bango's arms hardened and Bango went and took from his woman, the priestess, the poui stick mounted with the Amerindian spirit, and in his eyes shone that gleam that now, yes, there would be battle. And maybe that was the reason why, listening up the hill, Fleurs' wife heard the terrible silence settle and when they began for Fleurs, the drums beat with a new life as if they had all along been expecting him.

Mammie's Form at the Post Office

E. A. MARKHAM

She remembered it just in time and panicked; but there must be a way of getting the money there today. Her children were heartless, telling her it wasn't necessary: they had no respect for the dead.

At the post office, she went to the wrong end of the counter, and felt a fool when they directed her to the right queue, as if she couldn't read; so she tried to explain. There were a lot of openings but most of them said CLOSED, so she had to join a queue. It embarrassed her that all these post offices now had bullet-proof glass shutting out the customer: really, it was offensive to treat people like this – she was almost beginning to feel like a criminal. She thought of Teacher Tudy's post office at home where people from the village would come and stand in the yard with their back to the stables (which Tudy had converted to a garage) while their names were read out from the dining-room door. Of course, Mammie never had to stand in the yard; she would either send over Sarah or Franco; or if she didn't think of it, Tudy would put the letters aside, and probably bring them over herself the next night. Queuing behind the bullet-proof glass, Mammie couldn't help feeling that she'd been reduced to standing with her back to Teacher Tudy's stables, waiting for her name to be called out.

When it was at last her turn, she told the boy behind the counter that she wanted to send some money to the West Indies, she wanted to send $100 home. But the boy pretended he didn't understand what she was saying, and then asked if she wanted to send money *abroad*. She had to correct him and tell him she was sending her money *home*: that's where she was from. She was indignant that first they treated you like a foreigner, and then they denied you your home. He was just a child, and she wondered why they didn't have anyone bigger who could deal with the customers and understand what they wanted. She wanted to send $100 home.

'D'you want to send dollars?'

'Yes. Yes. A hundred.'

'$100. To the West Indies.'

'To Murial.'

'Yes. Not sure if you can do that, actually. Look, I'll just . . .'

'And I'm in a hurry.'

He was just moving off, apparently to look for something, and stopped. 'Look, I've just got to check on this, all right?'

'Yes. Go ahead. As long as it gets there in a hurry.'

'You'll have to send it by telegraph in that case. Can you . . . Just hang on . . .' He reached under the counter and took out a form. 'I'll just go and check on the rates. If you'll just fill out this meanwhile.' He slipped the form under the bullet-proof glass, and told her to fill out both sides.

Mammie took the form and started searching for her glasses. And after all that, the form didn't make sense. It was all to do with people sending money to Bangladesh and Pakistan, and not one word about the West Indies; so the young fellow must have given her the wrong form.

When he came back – with a big book – Mammie returned the form and asked for one for the West Indies; and he said it didn't matter: West Indies was the same as Bangladesh. It was the first time in her life she'd ever heard anyone say that the West Indies, where she was born and grew up and where all her family came from and where her mother and the rest of her relations died and were buried, was the same as Bangladesh which was some-where in India, where the people were Indian, and she'd never set foot in her life. But she kept all this to herself, and filled out the form nevertheless.

She put down Murial's name. Murial didn't live in a 'Road or Street'; she lived in the village (she had a lovely house in the village), so Mammie had to leave out that line and go right on to VILLAGE OR TOWN and COUNTRY OF DESTINATION having again left out DISTRICT, STATE OR PROVINCE. While she was doing this, someone pushed her to one side as if she was a beggar, and took her place; but she wasn't going to argue with any of them.

On the other side of the form, she had to make a decision. Murial wasn't a DEPENDANT, so that took care of that. She was tempted to sign her name under PURPOSE OF PAYMENT, but the money had nothing to do with:

a) for goods imported into the UK up to £50 in value . . . subject for the possession of an import licence if necessary;
b) of subscriptions and entrance fees to clubs/societies other than for travel services up to £50 per year per club/society;
c) of maintenance payments under Orders of Court;
d) in settlement of commercial and professional debts up to £50 (see paragraph below).

She was sending the money to repair her uncle's head-stone and to weed the family plot. As Murial was kind enough to look after her affairs at home, Mammie thought it might upset her if she sent the money as PAYMENT, for Murial wasn't someone she employed, Murial was a friend. So in the end, she entered it under CASH GIFT.

The boy took the form and said she'd have to send it in pounds, and they could change it at the other end. That was all right. Then he started filling out another form, checking with his book, and showing it to the man working next to him, so that the whole world would soon know her business. Then he looked up and smiled at her, and asked if it was urgent.

The boy was a fool, she had already told him it was urgent.

'Then, that'll be . . . £45.50 plus three and seven twenty. That would be . . . £55.20. OK?'

He was crazy. She had £30, which was plenty. He was joking.

'You joking?'

'Sorry . . .?'

'Last time it cost only £24. Or twenty-three.'

Then he said something that she didn't really follow. So she asked him to repeat it, because then he'd surely find out his mistake.

He was treating her like a child now. 'That'll be £45.50 for the $100. And there's *three pounds* charge for sending it urgently. You want it urgent, don't you . . .'

'Yes. Yes.'

'. . . and then there's the message, and that's going to cost you another . . .'

'Cut it out. Cut out the message.' The message wasn't important.

The message itself was all right, the message was free. But . . .

Mammie wanted the message out.

He read as he crossed it out: 'This is to weed the head-stones.'

'Not weed. To weed the *graves*.'

'Yes, well, it don't matter now, I've crossed . . .'

'It *does* matter. I'm not illiterate. You can't weed the headstones, you repair them.'

'It doesn't cost any more, it's the address that's expensive. Look, do you have to send it . . . It'd be cheaper by "telegraph letter".'

'Will it get there today?'

His friend working next to him made a comment and laughed, but the young lad himself didn't laugh. He came very close to the glass and she didn't like his look.

'It'll get there in a few days. I mean, it's not exactly *urgent*, is it?'

'All right, all right.'

'You'll send it the cheaper way?'

'It's all right, I'll go to another post office.'

This time he was very rude.

'It didn't cost so much last time,' Mammie wasn't going to be defeated. But by then he was dealing with another customer, complaining.

She was too busy to go to another post office now; she had to go home to put on the dinner, in case anyone dropped by; she had to look after the living as well as the dead, 'the quick and the dead': she smiled to herself. The joke pleased her. It occurred to her than that at the post office she had just said 'dollars' to the young lad; she didn't specify West Indian dollars which were only about four shilling and twopence, which would be less than 25p in the new money (at least, that's what it was in the old days). Last year, it had only cost her £24 to send the money to Murial. At the other post office. This year, she was prepared to allow for another £4 for inflation and for telegraphing it . . . Unless the boy was talking about some other dollar; but he must know she was West Indian, even though he wasn't qualified to work behind the bullet-proof glass. But what could she do; she was tired: her mother would have to wait another day, choking in grass.

The Duel in Mercy Ward

IAN McDONALD

Benjie and Beepat arrived in the ward at Mercy about the same time. This ward was for chronic, not exactly terminal, cases. One or two used to make a kind of recovery and totter out into the land of the living. But generally when you went in there you only came out on the long journey. Benjie was wheeled in one morning, Beepat the same afternoon, and ever afterwards Benjie made his seniority a point to emphasize and exaggerate.

'I was here long, long before you come in making trouble,' Benjie would say.

'You old fool,' Beepat would respond. 'We come in the exact same time.'

And that would be good for an hour or two of satisfying, acrimonious debate.

But that was just a very small bone in the huge pot of contention that Benjie and Beepat soon began to cook up. They argued about everything. They drove the nurses to distraction. They were in next-door beds at first but they soon had to be separated. They still found ample ways to meet and quarrel and suck teeth at each other's views.

They made as many as possible in the ward take sides, which added to the confusion. The halt and the lame and the nearly blind, not to mention the dying and the nearly dead, were summoned to make a choice. It was World Cup Final every day, Benjie's team against Beepat's team, and you better have helmets because bouncers bound to fly.

Everything was a case of competition between Benjie and Beepat. They had some big rows about politics – how the other one's party was full of vagabonds and fools. They had some big rows about religion – how Hindus have so many thousands and thousands of Gods they even have a God for water-snake and carrion-crow and how Christians like cannibals, wanting to drink the blood of Jesus Christ. And they had some big rows about race – how Indians mean and sly and can't take their liquor and how black people only like to fête and play with women. But somehow in these rows you had the feeling they were rowing for rowing's sake. It was Beepat so Benjie had to say one thing and it was Benjie so Beepat had to say the other thing. But they didn't seem to want to put their heart in it. Politics, religion, and race really were not worth getting worked up about. Life was too short.

Cricket was the cause of more important rowing. Right at the beginning they made a mistake and in one argument both said, while the other was also saying, how Kanhai was the greatest batsman in the world. So from then on they had to forget Kanhai in the rowing and row instead about who the second best was. And if Benjie selected a team not one man could be the same as in the team Beepat selected. And if a man had a good cover-drive for Benjie, no, he only had a good hook-shot for Beepat. And when they were listening to Test Match cricket there were always three commentaries – Benjie's commentary which was giving one view, Beepat's commentary which was giving a view as if it was a different game, and the real commentator's commentary which, to tell the truth, wasn't half so interesting or quarter so scandalous as Benjie's and Beepat's commentaries.

But even cricket wasn't all that much. What Benjie and Beepat really put their hearts into were rivalries that could be decided definitely and specifically right there in the ward on a daily basis.

Like the rivalry to see who was the most popular patient in the ward. This amounted to seeing who could get the most visitors to come at visiting hour. The story started when one of Beepat's cousins and five nieces and nephews happened to come and visit at the same time when his old brother and sister-in-law were there. That made eight people around Beepat's bed. And Benjie only had two people visiting him. So Beepat made a big thing about how some people so bad-natured they don't have any family or friends left to visit them while some other people at least could say a lot of friends and family still think highly of them and show their devotion.

Well, you can imagine Benjie's response. It only took about three days before ten people turned up around Benjie's bed at visiting hour and only four by Beepat's bed that same day. Benjie didn't forget to rub the salt in the wound, and what could Beepat say? He stayed quiet and planned his own counter-attack. He sent word out by his cousins and by his cousin's cousins. I am sure I don't have to describe all what happened then: more and more people coming in to visit Benjie and Beepat. Benjie drew from all over town and up the East Bank; Beepat drew from the East Coast mostly but as far away as Crabwood Creek too. Benjie even sent out and hired a bus to bring visitors in one day after competition was going about a month. By this time only a few of the visitors were actually getting in to see Benjie and Beepat, but that didn't prevent both of them getting a count of how many had turned up to visit and then each announcing, like an election official, the total number that had tried to pay a visit to their beloved Benjie/Beepat. It was a hard battle and visiting hour was an exciting time for the whole ward until a stop had to be put to all the nonsense, the authorities cracked down, and Benjie and Beepat had to find another contest in which to test wits and belligerence.

That ward is more often than not a place of anguish and despair where people at best lose their grip on life and quietly fade away and at worst die in a hopeless, lonely agony which shakes the soul to think about too long. But in the era of Benjie and Beepat a little more of something like a last vital spark was preserved a little longer in all those hopeless, discarded cases. It wasn't much and it wasn't for long but it was something and it was for a while and in life can you be sure that in the end there is much more than that? I don't know.

And that leads directly to by far the intensest rivalry between these two obscure but determined representatives of the life-force, Benjie and Beepat. Neither of them was going to be the one to die first. That was the ultimate competition. Benjie, you could say, would rather have died than pass away before Beepat. And Beepat felt exactly the same way. They put their last surge of will-power into this battle to the last breath not to be first to go.

They kept an eager eye on each other to see what signs of wear and tear might be appearing – further wear and tear, I should say, because you can imagine that Benjie and Beepat were both worn and torn a good bit already by the time they were brought in to the ward at Mercy. If one of them coughed an extra amount in the night the other started up at once and the next morning was sure to make a comment. They kept an eye on each other's bowel movements. Nothing they would have liked better than to get a sight of each other's urine samples to see if they were clear or cloudy. They each had ancient village remedies to supplement the despised hospital medicine and they both made sure the other knew a new and extra-potent cure was being smuggled in which would give the recipient an edge in the struggle to survive.

Twice they had to take Beepat down to the operating theatre.

'He gone now,' Benjie said. 'Old Beepat gone. I don't know how he last so long, he was so sickly-looking. But now he gone.'

But Beepat returned both times and continued the fight

to the death. Once Benjie in his turn had to be given blood and saline, right there in his bed. A doctor and some nurses bustled about setting up the apparatus and plastic bottles and Benjie in truth looked gone, lying with his eyes closed and a deadly waxen look in his face. It was Beepat's turn to intone the last rites.

'Benjie could never make it now. When you see those bottles hook up like that in a man, that is the end. The end. He can't make it any more. It was only mouth when he said he was feeling so good yesterday. Now look at that face, it could be in a coffin already.'

But Benjie pulled through.

One morning at crack of dawn Beepat was amazed to see Benjie trying to do what appeared to be push-ups on the floor by the side of the bed. The word went round that Benjie was feeling so good that he had decided to begin a regime of light exercises every morning and evening. It was good psychology, and had the effect of shaking up Beepat and putting him on the defensive for a while. But it turned out to be counter-productive. After a couple of mornings Benjie couldn't make the grade and had to put the get-fit regime in cold storage. In fact he had a bad relapse and couldn't even get out of bed for a few days, which gave Beepat the chance to make a special effort to walk around the whole place and show how strong he was.

It would be good to tell how the story ended with Benjie and Beepat walking out one fine day, good for a few more years rowing. But, in truth, life isn't like that, not for you, not for me, and not for Benjie and Beepat. The day came when Benjie began to go down. It was Diwali and Beepat had got some clay *diyas* and put them glimmering around his bed. It looked beautiful. Beepat was very proud. Normally Benjie would have had some comment to make, but he was silent and still. Beepat was surprised. From that time Benjie couldn't get out of bed anymore. He tried hard one or two more times but he couldn't raise himself to take the bait. Beepat began to get silent.

Benjie had a bad case of sugar and it had got to the time when the doctors couldn't even slow down the ravages of the disease. The legs were going bad. They had to operate and cut and try to keep the rest of Benjie whole. But the sickness was too far gone and Benjie was too old. You can't only live on strong will. In the last month they cut him down four times, but he still hung on. The first time Beepat made a joke at Benjie's expense, but after that he didn't make any more jokes. Every time they cut Benjie, Beepat grew more quiet. The whole ward grew silent: no more Benjie and Beepat rowing. The time for that was over.

When they cut Benjie for the fourth time they brought him back up to the ward with his legs cut off just above the knees. He was hardly living any more but he was still alive. Beepat lit a *diya* in front of the greatest of his Gods before he lay down for the night. During the night you could hear Benjie's breathing across the ward. The *diya* by Beepat's bed flickered out and he fed it with oil a few times. Beepat lay awake late and then he composed himself to sleep. It was strange. When the nurses made their second morning round, when the birds had just begun to sing, they found that Beepat's sleep had eased into dying. It was recorded that his heart gave out, after respiratory troubles, and he died at 9.02 a.m. Benjie lasted until noon that day.

Dry Bones

EARL McKENZIE

There was an old slave who was no longer of any use on the plantation and was left to fend for himself. In those days there was nobody more useless than an old man, an old woman could at least look after children, but a man who was no longer strong enough to work in the canefield or the sugar mill was no use. He cost more to feed than he could contribute, so he was set loose to make do any way he could.

At first some of the other slaves shared their food with him, but since they hardly had enough for themselves, this didn't go very far. Besides, the old man felt guilty accepting food from people who had to work so hard. So he began spending a lot of time wandering through the bushes and living off such fruits and roots as he could find. Since he was old and shaky and couldn't do much walking, sometimes he would spend long hours just sitting in the sun and warming himself. After a while he began spending all his time in the bushes not wanting to be a burden to anyone. People on the plantation began to forget him. His body withered until he was almost all skin and bones. Slaves were sold to other plantations and new slaves were bought. Many of those who once knew him thought he was dead, and when people saw him in the bushes they thought they were seeing a ghost. The story developed that there was a skin-and-bone ghost who lived in the bushes. They called him Dry Bones.

Many strange things can happen to an old slave dying in the bushes. Dry Bones heard familiar voices in his dreams instructing him how to prepare his soul for his return to his home in Africa. The voices said his soul must be completely transformed into the form of a bird. The voices instructed him and the process began.

One day a slave boy was walking in the bushes and he saw this huge white bird perched on the top of a tree with its wings outstretched warming itself in the sun. He took out his sling shot, loaded it, aimed for the bird's head and fired. The bird fell, bouncing from branch to branch, and finally landed on a guava tree where it rested with its head hanging down. The boy rushed to the tree and shook it until the bird fell to the ground. He noticed that the bird fell very lightly, almost without sound, and when he picked it up he was surprised to find that, in spite of its size, it was very light, almost weightless. Nevertheless he shoved the bird into the crocus bag he was carrying, slung it over his shoulder and began walking home.

As he walked along he noticed that the bag kept getting heavier and heavier, and bulges began forming in it. Then he felt hard things rubbing against his back and sharp points sinking into his shoulders. Quickly he threw down the bag. He heard a moan as the bag hit the ground, and he saw different parts of it sticking out as if something was turning over inside; the thing was quite big now, almost filling the bag. The boy was terrified and he turned and ran away as fast as he could. As he ran he kept repeating, 'Our Father! Our Father! Our Father!' When he got to a crossroads he marked an X in the middle of the road and continued running home to tell his mother what he had seen.

A few weeks later the slave master and one of his slaves went bird shooting. The master carried his gun slung over his shoulder and the slave walked behind him carrying a bag in which he put the birds the master shot. They got to a tree and saw a huge white bird sitting at the top with outstretched wings warming itself in the sun. The master cocked his gun and got ready to shoot.

'No, sah!' said the slave. 'Please don't shoot it, sah!'

'Why not?'

'Is an obeah bird, sah.'

The master chuckled. 'You people and your stupid superstitions!'

He aimed and fired. The bird fell, bouncing from branch to branch, and finally landed on a guava tree where it rested with its head hanging down. The master rushed to the tree and shook it until the bird fell to the ground. The slave noticed that it fell very lightly, almost without sound.

'Pick it up,' the master commanded.

'No, sah!' said the slave, his eyes wide with fright.

'Pick it up I say!'

The slave was trembling. 'Is a ghost-bird, sah!'

The master looked around for a stick. The slave dropped the bag of dead birds he was carrying and ran off into the bushes crying.

'The blasted fool!' said the master.

Then he picked up the bird. It was a bit light for its size but was heavier than it had appeared from the way it had fallen. He put it in the bag, threw the bag over his shoulder and began climbing the hill.

He had only gone a few yards when he felt the bag getting heavy. At first he thought it was just because he wasn't accustomed to carrying loads and because the hill was a bit steep. But he soon felt the bulges forming, the hard things rubbing against his back, and the sharp points sinking into his shoulders. He was about to drop the bag when he felt two bony hands fasten around his neck, and two bony legs gripping him around his waist. He cried out and tried to shake the thing off, but the weight kept increasing.

'Help!' he bawled out. 'Help! Help!'

'When you picked me up, you picked up your troubles,' said Dry Bones.

'Let me go!' the master panted. 'Let me go!'

He began to struggle again to get rid of Dry Bones. They fell to the ground and rolled over but Dry Bones held on. The dead birds from the bag were now strewn all over the grass. In his fright the master had almost lost hold of his gun.

'When you picked me up, you picked up your troubles!' repeated Dry Bones.

'What do you want from me?' the master pleaded.

'Take me back to your house and feed me.'

'But I can't walk with you on my back, you're too heavy.'

'But it is easy for you to carry a bird.'

The weight lessened, and when the master turned around he saw the white bird standing in the grass and watching him. He picked up the dead birds and returned them to the bag; the white bird then slipped into the bag by himself. The master threw the bag over his shoulder, picked up his gun and began walking towards his home, not certain whether he was awake or dreaming.

After about a quarter of a mile he met his overseer on a horse. His overseer was his own son that he had had with one of the slave women.

'Seems you had a good day's shooting, sir,' said the overseer.

'And I'm dog-tired too. Why don't you help me carry them? You may have a few of them if you like.'

'Sure, sir,' said the overseer, 'and thank you very much.'

The master gave him the bag. 'I'm going across to the mill,' he said as he started walking in the opposite direction.

The overseer slung the bag over his shoulder and rode off.

Suddenly he felt the bag getting heavier.

'What the rahtid is this?' he said.

Then he felt the bulges forming, the hard things rubbing against his back, and the sharp points sticking into his shoulders. Suddenly the bony hands gripped his neck and the pair of bony legs folded around his waist. The overseer began struggling to free himself. With the increased weight and the struggle above him, the horse began galloping.

'Let me go!' cried the overseer. 'Me say let me go!'

'When you picked me up, you picked up your troubles,' said Dry Bones.

The horse was galloping faster now, and in their struggling they lost their balance and fell to the ground. They rolled and tumbled in the road. The overseer began cursing a lot of bad words but Dry Bones wouldn't let go.

'Is what the hell you want with me?' said the overseer.

'Take me home and feed me.'

'But why should I feed you?'

'Because I am Dry Bones.'

'Dry Bones!' breathed the overseer. New sweat broke out all over his body and he trembled. 'You're Dry Bones the jumbie! Oh, let me go! What do you want with me?'

'Right now I am half man and half spirit,' said Dry Bones. 'Take me home and feed me.'

With his head bowed and tears rolling down his cheeks the overseer began walking toward his house with Dry Bones fastened to his back.

The overseer's wife didn't like the idea of her husband taking this emaciated old man into their home and she showed her resentment openly. The overseer put Dry Bones in the storeroom and gave him food. He didn't tell his wife how he had come by Dry Bones because he felt sure she wouldn't believe him. She would think he was crazy. So he told her he found the old man in the bushes starving. In fact he was even afraid of mentioning it to his boss for fear of being laughed at and declared mad. The whole thing was like a bad dream and he kept hoping he would wake up and be rid of it. But the old man in the storeroom was real enough and had the appetite to prove it; he couldn't get enough to eat. He often complained of being cold, and at his request, the overseer put him in an armchair in the yard every morning so he could warm himself in the sun. Flesh began to appear on his bones. The overseer was afraid to raise the question of the old man's mysterious appearance in the bird-shooting bag; it was as if he felt that by not discussing it, it would simply go away. But there was no way he could just rationalize away the old man's presence in his house, for everytime Dry Bones looked at him the message in his eyes was clear – 'Try to get rid of me and there will be trouble.'

Finally the overseer decided he couldn't live with the strange situation any longer. He had to discuss his problem with somebody. So late one night, after everybody in the house had gone to bed, he crept quietly out of the house and went to seek the services of an obeah man. The obeah man lived alone in a little wattle-and-daub house beside a river. There was a light in the house when the overseer got there. He knocked on the door and the obeah man opened it. He was jet black, had thick uncombed hair, and was stripped to the waist. A small wooden carving of a grotesque head hung from the necklace of red cloth he had around his neck. In the middle of the floor a black candle burned surrounded by bones and various kinds of herbs. The obeah man told the overseer to sit on the other side of the candle, and then he sat down facing him. The overseer explained that he wanted to get rid of Dry Bones.

'You want me to kill him?' asked the obeah man.

The overseer shivered. 'No, I just want to get rid of him.'

'But how you going to get rid of him unless you kill him?'

The obeah man's eyes shone in the candlelight.

'If he was just an ordinary man I wouldn't mind too much,' said the overseer, 'but he has these powers.'

'Powers!'

The overseer explained how he had come by Dry Bones.

'Ah!' said the obeah man. 'Everything is perfectly clear

now. You will have to get rid of him.'

'But how?'

'Return him to the bushes.'

'But he will starve to death. He's been eating like a glutton since he came to my house.'

'That is bad,' said the obeah man shaking his head. 'He is trying to return to this world but it is too late. You don't begin the journey he has started and turn back.'

'What do you mean?'

'Never mind. This is not a matter of too much importance to you. But that old man began learning something important in the bushes. People always learn something important in the bushes. Jesus. Moses. You must take him back to the bushes. It is the only way to save both him and yourself.'

'But what am I to do?'

'Leave it to me. It is my business to see to it that he makes his journey home.'

The overseer paid the obeah man and set off for his home.

The following morning, at the usual time, he put the old man in the yard to warm himself in the sun. Dry Bones leaned back in the armchair and began enjoying the warmth of the sun on his skin. He had just eaten a big breakfast of roasted breadfruit, fried pork with ackee, and rich coffee sweetened with coconut milk. The sky was clear and blue with a few puffs of white clouds pushing up from behind the mountains. Dry Bones stretched and relaxed again. Then he began daydreaming about his concept of a perfect lunch: mackerel and ochroes cooked in coconut gravy, boiled green bananas and tender St Vincent yam, followed by a tall glass of soursop juice.

Suddenly the sky darkened and he looked up. A huge hawk was circling the sky above him. It passed over the sun again, darkening the yard momentarily. It came closer and perched on a branch of the avocado pear tree at the edge of the yard. It stared down at Dry Bones and pointed its head at him as if taking aim before swooping down at him.

'Pin-ya!' it cried in a harsh piercing voice. 'Pin-ya! Pin-ya!'

Then it swooped.

Dry Bones cried out as he saw the opened talons coming swiftly toward his face. But they didn't scratch him, they just brushed his face as the hawk rose in the air again and perched on a branch of the breadfruit tree at the other side of the yard. Before Dry Bones could catch his breath the hawk swooped again. This time the wings brushed hard against his head and the talons ripped his forehead. Dry Bones tried to get up but his body wouldn't obey his will. The hawk was perched on the pear tree, again its head pointing at him, preparing to swoop again. Dry Bones stared into its fierce eyes. Suddenly he realized with horror that the eyes were those of his old slave master, and he noticed that the bird's entire head was being transformed into that of the man who had once owned him, and who had worked him to the wreck he had become. The hawk swooped and Dry Bones cried out, beating it away with his hands. The hawk was on the breadfruit tree now, and when Dry Bones looked at it he saw its face was becoming that of the book-keeper whom he had once caught raping his woman. The hawk swooped and he cried out again. From the pear tree the hawk aimed at him again. Its neck stretched toward him, and it became so long it was like the whip with which he had been beaten so many times. The hawk swooped and he struggled to fight it off, but he was getting weaker and weaker, and he didn't feel he could withstand it much longer. He raised his eyes to the breadfruit tree. The hawk's face was now that of the overseer. It swooped and Dry Bones cried out with all his heart.

'Is what do you?' a voice came from the door of the house.

He turned and saw the overseer's wife standing at the door with a dish in her hand.

'The hawk!' he cried, 'the hawk!'

'Which hawk?'

He looked up at the tree but the hawk was gone.

'There was a hawk there mad to kill me,' said Dry Bones.

The woman hissed her teeth and went back into the house.

Dry Bones looked up into the tree and the hawk had reappeared. It stretched its head toward him and again took on the appearance of the overseer. Then it swooped. Dry Bones fell into a dead faint. When he came out of it the overseer's wife and her servants were standing around him, and they were saying that he was out of his mind.

The following morning he did not want to be left alone in the yard but no one would stay with him. As soon as the servants left, the hawk appeared and resumed its torture. It kept swooping from tree to tree, and before each swoop it took on the image of some painful association from his wretched life. It also began scratching him persistently, and when he rubbed his face with his hands he saw blood. He wished he could faint but he was unable to. The hawk kept reappearing at intervals throughout the entire day. By evening Dry Bones was a mass of blood and pain.

The following morning he pleaded not to be put out in the sun.

'Put him out,' said the overseer's wife. 'Is he begged to be put out, so he must be put out.'

The hawk reappeared as soon as they left. Dry Bones struggled out of the chair and began dragging himself across the yard toward the protection of the bushes. The hawk followed him and kept up its attack to the edge of the yard, but it did not follow him into the bushes. Dry Bones turned to see if it was watching him but everything was quiet and the bird was nowhere to be seen. He waited for a few minutes and then began re-entering the yard. Suddenly he heard the screeching of the hawk in one of the trees, and he felt it on his back tearing him savagely with its beak and talons. He cried out and began dragging himself toward the bushes again. Each time he tried to re-enter the yard the bird attacked him. Finally he gave up the struggle and resigned himself to the bushes once again. He began dragging himself toward a nearby clump of trees. As he hauled his body over the grass and stones his tears mixed with the blood that streamed from the scratches on his face.

Dry Bones returned to living off fruits and roots. He shrank again to skin and bones. And soon he began hearing the voices in his dreams again, telling him how to come home.

Late one quiet night, he died while sleeping on his bed of dried leaves in a bamboo walk. And as he died a white bird rose up through the bamboo leaves and began following the path of the valley toward the sea. It got to the coast and soon was moving across the large, dark blue ocean.

His bones are still scattered through the bushes, and many people see them without knowing what they are. But once a year, very late at night, a white bird can be seen in these bushes; it is the ghost of the old man come to collect another splinter of his bones.

Visiting

ROGER McTAIR

'There should be bridges between islands,' Solomon said, looking over the bay. Clapham wiped the bar's counter thoughtfully, and said, 'Yes, sir.'

'Hey! Cut out the "sir" business,' Solomon said, 'all my friends call me Sol, or Sol-oh; get it, sol-oh. I'm just a Trinidadian from over the sea; one hour by plane. If we had a bridge between Bridgetown and Port of Spain you could drive in eight hours.'

'Can't drive,' Clapham replied. 'All I have is an old Raleigh bicycle.' He wiped the already spotless bar again and again.

A light warm breeze agitated the palm trees and well-cut decorative shrubs and the hot scent of flowers mixed with the salt tang of the sea. The music from the hotel stopped and the sound of the rolling sea took its place. Clapham stopped wiping the counter and waited, attentively.

A small group of men and women walked down the gravel path that led from the hotel grounds and parking lot. They sat on the other side of the circular outdoor bar, exchanging jokes, laughing and talking. Solomon turned on his stool to contemplate the bay. This was the last day of his vacation and he felt a little melancholy. He wished there was a moon over the bay. He whistled some bars from 'Mood Indigo'. There were lights twinkling out to sea. Must be an ocean liner touring the islands, Solomon thought.

'That's Ellington, isn't it?' Clapham asked under his breath.

'Yes,' Solomon said. 'The Duke himself.'

Clapham moved smoothly and quietly in his limited space. His voice was soft and soothing as he served the laughing tourists. The three men and four women joked loudly with the old barman. He just smiled. There was a whining, nasal twang to their voices. Solomon could not decide if the accents were mid-western or southern. Not that he was an expert on American accents, he told himself. He kept his back to the thatched bar and watched the waves rush on the sand. He tried to block out their voices. It was his first visit to another island. The damn place felt like home; somewhat. This bay could be Salybia, or Point Cumana, but it wasn't, it was in another island, 200 miles away, Clapham's soft accent reminded him.

A white-haired white man, immaculate in evening wear, leaning on the arm of a middle-aged black man walked slowly down the gravel path. He sat on a bench under a palm tree some yards from the bar. He wore a red carnation in his lapel. His manservant was dressed in a black chauffeur's tunic from a thirties English movie. The old man settled himself on the bench and leaned his hands on his cane. He stared out to sea. His manservant stood impassive and erect a little distance behind the bench.

Ah, the Antilles, Solomon thought, sipping his rum and closing his eyes. He had intended to go to New York for this vacation, until Beckles had asked him if he had ever been to Grenada. No, he had said. You ever been to Barbados? You ever been to Jamaica? No! Beckles smiled. You ever been to Toronto? Yes, he had said. Montreal? Yes! Brooklyn? Yes! Beckles smiled again.

Solomon booked for three weeks in Barbados.

He was about to whistle the Ellington tune when someone sat next to him. He opened his eyes, it was an attractive blonde woman. She smiled at him. Solomon smiled back. She had very good teeth and looked thirtyish. Solomon caught a pleasant whiff of cologne. She was tastefully dressed in a light summer dress that moved lightly when she moved. Her hair was cut short and looked as if it had just been styled. She kept putting her hand to her head as if she had more hair to feel. Then she would gingerly touch the short cropped cut. Clapham came over and took her order. Solomon nursed his drink.

She made small-talk with Clapham. Solomon watched the dark expanse of sea.

'Do you work around here?' she said, looking at Solomon. Solomon swung around very slowly on the stool. Clapham wiped the formica counter again with clean precise motions. Solomon thought he saw a hint of a smile on his face.

'This is my third visit here. You do have a very lovely island.'

Solomon said nothing.

'Sometimes, in winter? In Ottawa; I'm from Ottawa,' she paused, looking intently into Solomon's face. 'In Canada . . .?' Solomon nodded.

'Sometimes in winter, in Ottawa . . .'

'In Canada . . .' Solomon said helpfully.

'. . . yes, in Canada! I see these people eh! Immigrants? You know, not only like Negroes eh? Black? But East Indians, Latin Americans, even Portuguese, like they are from a warm climate eh. And they look so miserable in the cold and snow, and I always wondered . . .'

Solomon smiled. He knew the old barman was smiling behind his straight face and lowered eyes.

'. . . how they could leave their lovely warm countries . . .' She seemed relieved to have spilled it out. Solomon was relieved too. He had heard the sentiment many times before.

Three more people joined the Americans, a thin man in a white safari outfit and two women in evening dress. 'We've been doing the limbo,' the thin man said. There was another exchange of banter, and laughter. One of the party ordered more drinks. The newcomers stood in a knot behind the seated group. They laughed loudly at any remark one of their number made.

The old man in evening dress looked over reprovingly. His manservant's face was blank.

Clapham served their new drinks. The men made a great fuss about getting the check. 'Noisy, aren't they,' the woman from Ottawa said to Solomon. The band from the hotel began playing again. A calypsonian sang along with the band. The calypso was the hit of the season. The Americans began singing too:

> She say she don't like bamboo
> but she don't mind meh cane
> She say cane juice real sweet
> It does reach to she brain.
> The cane getting soft
> the juice pulping out
> sweet cane juice dripping
> all over she mouth.
> We jump in a taxi
> She get on the plane
> She say next year she coming
> ForCane again and again.

One of the Americans did not sing. He just danced on his stool. His hair fell in his face as he moved to the music. He waved his hands a lot. His hands and his forearms were really big. His friends thought he was very funny.

The thin man in the safari suit began doing a limbo on the sand. The others followed in a twisting line, laughing, dancing around the bar, kicking up sand, singing loudly:

> She say next year she coming
> ForCane again and again.

Clapham impassively washed glasses. Occasionally he glanced at the revellers. He moved in the cage of the enclosed bar like a grey-haired ghost.

The old man in the evening dress whispered something to his manservant. The manservant walked briskly down the gravel path toward the hotel. The old man leaned forward on his walking stick, frowning. The Americans did not notice.

'This is really disgusting,' the woman from Ottawa said, 'do you want to go to the hotel bar?'

'No,' Solomon said, 'I'm OK here. I'm talking with Clapham.'

'I came with some people,' she said. 'They are all in there dancing to that.'

'You'd better get accustomed,' Solomon said. 'You'll be hearing it every day until you leave.'

She pulled her mouth down in a little gesture of distaste. Solomon smiled a little to himself.

The Americans danced down the beach and to the edge of the surf. They formed a conga line, high stepping and laughing. They were breathing heavily when they returned.

'I don't know your name,' the woman from Ottawa said.

'Solomon,' he said. 'Eric Solomon.'

'Mine's Margaret, Margaret Robinson. I'm staying at the Hilton. Do you live around here? Are you, ah, connected with the hotel?'

'I suppose,' Solomon said, 'I'll have to be nice and let you know that I'm a visitor, just like our happy friends over there, just like yourself.' She didn't say anything for a while. Solomon spun on his stool and watched the sea. The twinkling lights had gone. The hotel band played 'Big Bamboo', 'Dick the Handyman', 'Benwood Dick', 'My Pussin'', 'Miss Tourist', 'No Money No Love'. Then they played 'Sweet Cane Juice' again.

'I've made a fool of myself, haven't I?' she said.

'Why . . .'

'You come to Barbados, and I guess you expect . . .'

'And I'm black, male, sitting here . . .' He thought he might as well bring it into the open.

The band swung into 'Big Bamboo'.

'No! No!' she said. 'It wasn't that.' She looked embarrassed. 'I'm sorry.'

'Don't be sorry,' Solomon replied. 'It's an easy mistake. It happens often in these islands.'

She shook her head in dismay as if she thought Solomon had misunderstood.

A young man and woman walked down the path to the bar. The woman slowed as the couple reached the edge of the path. The man had already stepped towards the bar. She stopped and whispered urgently to her companion. He nodded his head, urging her forward. She followed him reluctantly. They sat next to Margaret and Solomon, leaving empty stools between them and the Americans. The woman was dressed up as if she had just left a wedding reception. The man wore a dark grey suit, the jacket cut high and open at the neck in the appropriate tropical formal style. Margaret ordered another drink. The Americans waved Clapham over just as the couple sat. Clapham begin mixing and serving them drinks. He turned towards the newcomers. As the man opened his mouth to order Clapham reached under the counter searching for a bottle of something.

The young man raised his voice, 'Like you ignoring me. I've been waiting here for service and you ignoring me.'

Clapham turned to him and said, 'I'll be with you in a minute, sir, I am serving these people.'

'Don't give me that, mahn, I've been here five minutes and you ain't piss on me, mahn. You ain't even look at me, mahn. You serving all these blasted white people and have we here hole-up waiting.' He looked significantly at his companion. She looked straight across the bar into the shadows. Solomon noticed her fingers were locked tightly together.

The Americans got very quiet and very serious. They stared at the young man. They stared at Margaret and Solomon. They looked at each other.

'This is my blasted country,' the young man shouted.

One of the Americans vaulted into the bar and said, 'I'll serve you . . .' One of the women laughed; a nervous laugh. 'It's OK,' the American said to Clapham, moving him out of the way, 'I'll serve him.'

He spread his hands wide and leaned over the counter. Clapham looked horrified and dumbfounded. The young man was taken aback, groping for words.

'Whaddya want,' the American said quietly. 'I'll serve ya.' He was big. Eric thought he had the biggest neck he had ever seen. It was like a tree trunk. 'Well, what do you want? Whaddaya drinking?' the American said again; he was leaning, huge hands on the counter, 'Tom Collins, Martini, on the rocks, rum and water, planter's punch, bourbon and water, daquiri, Black Russian.'

'You hear that, you hear that,' the young man said to his girl, 'I don't have to stay here in my own country and take these insults, mahn.'

Just as he got up to leave, three uniformed policemen came crunching down the gravel path. The uniformed manservant was with them trying to keep up. The couple looked up, the woman uncomfortable, the man defiant. Two of the policemen headed straight for them. The other strode around the bar and took up a position behind Solomon. Solomon noticed he was big too, not as massive as the American but certainly not inconsequential. He held a baton in his hands, slapping it occasionally in his palm: thwack. thwack. thwack. thwack. Solomon kept a watch on him out of the corner of his eye.

'What's the matter here?' the senior policeman asked.

'This is my country. They can't come here and insult me

in my own country.' There was a hint of pleading under the defiance in the young man's voice.

The American still leaned over the bar. 'He said he wanted a drink, I offered him a drink, I was going to serve him. It's his country.' His face was very blank; his eyes were cold, hard and grey.

The senior policeman said to the angry man, 'We don't want any trouble, why don't you find a nice local place to drink and leave these people alone?'

'They don't have to go, officer,' the American said. 'I'll serve 'em. I'll serve 'em whatever they want.'

The policeman looked betrayed. The man and woman began moving away.

'Isn't this a local place?' Margaret from Ottawa whispered to Solomon.

'I'll explain later,' Solomon replied.

'Hey,' the big American called, 'you too good to drink with us, fella? We're not good enough for you? C'mon, I'll buy you a drink. You don't have to go. I'll drink with you. I'll drink with anybody.'

The senior policeman looked nonplussed. The manservant moved to take up his position behind the old man in evening wear. The young couple quickly walked down the path, the man striding, head held high, the woman scurrying, chased by the sound of the sea.

They disappeared into the dark. The policeman turned from their wake to look at Solomon sitting suspiciously silent at the bar. Solomon stared back. He was very aware of the third policeman somewhere at his backside. The thick-necked American turned and looked directly at him. His eyes are battle-dress green, Solomon thought.

'I'll serve you too if you want.'

Solomon smiled. He kept his gaze on the two policemen in front, thinking the island uniforms are different, but the faces are just the same. He wished he could see the big policeman at his back. He had moved behind Solomon's stool. Solomon's head and neck felt very tense and exposed.

Margaret from Ottawa got very angry. 'Why don't you stop making a fool of yourself.' She glared at the American, then at the policemen. 'He's not a beachboy. He's a visitor. A tourist, just like me, just like you.'

The policemen looked very dubious. Solomon could hear the one at his back breathing and slapping the baton; thwack. thwack. thwack. thwack.

The other Americans looked on bemused. They seemed to be waiting to see what would happen next. A gust of wind shook the palm trees. Solomon felt an urge to pucker his lips and whistle 'Mood Indigo'. He pressed them together instead.

'That's right,' Clapham said. 'He's staying at the hotel, he's a visitor. He's been here more than a week.'

'Well, as long as he doesn't give any trouble,' the senior policeman said, looking imperious.

'Gor blimey,' Clapham said, his eyes on fire. 'He's been sitting here talking to me for two hours. What you mean coming now talking about trouble, what trouble? He don't have anything to do with this.'

'Easy old man, easy,' the American said, holding up his hands in mock terror. Clapham turned on him and said, 'Can you leave my bar now please.' The American said 'Yes sir, if you want, sir. It's your country.' He vaulted one hand over the counter. His friends laughed heartily.

The policemen marched away, heels crunching into the gravel path. Just as they left the one behind him stared Solomon over from head to toe. His forehead was furrowed in a hard fleshy knot. He kept slapping the baton in his palm as he walked away. Solomon felt a cold bead of perspiration roll down his armpit and settle in his shirt.

The old man and his manservant got up slowly and walked past the bar. 'Good night, Major,' Clapham said. The old man tipped his forehead.

'Can you believe it?' Margaret said. 'Black Russian indeed.'

Solomon just tried to quiet his breathing.

Clapham emptied and washed the glasses the Americans had left. It was nearly midnight. The band had stopped.

The woman from Ottawa said, 'I've never been down south alone. I've always come with my husband. We've had a lovely time. We got divorced two months ago, just like that.'

'Sorry,' Solomon said.

'I'm sorry about tonight too.'

'Don't be sorry.'

'Could we do something tomorrow? Sightseeing? Touring? I've never seen much of the island.'

'I'm leaving tomorrow morning at eight,' he said, 'and there's nothing much to see. Plantation house, plantation mansion, rum distillery, sugar mill, sugar windmill.'

'There must be more,' she said.

'Well, it isn't all Carnival and Crop-over, but they won't show you the slave-breeding stations in the countryside. None of them advertise that.'

'Don't say that,' she said. 'I'm so sorry.'

'No need to be,' Solomon said, draining his drink. 'It has nothing to do with you. You're just visiting.'

She reached out and touched him on his arm. Her hand lingered. He looked at her and she made a funny little face. They looked at each other, her hand still resting on his arm.

'You should go,' he said, nodding past the lighted pathway to the hotel. 'Isn't it past your bedtime?'

Clapham said nothing for about five minutes after she left. He closed the counters, measured the bottles, washed the sink and rang up the register. Solomon sat watching him work.

'I remember when they wouldn't allow coloured people

to come to these bars,' he said at last, 'no coloured people at all.'

'Black people,' Solomon corrected him.

'Gor blimey, I been saying coloured people all my life. I can't change; too old, Sol-oh man, too old. Too kiss meh rass old,' he laughed.

'You know,' Solomon said, 'I know a beach just like this in Trinidad.'

'Coming back next year?' Clapham asked.

'I dunno. We need a bridge. My mother never been to Barbados and she's nearly sixty; been to England though; twice.'

Clapham laughed a little louder. 'Damn it, mahn, I been to England and New York.'

'Never been to Trinidad, eh?'

'No man, I got children and grandchildren in Brooklyn, Queens, Leeds, Manchester and London. Big children, big grandchildren. Don't know a soul in Trinidad, though.'

'You know me, man.'

'Some time nuh, I going to check out Trinidad . . . check out your big-able island.'

'Well, I have to pack,' Solomon said.

They shook hands. Solomon walked along the beach to the hotel. There was a new security guard on duty. He took a precautionary step toward Solomon. 'Visitor,' Solomon said. 'Room 1009,' making himself very clear. The guard let him pass. He looked confused and anxious.

Across the hotel lobby Solomon saw the Americans waiting for an elevator. They were still happy. He walked to the front desk. There were no messages. He wasn't expecting any.

He had the elevator to himself.

A light warm wind blew the sea-smell into his room. From his balcony he could hear the sea. That and the sound of insects were the only sounds. Everything was asleep. The sky was overcast and heavy, light spilled half-heartedly from the hotel gardens to the beach. There was an outline of beach and surf, silhouetted trees and a dark dense mass he knew to be water.

Goddam Antilles, he thought, leaning over the balcony. The fear and anger he had felt at the outdoor bar exploded in his temples. He wondered if there was any escape. Goddam Antilles. Maybe he should go live in Canada. Then he thought of Margaret, divorced, excursion fare from Ottawa. Not unattractive either.

It was an hour's flight to Trinidad; he slept all the way. Waiting, it seemed forever, for his luggage at Piarco Airport he thought he should have made Clapham a firm invitation to visit Trinidad.

'. . . If there was a bridge . . .' He whistled a bit of 'Mood Indigo' under his breath.

Someone waiting for luggage began humming 'Sweet Cane Juice'. Two or three others picked up the melody. Solomon got his bags. There was a line-up. It seemed the whole line was humming 'Sweet Cane Juice'.

It took two hours to clear customs and immigration.

The Night Watchman's Occurrence Book

V. S. NAIPAUL

November 21. 10.30 p.m. C. A. Cavander take over duty at C— Hotel all corrected. *Cesar Alwyn Cavander*

7 a.m. C. A. Cavander hand over duty to Mr Vignales at C— Hotel no report. *Cesar Alwyn Cavander*

November 22. 10.30 p.m. C. A. Cavander take over duty at C— Hotel no report. *Cesar Alwyn Cavander*

7 a.m. C. A. Cavander hand over duty to Mr Vignales at C— Hotel all corrected. *Cesar Alwyn Cavander*

This is the third occasion on which I have found C. A. Cavander, Night Watchman, asleep on duty. Last night, at 12.45 a.m., I found him sound asleep in a rocking chair in the hotel lounge. Night Watchman Cavander has therefore been dismissed.
Night Watchman Hillyard: This book is to be known in future as 'The Night Watchman's Occurrence Book'. In it I shall expect to find a detailed account of everything that happens in the hotel tonight. Be warned by the example of ex-Night Watchman Cavander. *W. A. G. Inskip, Manager.*

Mr Manager, remarks noted. You have no worry where I am concern sir. *Charles Ethelbert Hillyard, Night Watchman*

November 23. 11 p.m. Night Watchman Hillyard take over

duty at C— Hotel with one torch light 2 fridge keys and room keys 1, 3, 6, 10 and 13. Also 25 cartoons Carib Beer and 7 cartoons Heineken and 2 cartoons American cigarettes. Beer cartoons intact Bar intact all corrected no report. *Charles Ethelbert Hillyard*

7 a.m. Night Watchman Hillyard hand over duty to Mr Vignales at C— Hotel with one torch light 2 fridge keys and room keys 1, 3, 6, 10 and 13. 32 cartoons beer. Bar intact all corrected no report. *Charles Ethelbert Hillyard*

Night Watchman Hillyard: Mr Wills complained bitterly to me this morning that last night he was denied entry to the bar by you. I wonder if you know exactly what the purpose of this hotel is. In future all hotel guests are to be allowed entry to the bar at whatever time they choose. It is your duty simply to note what they take. This is one reason why the hotel provides a certain number of beer cartons (please note the spelling of this word). *W. A. G. Inskip*

Mr Manager, remarks noted. I sorry I didnt get the chance to take some education sir. *Chas. Ethelbert Hillyard*

November 24. 11 p.m. N. W. Hillyard take over duty with one Torch, 1 Bar Key, 2 Fridge Keys, 32 cartoons Beer, all intact. 12 Midnight Bar close and Barman left leaving Mr Wills and others in Bar, and they left at 1 a.m. Mr Wills took 16 Carib Beer, Mr Wilson 8, Mr Percy 8. At 2 a.m. Mr Wills come back in the bar and take 4 Carib and some bread, he cut his hand trying to cut the bread, so please dont worry about the stains on the carpet sir. At 6 a.m. Mr Wills come back for some soda water. It didn't have any so he take a ginger beer instead. Sir you see it is my intention to do this job good sir I cant see how Night Watchman Cavander could fall asleep on this job sir. *Chas. Ethelbert Hillyard*

You always seem sure of the time, and guests appear to be in the habit of entering the bar on the hour. You will kindly note the exact time. The clock from the kitchen is left on the window near the switches. You can use this clock but you MUST replace it every morning before you go off duty. *W. A. G. Inskip*

Noted. *Chas. Ethelbert Hillyard*

November 25. Midnight Bar close and 12.23 a.m. Barman left leaving Mr Wills and others in Bar. Mr Owen take 5 bottles Carib, Mr Wilson 6 bottles Heineken, Mr Wills 18 Carib and they left at 2.52 a.m. Nothing unusual. Mr Wills was helpless, I don't see how anybody could drink so much, eighteen one man alone, this work enough to turn anybody Seventh Day Adventist, and another man come in the bar, I dont know his name, I hear they call him Paul, he assist me because the others couldn't do much, and we take Mr Wills up to his room and take off his boots and slack his other clothes and then we left. Don't know sir if they did take more while I was away, nothing was mark on the Pepsi Cola board, but they was drinking still, it look as if they come back and take some more, but with Mr Wills I want some extra assistance sir.

Mr Manager, the clock break I find it break when I come back from Mr Wills room sir. It stop 3.19 sir. *Chas. E. Hillyard*

More than 2 lbs of veal were removed from the Fridge last night, and a cake that was left in the press was cut. It is your duty, Night Watchman Hillyard, to keep an eye on these things. I ought to warn you that I have also asked the Police to check on all employees leaving the hotel, to prevent such occurrences in the future. *W. A. G. Inskip*

Mr Manager, I don't know why people so anxious to blame servants sir. About the cake, the press lock at night and I dont have the key sir, everything safe where I am concern sir. *Chas. Hillyard*

November 26. Midnight Bar close and Barman left. Mr Wills didn't come, I hear he at the American base tonight, all quiet, nothing unusual.

Mr Manager, I request one thing. Please inform the Barman to let me know sir when there is a female guest in the hotel sir. *C. E. Hillyard*

This morning I received a report from a guest that there were screams in the hotel during the night. You wrote All Quiet. Kindly explain in writing. *W. A. G. Inskip* Write Explanation here:

EXPLANATION. Not long after midnight the telephone ring and a woman ask for Mr Jimminez. I try to tell her where he was but she say she cant hear properly. Fifteen minutes later she came in a car, she was looking vex and sleepy, and I went up to call him. The door was not lock, I went in and touch his foot and call him very soft, and he jump up and begin to shout. When he come to himself he said he had Night Mere, and then he come down and went away with the woman, was not necessary to mention.

Mr Manager, I request you again, please inform the Barman to let me know sir when there is a female guest in the hotel. *C. Hillyard*

November 27. 1 a.m. Bar close, Mr Wills and a American 19 Carib and 2.30 a.m. a Police come and ask for Mr Wills, he say the American report that he was robbed of $200.00c, he was last drinking at the C— with Mr Wills and others. Mr Wills and the Police ask to open the Bar to search it, I told them I cannot open the Bar for you like that, the Police must come with the Manager. Then the American say it was only joke he was joking, and they try to get the Police to laugh, but the Police looking the way I feeling. Then laughing Mr Wills left in a garage car as he couldn't drive himself and the American was waiting outside and they both fall down as they was getting in the car, and Mr Wills saying any time you want a overdraft you just come to my bank kiddo. The Police left walking by himself. *C. Hillyard*

Night Watchman Hillyard: 'Was not necessary to mention'!! You are not to decide what is necessary to mention in this night watchman's occurrence book. Since when have you become sole owner of the hotel as to determine what is necessary to mention? If the guest did not mention it I would never have known that there were screams in the hotel during the night. Also will you kindly tell me who Mr Jimminez is? And what rooms he occupied or occupies? And by what right? You have been told by me personally that the names of all hotel guests are on the slate next to the light switches. If you find Mr Jimminez's name on this slate, or could give me some information about him, I will be most warmly obliged to you. The lady you ask about is Mrs Roscoe, Room 12, as you very well know. It is your duty to see that guests are not pestered by unauthorized callers. You should give no information about guests to such people, and I would be glad if in future you could direct such callers straight to me. *W. A. G. Inskip*

Sir was what I ask you two times, I dont know what sort of work I take up, I always believe that nightwatchman work is a quiet work and I dont like meddling in white people business, but the gentleman occupy Room 12 also, was there that I went up to call him, I didn't think it necessary to mention because was none of my business sir. *C. E. H.*

November 28. 12 Midnight Bar close and Barman left at 12.20 a.m. leaving Mr Wills and others, and they all left at 1.25 a.m. Mr Wills 8 Carib, Mr Wilson 12, Mr Percy 8, and the man they call Paul 12. Mrs Roscoe join the gentlemen at 12.33 a.m., four gins, everybody calling her Minnie from Trinidad, and then they start singing that song, and some others. Nothing unusual. Afterwards there were mild singing and guitar music in Room 12. A man come in and ask to use the phone at 2.17 a.m. and while he was using it about 7 men come in and wanted to beat him up, so he put down the phone and they all ran away. At 3 a.m. I notice the padlock not on the press, I look inside, no cake, but the padlock was not put on in the first place sir. Mr Wills come down again at 6 a.m. to look for his sweet, he look in the Fridge and did not see any. He took a piece of pineapple. A plate was covered in the Fridge, but it didn't have anything in it. Mr Wills put it out, the cat jump on it and it fall down and break. The garage bulb not burning. *C. E. H.*

You will please sign your name at the bottom of your report. You are in the habit of writing Nothing Unusual. Please take note and think before making such a statement. I want to know what is meant by nothing unusual. I gather, not from you, needless to say, that the police have fallen into the habit of visiting the hotel at night. I would be most grateful if you could find the time to note the times of these visits. *W. A. G. Inskip*

Sir, nothing unusual means everything usual. I dont know, nothing I writing you liking. I don't know what sort of work this night watchman work getting to be, since when people have to start getting Cambridge certificate to get night watchman job, I ain't educated and because of this everybody think they could insult me. *Charles Ethelbert Hillyard*

November 29. Midnight Bar close and 12.15 Barman left leaving Mr Wills and Mrs Roscoe and others in the Bar. Mr Wills and Mrs Roscoe left at 12.30 a.m. leaving Mr Wilson and the man they call Paul, and they all left at 1.00 a.m. Twenty minutes to 2 Mr Wills and party return and left again at 5 to 3. At 3.45 Mr Wills return and take bread and milk and olives and cherries, he ask for nutmeg too, I said we had none, he drink 2 Carib, and left ten minutes later. He also collect Mrs Roscoe bag. All the drinks, except the 2 Carib, was taken by the man they call Paul. I don't know sir I don't like this sort of work, you better hire a night barman. At 5.30 Mrs Roscoe and the man they call Paul come back to the bar, they was having a quarrel, Mr Paul saying you make me sick, Mrs Roscoe saying I feel sick, and then she vomit all over the floor, shouting I didn't want that damned milk. I was cleaning up when Mr Wills come down to ask for soda water, we got to lay in more soda for Mr Wills, but I need extra assistance with Mr Wills Paul and party sir.

The police come at 2, 3.48 and 4.52. They sit down in the bar a long time. Firearms discharge 2 times in the back yard. Detective making inquiries. I dont know sir, I thinking it would be better for me to go back to some other sort of job. At 3 I hear somebody shout Thief, and I see a man running out of the back, and Mr London, Room 9, say he miss 80 cents and a pack of cigarettes which was on his dressing case. I don't know when the people in this place does sleep. *Chas. Ethelbert Hillyard*

Night Watchman Hillyard: A lot more than 80 cents was stolen. Several rooms were in fact entered during the night, including my own. You are employed to prevent such things occurring. Your interest in the morals of our guests seems to be distracting your attention from your duties. Save your preaching for your roadside prayer meetings. Mr Pick, Room 7, reports that in spite of the most pressing and repeated requests, you did not awaken him at 5. He has missed his plane to British Guiana as a result. No newspapers were delivered to the rooms this morning. I am again notifying you that papers must be handed personally to Doorman Vignales. And the messenger's bicycle, which I must remind you is the property of the hotel, has been damaged. What do you *do* at nights? *W. A. G. Inskip*

Please don't ask me sir.

Relating to the damaged bicycle: I left the bicycle the same place where I meet it, nothing took place so as to damage it. I always take care of all property sir. I don't know how you could think I have time to go out for bicycle rides. About the papers, sir, the police and them read it and leave them in such a state that I didn't think it would be nice to give them to guests. I wake up Mr Pick, room 7, at 4.50 a.m. 5 a.m. 5.15 a.m. and 5.30. He told me to keep off, he would not get up, and one time he pelt a box of matches at me, matches scatter all over the place. I always do everything to the best of my ability sir but God is my Witness I never find a night watchman work like this, so much writing I dont have time to do anything else, I dont have four hands and six eyes and I want this extra assistance with Mr Wills and party sir. I am a poor man and you could abuse me, but you must not abuse my religion sir because the good Lord sees All and will have His revenge sir, I don't know what sort of work and trouble I land myself in, all I want is a little quiet night work and all I getting is abuse. *Chas. E. Hillyard*

November 30. 12.25 a.m. Bar close and Barman left 1.00 a.m. leaving Mr Wills and party in Bar. Mr Wills take 12 Carib, Mr Wilson 6, Mr Percy 14. Mrs Roscoe five gins. At 1.30 a.m. Mrs Roscoe left and there were a little singing and mild guitar playing in Room 12. Nothing unusual. The police came at 1.35 and sit down in the bar for a time, not drinking, not talking, not doing anything except watching. At 1.45 the man they call Paul come in with Mr McPherson of the SS Naparoni, they was both falling down and laughing whenever anything break and the man they call Paul say Fireworks about to begin tell Minnie Malcolm coming the ship just dock. Mr Wills and party scatter leaving one or two bottles half empty and then the man they call Paul tell me to go up to Room 12 and tell Minnie Roscoe that Malcolm coming. I don't know how people could behave so the thing enough to make anybody turn priest. I notice the padlock on the bar door break off i hanging on only by a little piece of wood. And when I went up to Room 12 and tell Mrs Roscoe that Malcolm coming the ship just dock the woman get sober straight away like she dont want to hear no more guitar music and she asking me where to hide where to go. I dont know, I feel the day of reckoning is at hand, but she not listening to what I saying, she busy straightening up the room one minute packing the next, and then she run out into the corridor and before I could stop she she run straight down the back stairs to the annexe. And then 5 past 2, still in the corridor, I see a big red man running up to me and he sober as a judge and he mad as a drunkard and he asking me where she is where she is I ask whether he is a authorized caller, he say you don't give me any of that crap now, where she is, where she is. So remembering about the last time and Mr Jimminez I direct him to the manager office in the annexe. He hear a little scuffling inside Mr Inskip room and I make out Mr Inskip sleepy voice and Mrs Roscoe voice and the red man run inside and all I hearing for the next five minutes is bam bam bodow bodow bow and this woman screaming. I dont know what sort of work this night watchman getting I want something quiet like the police. In time things quiet down and the red man drag Mrs Roscoe out of the annexe and they take a taxi, and the Police sitting down quiet in

173

the bar. Then Mr Percy and the others come back one by
one to the bar and they talking quiet and they not drinking
and they left 3 a.m. 3.15 Mr Wills return and take one
whisky and 2 Carib. He asked for pineapple or some sweet
fruit but it had nothing.

6 a.m. Mr Wills come in the bar looking for soda but it
aint have none. We have to get some soda for Mr Wills sir.

6.30 a.m. the papers come and I deliver them to Doorman Vignales at 7 a.m. *Chas. Hillyard*

Mr Hillyard: In view of the unfortunate illness of Mr
Inskip, I am temporarily in charge of the hotel. I trust
you will continue to make your nightly reports, but I
would be glad if you could keep your entries as brief as
possible. *Robt. Magnus, Acting Manager*

December 1. 10.30 p.m. C. E. Hillyard take over duty at C—
Hotel all corrected 12 Midnight Bar close 2 a.m. Mr Wills 2
Carib, 1 bread 6 a.m. Mr Wills 1 soda 7 a.m. Night
Watchman Hillyard hand over duty to Mr Vignales with
one torch light 2 Fridge keys and Room Keys 1, 3, 6 and 12.
Bar intact all corrected no report. *C. E. H.*

Dog Food

MICHAEL RECKORD

A small security guard with a huge German Shepherd on a leash barred my way into the supermarket.

'I just need a bag of corn meal,' I told him.

'Yu can't go een.'

'For the dogs,' I said. I put out my hand to pat his animal.

'Hey!' He dragged the dog away. 'Him wi' bite yu.'

'Not me,' I said. 'He'll bite if you order him to; or if he smells fear. But I'm not afraid of dogs.'

I patted the dog's head and its tail twitched, a mere suggestion of a wag. The guard looked at me incredulously. I smiled down at him.

'Please let me pass.'

He glanced behind him into the supermarket, then back at me. 'A riot goin' on in dere, yu know.'

'I'm not afraid.'

He scratched his head. 'Ah don't even tink dem have any corn meal.'

'Allow me to go and find out for myself, officer. The manager knows me and usually keeps back a few scarce items in the storeroom for me. I'm Mrs Gregory.'

'Mrs Gregory?' he echoed. Clearly didn't know me. Probably didn't read the newspapers.

I told him who I was, or rather who my husband was. Reluctantly he stepped aside.

'Well, try yu luck, Mrs Gregory. But ah don't tink yu can get pass dem women inside just now. Maybe when de police come.'

'The police have been sent for?'

The little man nodded. 'Is only police can control dem women when dem start gwaan like – like – animals.'

'What's the problem?' I asked.

He shrugged. 'Dem tink de manager hoarding scarce goods in de storeroom, Flour, an rice, an soap. So dem trying to bruk down de door.'

'I'm sure the manager bought whatever goods he has with hard-earned cash,' I said. 'They're his, and he's entitled to do whatever he wants with them. I'll bet if their neighbours tried to break down their walls to get their goods they'd be extremely annoyed.'

I went inside and walked over to the manager, a pleasant, well-dressed Chinese gentleman of about forty – a second-generation Jamaican. From the little elevated cubicle that served as his office, he was watching – with typical Chinese inscrutability – the dozen or so women who were yelling at the top of their voices while they beat against the storeroom's drawn steel shutter.

'Good morning, Mr Lowe,' I said. 'I'm sorry about this little trouble you're having.'

'Lue,' he said. 'Good morning, Mrs Gregory.'

'You know, Mr Lue,' I continued, 'the one thing that's wrong with this country is that it's overpopulated.'

He glanced at me briefly, then back at the howling pack of women. They weren't harming the shutter, but I suspected he was worried about them turning to the goods on the shelves.

'Really, Mrs Gregory?' he said.

'Sure. You have a big supermarket here. If you didn't have so many hungry-belly creatures to cater to –' I indicated the mob '– and their hungry-belly offspring, the goods you store here would be quite adequate.'

He glanced at me again. Inscrutably. I wondered if he hadn't understood my point.

'In other words,' I explained, 'your goods are only

scarce because so many people want them.'

He smiled. 'You may be right. And how can I help you today?'

'I need about ten pounds of corn meal,' I said. 'For the dogs.'

He looked grave. 'We have only a little corn meal left, you know, and *they* want it.' He glanced at the women and hesitated. 'Couldn't you buy some of the tinned dog food for today?'

'Oh, I have lots of the tinned stuff. But I need the meal to mix with it. At three dollars a tin, it's too expensive to feed my four dogs with tinned meat alone.'

'I see. Well, could you wait awhile? As soon as the police get those women out of the store, I'll be able to get to the corn meal.'

'They won't be long, will they?'

'I hope not,' he said, eyeing the women.

I frowned. 'You can never tell with the police though, can you? They might be in the middle of a domino game or something. Tell me, is anyone in the storeroom?'

'A couple of packers. Why?'

'I wonder if I could persuade them to pass me the corn meal?'

He shook his head 'You'd never get past those viragos. I think you should wait.'

Smiling at him, I said, 'My husband's favourite adage is: "Nothing tried, nothing done".'

I walked across four aisles to the mob. It was then I noticed that there were three young men – two were boys under twelve, really – in the group. While the women were deadly serious about what they were doing – screaming through the shutter or hammering with their fists or feet upon it – the boys were having fun, grinning at each other and shouting for shouting's sake.

The din was terrific. 'Open de damn door!' Bam! Bam! Bam! 'Pass out de rice!' Buff! Buff! Buff! 'Mi have pickney fi feed!' Wham! Slam! Bang! 'Gimme some soap powder, or ah wi bruk up yu - !' Biff! Baff! Boff! 'De damn Chinee man tief wi when de goods plentiful, an im won't sell wi dem when dem scarce. An oonu tekking him side 'gainst yu own people!' Buff! Slam! Bang! 'Mi seh open de door!'

The women were of all shapes and sizes – short, tall, fat, slim. Some were colourfully, some drably dressed. Most were very black, though there were a couple who were brown-skinned, like me. One was even fairer than I was, but otherwise quite ugly.

'Ladies,' I said, quietly but firmly, 'may I have just a word with one of the storemen in there.'

No one paid me the slightest attention. I tried again, a little more loudly. 'Ladies, if you'd excuse – '

It was like talking to a wall, except this was a moving, heaving, punching, kicking, screaming wall of human bodies. But they *were* all deaf.

'I'm addressing you women,' I shouted. Again in vain, except that two of the boys looked at me, grinned, and went back to assisting the women in making noise and uselessly battering at the shutter.

I can't stand being ignored, never could, and I felt myself losing my temper. But that would have been unseemly. So I decided against shouting any more and against trying to push through the women to get to the shutter.

Breathing deeply, willing myself to be calm, I retreated a few paces from the pack. Which was lucky for me, for that was when the police arrived.

Five of them, gas-masks around their necks, revolvers in their holsters, batons drawn and waving, rushed through the door, shouting. I heard them, but I doubt if the women did until the cops were right on them. Two of the policemen grabbed one boy each and hauled them from the crowd. Depositing the youths a little distance away, the cops then rushed back to assist their colleagues in their efforts to quell the women.

'Bruk it up. Stop dis noise. Oonu go home. Outa de man store!' and similar instructions were shouted to the women, while the cops pulled with hands and pushed with batons at the human wall. But the women, angry and desperate, were not easily moved. At first they resisted the policemen passively, then they started pushing back, so that for several minutes there was more confusion around the shutter, not less.

Then, gradually, the superior strength and fighting technique of the officers caused a breaking up of the solid mass into smaller, discrete groups of fighters. Mostly there was one policeman to two or three women, except in one instance where a young cop was tackling a large, dark woman in a floral dress and blue tie-head.

'Cool down yuself, and come outa de man shop,' yelled the policeman, pushing the woman in the general direction of the door.

'Come out yuself. Mi haffi get rice an flour fi mi family dinner,' the woman shouted back. And she pushed the lighter constable back toward the shutter.

'Yu resisting an officer of de law. Ah can arrest yu.'

'Boy, move outa mi way. Mi pickney haffi eat.'

'Ah warning yu!' The policeman raised his baton high in the air.

'Don't lick her!' The yell came from behind me. I turned. It was the oldest of the young men, a youth of about seventeen.

He rushed forward, but the baton landed with a loud crack on the woman's skull. Blood gushed from a large cut that suddenly appeared on her forehead. She staggered and bent low, both hands holding her head.

'Aunt Ivy! Aunt Ivy!' The youth was screaming, his agonized voice blending with the woman's wail. He rushed to her and held her around the shoulders, preventing her, it seemed to me, from falling.

Glaring at the young policeman, who looked a little

scared at what he'd done, the youth snarled: 'Yu son of a bastard! Yu piece of nastiness! Yu lick Aunt Ivy! Ah going fix yu – '

He kicked at the policeman, caught him in the crotch and the cop doubled up in pain. The boy drew back his foot again. 'Yu bitch!' And he was aiming another kick at the constable's face when another policeman walked away from the women he'd been struggling with, drew his gun and, quite coolly, pressed it against the youth's chest and pulled the trigger.

A loud report. Then dead silence. The youth fell like a full sack of corn meal. Pieces of flesh scattered. Blood gushed suddenly, then just as suddenly stopped. I glimpsed the stunned faces of the policemen and crowd alike as I turned away.

It was quite distressing. Nauseating, in fact. But I looked on the bright side: there was one less hungry belly to feed. The manager, still in his cubicle when I reached him, looked sick, not inscrutable anymore.

'Do you think I could get my ten pounds of corn meal now?' I asked.

He stared at me, as if he hadn't heard.

'My corn meal,' I repeated. 'The mob's dispersed. Would you have one of the store men bring it to my car?'

'Yes,' the manager said slowly, apparently in a daze. 'Yes, Mrs Gregory. Please pay the cashier.'

I did so and walked to the door. The little guard and his large dog were both staring through the glass. I patted the dog on the head again and turned to the guard.

'See, I'm not afraid of dogs,' I said.

Anti-Apartness Anancy
ANDREW SALKEY

Special, sweet truth (*not* history truth) is that Caribbea is a deep sea woman, broadminded when mostly everybody inside her have narrow heart and tight ways. She stay so, from time. Back when pirate prancing and spinning doubloon on her foam, she lick up a class of storm that quiet the direct hooligan buccaneer grabbaliciousness. Back when the islands them catching hard miseries from slavery, she send hurricane, and wash way some of the brutality and savagery off slave back, for a day or so, from year to year, August, September, October time.

So, you see, Caribbea have a long, long tradition-culture of serious risk-taking and rescueation. But, you must know this: Caribbea truly native to more than the islands them in her water; she hinternational, too.

Anywhere, she spy out justice-lack, equality-lack, imperial parangles, and so, she ups and send a daughter or a son to do her name and intention proud; look the heaps of daughter and son did go do Caribbea bidding in Nigeria, Sierra Leone, ol' Gold Coast, Algeria, the US. . . !

Well, now then, Caribbea send for Brother Anancy, a key-ace son who first come out of Africa himself when Europe economics-ting-an-ting salt bad, and nough tiefing had was to devil-support expansion, and slavery was a bunch of khus-khus grass for Europe, and slave leave with plenty ashes in them mouth, on the Middle P, and after.

So, right now, Caribbea send for Anancy because she feel him could well use some of the back-home tactics to help out the township folks in South Africa.

Caribbea understand that Afrikaner *baasskap* days nearing time when it going take tail and lap it between Sam Browne buckle and oak tree branch, but that, as facts, it going need a shove from somebody tactical like Anancy.

All the same though, Anancy, who is a proper African New World spider and a natural man, fuse up with a clench fist of high cunny, usual cause bafflement and perplex head mongst every enemy he got. Don't forget, now, Anancy is a craft of dutty low blows is a barrow of brigand help for poor people who dispossess total is a particular fighter against wretched earth is a duppy conqueror of all conquerors is a nut shell giant of world jinalship versus darkness.

When Anancy land up in the thick apartness of South Africa, and he remember the must-trust words Caribbea breathe into him, the ones that make him out to be a tactical spider-man, he take foot and visit a nearby township.

Anancy start to talk to a leader-woman. She have a real vital name. everybody call her Nomzamo, and that mean She Who Born To Persevere, a most correct name, seeing as how South Africa and the whole world stay collapse-sided for that matter of frightration fact.

Nomzamo say, 'Amandla!' And she teach Anancy to say, as a proper answer, 'Awethu!'

And that short word-ritual add up to: Power! Power is ours!

So, Anancy tell Nomzamo what he come to do, and that a next woman send him.

And Nomzamo say that she hear about Caribbea and that she is a far-away good conscience woman who know about total deep suffering, as ages.

Nomzamo and Anancy talk and drink some peas soup with meat kind in it, and talk some more. She say a certain something that heart touch Anancy tactics, urgent special.

She mention in a soft voice that whatever tactics Anancy coming with, he must get approve from the Black, Green and Gold (BGG) before he make a move into movement.

He promise her that that is that, that, in fact, Caribbea warn him about that, direct.

Nomzamo set up a meeting with Anancy and two BGG official, for the next day, and she invite Anancy to stay in her house, for the night. But Anancy say, 'If you give me a blanket, I could stay up in a tree branch, outside you house.'

'But why so?' Nomzamo ask him, puzzle frown.

'Well, I could tighten up and spin a small web and settle down in a nook in the tree.' Anancy twinkle one eye, and touch the top part of the green waistcoat he like to wear on jobs that call for tactics. 'Besides, if the police and army come to search you house, early morning, they won't find no stranger to get you into bothers.'

Nomzamo still puzzle frowning, but she nod sweet understanding, when she hook into the compassion part of Anancy reasoning. She not a world class leader-woman for nothing.

Case as may be, Anancy leave Nomzamo house, and he scout out the township, drink a big head rich foam beer down by a working people open air set-up, and decide to make a call on some apartness people, in the salube suburbs not all that distance from the township proper.

He coil up himself into a spider form, and flit over the house-tops, listening to the anxiety talk of the apartness people. They conversating about the township killings that the police and army doing everywhere, and they feeling secure gratis and powderful that force is brute force, and that *baasskap* life continuing, sweet and syrupy.

Anancy swoop down on one certain apartness person house-top in the salube suburbs, and he get a *bragadap* shock when he pick up what one woman saying, in a nose-and-throat scrape voice that Dutch Cape up, bad, to a next woman, 'If only we could go back and set up this country in a different way. From the time the South African Act of 1913 was passed and the Africans were forbidden to acquire property, the system was clinched.'

Anancy stare down at this wagga-wagga confession, and nod pure so-so disbelief. He well know that Caribbea understand the 1913 thing but to hear it plain regretful from a salube suburbs person was something extra voops.

As Anancy flit off to a next part of the city, he considering that these apartness people and the murder government truly know what they causing to happen to millions and millions of folks. But, one conscience that guilty don't even make ripple whisper.

Still coil up tight spider, Anancy flit plenty miles to East London, and perch on a beam in a house that having regular discussion about revolute or stay-same-way. Revolute hold the night, big. Mind, heart, voice, one.

Anancy hear that '50 was the time when the pressdown on sovietics happen, with beat up and arrest; and more of that in '55, '56, '57 and '58; and then the murderation in Sharpeville '60; and the stay-home demo and banning of the BGG in '61; and the sabotage thing in '62, with more beat up and arrest; and passbook protest '64, when police shoot people in them back; then they pass the Group Areas tra-la-la in '65; and eleven years of white bandage state 'pression and terror, right up to '76 and the Soweto 'rising when they kill school children and other innocent folks. And then, a next ten years with the same justice-lack and brutality and murderation.

After that, Anancy s-back to Nomzamo house, about five morning time, and grab some shut eye on the tree branch, until the meeting with Nomzamo and the two BGG official.

He dream a dread dream, nook up on the tree branch: *Fire into every space he seeing. Fire on the land. Fire in water. Fire in the sky. Even fire was into shadow. He glimpse Table*

Mountain, and it have fire all round it and on top, too. Plenty crick-crack coming from heaps and heaps of run-an-stan-up fire. Then, sudden so, fog everywhere. Like it was a wicked smoke covering the world. Only one place escape the buffootoo *shroud: the space around Nomzamo house. Only thing is that hanging down low over the house is a bunch-up spread of searchlight sjambok beam and bullet belt.*

Morning dawn innocent lamb. The township lay down, wrongful peaceful but natural-like. Nomzamo yard looking spruce and spacious. The light make everything look stocious. Everything clean and clear-off and waiting.

Anancy study the z-bend brains he born with, while he walking ginger-foot round Nomzamo yard. What and what not to expect from the meeting with the BGG flip-flip in him mind the whole time. He know what he going suggest, but the BGG might come to consider it too *cut-capoose*.

Going worry bothers about that later when time come, Anancy say to himself, and sit down as a human self on Nomzamo back door step.

He head count the six tactics he feel he going drop on the BGG. They rightful extreme but they fit the wicked apartness disease to a small knife-twist t.

He turn mind to Nomzamo. When he consider the *baasskap* tormentation that she and her millions facing full face, every day, he know for sure that the six tactics-remedy not too extralandish.

Then, he turn mind to Caribbea. And when he ponder the serious job she give him to do, he well know that he must and bound to use more than the two-sided z-bend brains he got. Maybe even three or four could be the sides-number he going have ace cause to haul down into service. Whatever it take, Caribbea Anancy going do it with more than nough mind-and-heart contact-fusion. Anancy take mission make it into endless passion, constant for ever.

Meeting time come. Nomzamo and the two BGG official

them and Anancy sitting down, peas pod. Not a ripple is a ripple. Talk now coming to where Anancy apartness-remedy have to get airing in direct style.

So, Anancy clear him throat-hole, cock him head slantwise serious, bat him eye two time, and commence to deliver: 'The tormentation and torturation you all suffering in you own Azania, right here so, is a thing that I could maybe help you with, you know. It have due remedy, but the remedy not easy cheese.'

'Talk you talk,' Nomzamo tell him. 'We listening good.'

'I come with humble heart and ready head,' Anancy say. 'You must know that, from start, yes?'

'We understand the difficult twin that humble and ready making into one,' Nomzamo say.

The two BGG official nodding behind Nomzamo words. Then, they smile a perfecto brotherly smile in the space between Anancy and Nomzamo, where the two face ups and making frame picture.

Just about that said same time so, Anancy hearing Caribbea voice talking soft, soft, right under the table the meeting taking place around, and her sea-song voice saying, 'Don't only talk humble, Anancy, but beg you talk helpful, you hear? No gangplank grand charge. No big sermon speechifying. No twist arm. You hearing me, Anancy?'

Anancy say yes, quiet.

One BGG official ask him, 'How you plan stay?'

Anancy say, 'It hard but it have plenty hope inside it.'

The next other BGG say, 'We been waiting years to finish this leggo beast apartness plague. Hard not no obstacle, man. Hard is friend.'

Anancy hearing a funny leaf swirl sound outside in the yard but it look as if nobody else hearing it, at all, same thing like with Caribbea voice under the table.

Anancy take time and get up, beg pardon, and go by the window and look out.

Nomzamo and the two BGG official come to understand

that maybe why Anancy get up is because he cautious or because he needing to move stylish before he start to finger-jab down and chat up the tactics-remedy. So, they don't say nothing. They only waiting polite political and hunch shoulder.

Anancy, meantime, seeing a thing through the window that fantasticating him brains, total. A big heap of dry leaf and small bramble turning round and round in a tight circle in the middle of Nomzamo yard. Same time so, a giant billboard white hand, cut off by the elbow, floating free, come up to the window and pull Anancy out into the yard.

Nomzamo and the two BGG official still hunch up round the table.

The giant billboard hand cuff down Anancy into the turning heap of dry leaf and small bramble, and fly way, cool doctor breeze.

Rawtid! Anancy z-bend brains, two, three, four sides, contact Anancy mission-passion, and deciding now to struggle, gully mout' and macca precipice. Is what he make for, to rass! So, Anancy start a kicking-and-a-bucking thing mongst the leaf-and-bramble, and send some Ali upper-cut and Kong elbow blow into it, plus some Fu stranglehold and finger gouge. He spy say that this leaf-and-bramble is nothing else but *baasskup* turn into special devilment. The giant billboard white hand, chop off by the elbow, that fly way, is another shape that *baasskap* take to mince up him mind and mash up him anti-apartness tactics-remedy.

The leaf-and-bramble reach up to a storm swirl speed, and Anancy wedge down inside it, bury up into it, deep, deep, in spite of the ol'-time Maroon moves he making, after the Fu gouge.

He trying hard to raise up himself out of the storm swirl that bending up him body like Q, but he sinking down, every time. He make a next hard try, and he windmill all the leaf and bramble them, slap into the four corners of Nomzamo yard.

Anancy hush a laugh. He straighten the green waistcoat and he walk boasify up to Nomzamo back door step. And he grab the door-knob, baps.

Seconds, and the storm swirl gather power, come out of the four corner, join up, pick Anancy off the door step, lift itself off the ground, and take off cross the Atlantic and fling Anancy like a spider-star straight back into Caribbea sea water.

But, you see, what the giant billboard white hand, chop off by the elbow, and the leaf-and-bramble storm swirl didn't see was when Anancy drop a longish piece of paper, cute, inside the meeting room, before the white hand pull him outside.

Nomzamo and the two BGG official find it and pick it up when they notice Anancy well gone. They spread it out flat on the table and Nomzamo start to read it:

SIX TACTICS

1. GENERAL STRIKE OUT CALL BY BGG.
2. AZANIAN FOLKS TO PILE UP FOOD, SHARE IT MONGST OTHER SUFFERERS, STAY HOME, AND DON'T SHOP NOWHERE.
3. CAUSE STOCK EXCHANGE AND ALL TOURISM AGENCY TO CLOSE PRONTO, WITH PLENTY HEAVY BGG BOMBARDMENT-MOVES.
4. BGG TO DROP A MOST DEEP SLEEP SOMETHING INTO ALL THE RESERVOIR THAT SERVING THE APARTNESS SUBURBS AFRIKANER PEOPLE WITH DRINKING AND COOKING WATER.
5. BGG TO MASH UP AND BURY DOWN ALL VARIOUS NUCLEAR DEVICE AND PLUTONIUM CRUTRIMENTS IN THE PROFOUND EARTH BACK O' TABLE MOUNTAIN.
6. THEN, FINAL, BGG TO SHIP OUT OF THE COUNTRY ALL THE SLEEPING AFRIKANERS, AND LAY THEM DOWN SNUG IN THE ANTARCTIC.

And that is how Caribbea and Brother Anancy come to 'tribute a little something to the way apartness going vanish total from the *baasskap* world.

Jack Mandora, me no tell what not possible in a mostly impossible set-up!

Brackley and the Bed

SAMUEL SELVON

One evening Brackley was cruising round by the Embankment looking for a soft bench to rest his weary bones, and to cogitate on the ways of life. The reason for that, and the reason why the boys begin to call him Rockabye, you will find out as the ballad goes on.

Brackley hail from Tobago, which part they have it to say Robinson Crusoe used to hang out with Man Friday. Things was brown in that island and he make for England and manage to get a work and was just settling down when bam! he get a letter from his aunt saying that Teena want to come England too.

Teena was Brackley distant cousin and they was good friends in Tobago. In fact, the other reason why Brackley hustle from the island is because it did look like he and Teena was heading for a little married thing, and Brackley run.

Well, right away he write aunty and say no, no, because he have a feeling this girl would make botheration if she come England. The aunt write back to say she didn't mean to say that Teena want to come England, but that Teena left Tobago for England already.

Brackley hold his head and bawl. And the evening the boat train come in at Waterloo, he went there and start 'busing she right away not waiting to ask how the folks at home was or anything.

'What you doing in London?' Brackley ask as soon as Teena step off the train. 'What you come here for, eh? Even though I write home to say things real hard?'

'What happen, you buy the country already?' Teena sheself giving tit for tat right away. 'You ruling England now? The Queen abdicate?'

'You know where you going?' Brackley say. 'You know where you is? You know what you going to do?'

'I am going straight to the Colonial Office,' Teena say.

'What you think the Colonial Office is, eh? You think they will do anything for you? You have a god-father working there?'

Well, they argue until in the end Brackley find himself holding on to Teena suitcase and they on the way to the little batchy he have in Golders Green at the time.

When they get there Teena take one look at the room and sniff. 'But look at the state you have this room in! You ain't ashamed of yourself?'

'Listen,' Brackley say, 'you better don't let me and you have contention. I know this would of happen when you come.'

Teena start squaring up the room brisk-brisk.

'It making cold,' she say, putting chair this way and table that way and turning everything upside down for poor Brackley. 'How you does keep warm? Where the gas fire I hear so much about?'

Brackley grudgingly put a shilling in the meter and light the gas.

'What you have to eat?' But even as she asking she gone in the cupboard and begin pulling out rations that Brackley had stow away to see him through the winter. Brackley as if he mesmerize, stand up there watching her as she start up a peas and rice on the gas ring.

'You better go easy with them rations,' he say. 'I not working now and money don't grow on tree here as in Tobago.'

When they was eating Teena say: 'Well, you have to get a job right away. You was always a lazy fellar.'

'Keep quiet,' Brackley say, enjoying the meal that Teena

cook in real West Indian fashion – the first good meal he ever had in London. 'You don't know nothing.'

'First thing tomorrow morning,' Teena say. 'What time you get up?'

'About nine – ten,' Brackley say vaguely.

'Well is six o'clock tomorrow morning, bright and early as the cock crow.'

'You don't hear cock crowing in London,' Brackley say. Then he drop the spoon he was eating with. 'Six o'clock! You must be mad! Six o'clock like midnight in the winter, and people still sound asleep.'

'Six o'clock,' Teena say.

Brackley finish eating and begin to smoke, whistling a calypso softly, as if he in another world and not aware of Teena at all.

'Ah well,' he say, stretching by the fire, 'that wasn't a bad meal. Look, I will give you some old blankets and you could wrap up that coat and use as a pillow – you could sleep on the ground in that corner . . .'

'*Me*? On the floor? You not ashamed?'

'Well, is only one bed here as you see . . .'

'I using the bed.'

'Girl, is winter, and if you think I going to sleep in the corner with two old blanket and wake up stiff . . .'

But, in the end, was Brackley who crouch up in the corner, and Teena sound asleep in the bed.

It look to Brackley like he hardly shut his eyes before Teena was shaking him.

'Get up,' Teena say, 'six o'clock.'

Brackley start to curse.

'None of that,' Teena say. 'No bad language when I around.'

Teena move around fast and give Brackley breakfast and make him dress and get out on the cold streets mumbling, 'Get a job, get a job,' before he knew what was happening.

It was only about ten o'clock, when he was washing

dishes in a café where he get a work, that Brackley realize what was happening to him.

When he get home in the evening, Teena have screen put up around the bed and everything spick and span, and Brackley don't know where to look even for chair to sit down.

'I see you make yourself at home,' he say maliciously.

'And what you think?' Teena flares.

'The boys come here sometimes for a little rummy.'

'None of that now.'

'And sometimes a girl-friend visit me.'

'None of that now.'

'So you taking over completely.'

'Aunty say to look after you.'

'Why the hell you come England, eh?'

Well, a pattern begin to form as the weeks go by, but the main thing that have Brackley worried is the bed. Every night he curl up in the corner shivering, and by the time he doze off: 'Six o'clock, get up, you have to go to work.'

Brackley ain't sleep on bed for weeks. The thing like an obsession with him. He window-shopping on the way home and looking at them bed and soft mattress on show and closing his eyes and sighing. Single divan, double divan, put-you-up, put-you-down – all makes and sizes he looking at.

One night when frost was forming on the window pane Brackley wake up and find he couldn't move.

'Teena.'

'What?'

'You sleeping?'

'Yes.'

'Teena, you want to get married?'

'Married? To who?'

'To me.'

'What for?'

'So-I-could-sleep-in-the-bed – I mean, well, we uses to

know one another good in Tobago, and now that you are here in London, what do you think?'

'Well, all right, but you have to change your ways.'

'Yes, Teena.'

'And no foolishness when we married. You come home straight from work. And I don't want you looking at no white girls.'

'Yes, Teena.'

No sooner said than done. Brackley hustle Teena off to the registry office as soon as things was fixed, thinking only how nice the bed would be after the hard floor and the cold, with Teena to help keep him warm.

'What about honeymoon?' Teena say after the ceremony.

'In the summer,' Brackley say. 'Let we go home. I am tired and I feel I could sleep for weeks.'

'Bracks,' Teena say as they was coming away. 'I have a nice surprise for you. Guess who coming to London this evening?'

'Father Christmas,' Brackley says yawning.

'No. Aunty. I write telling her to come up, as the room not so small and we could manage until we get another place. And then she and me could get a work too, and that will help.'

'You putting hell 'pon jackass back,' Brackley moan. But it was only when they reach home that a great fear come to Brackley. He had was to sit down in a chair before he could talk.

'But Teena,' he say quietly, 'we ain't have no place for Aunty to sleep?'

'Don't worry,' Teena say. 'She can sleep with me until we find another place.'

Ballad

OLIVE SENIOR

1

Teacher ask me to write composition about The Most Unforgettable Character I Ever Meet and I write three page about Miss Rilla and Teacher tear it up and say that Miss Rilla not fit person to write composition about and right away I feel bad the same way I feel the day Miss Rilla go and die on me.

When Miss Rilla die I wish I could make up a Ballad for her like they do for famous people in the old days. Dont ask me why only when we sing ballad song in school I get sad and think of Miss Rilla. But I cant sing or play guitar and nobody make music round here since that Blue Boy gone away and beside this whole thing too deep and wide for a little thing like a Ballad. So I will just tell you the story of Miss Rilla and Poppa D, Blue Boy and me though it is really about Miss Rilla. And when we come to the sad part we can have something like a chorus because they have that in all the ballad song they sing but I dont think bout the chorus yet.

Miss Rilla die on truck that was carrying her to market and they bring her body back down but I never see it before they make it one with the Springville ground for all day I down by the river crying and not crying, laughing and not laughing.

O my Lord. Miss Rilla dont laugh round here anymore and it seem like all the laughing in the world come to a stop and everybody talking nice bout her. Eh-eh everybody talking like they never once say any nastiness and like Blue

195

Boy would say if he was here, 'It grieve me so Lord.' Is same way Blue Boy would say only he dont talk much because all the time he there playing music on one fife he did make himself and this music tall and pale and thin just like him and not like anything you ever hear over Mass Curly radio.

To show you how Blue Boy never talk much: the night Joe Amos come from town with news that Miss Rilla drop dead on truck every jack man in Springville have something to say. Except Blue Boy. He never say anything at all. Blue Boy just stick him fife in him pocket and he leave only I dont know is gone he gone forever till him mother come from over Laplands the Sunday and say nobody see him anywhere and where he is. And when I say I dont know she give me bad eye for me and Blue Boy always keeping company but it wasnt what anybody think at all so I dont pay her no mind. And nobody see him to this day although I have strong feeling he gone Kingston to get on Talent Show on radio and if he ever come back to this place at all he will change change.

So now Blue Boy sort of walk through my mind but not Miss Rilla. Blue Boy pass through my mind because I dont remember music in my mind. But every now and then when something really sweet me I will break into a loud loud laugh and sometimes when I listen back to this laugh is just like Miss Rilla herself laughing.

Even MeMa notice it for the other day she say to me, 'Lenora, cut out that nasty piece of laughing for you beginning to sound just like Rilla Dunvil' only by the time she say it I not laughing any more I crying but not so she can see.

MeMa never cry for Miss Rilla. MeMa never cry for nobody. And she did have some harsh word to say about Miss Rilla and Blue Boy – the only people in the world that I love.

Bwoy, hear what she say about Blue Boy when she see him passing on roadside:

'Look at that wutless good-fe-nutten a gwan there nuh.

Whoever hear bout a big man a-play on a half-ass piece of bamboo all day long, tell me nuh? But what you expect no Laplands he come from? An' let me tell you that nutten good ever come out of that backward place and that is the Lord own truth. Is pure Coromantee nigger live over there like that bwoy Zackie that did tief Mass Curly goat yu no see how the lot of them redibo and have puss eye? Just like that musicman friend of yours there. He might be yu cousin out of wedlock that yu father brother Rennis did have on the side with that Coromantee woman and blood thicker than water but I still dont see why you have to mix yuself up with that trash because everybody trying hard to bring yu up in a good Christian home with decent people children. Anyway bird of a feather flock together and everybody know your pedigree not so hot so if is that class of people yu want to mix up wid dog nyam yu supper. Yu can gwan yu is yu father pickney and he will have to deal with yu I not going worry myself no more.'

When MeMa go on so I just sit quiet quiet till she forget what she talking bout because if I make any sound she quick to fire me a box hot-hot. I call her MeMa though she really not my mother at all. She is the mother of Elsie and George and Rainey and Marshall and Petey and Dulcie and Gabriel but their pa Mass George is my Pa too only he did have me with a lady friend he was keeping one time over at Morningside. But she did have other children from before I born and MeMa did take me from I small and raise me up in her house because she say she couldnt stand the embarrassment that it cause with her church sister and all to see me as a Barstard round the place. And generally she not so bad though she say some word that really hurt sometime and I know that she dont love me like her own children but that Miss Rilla love me because she dont have no other children to love.

So whenever MeMa done quarrel and gone round the back I wait until her attention distracted and I run down to

Miss Rilla yard where I know Blue Boy waiting under the jacaranda tree and Miss Rilla sitting in her rocking chair eating her own sweet things she bake in the oven that Poppa D make for her round the back and I so happy my two people in the world waiting for me.

O God but sometime MeMa go on bad about people so, especially about Miss Rilla. Miss Rilla will walk past in her pretty red dress and her new head tie and some big gold earring hanging down and Poppa D new boots and I think she looking like a million pound and like Missis Queen herself.

'Aie there Miss Grett, w'appen,' she call out smiling and waving her hankie at MeMa who there hanging out clothes on the line.

'Holdin steady me darling, holdin steady me chile,' MeMa call out in her sweet-sweet voice and the clothes pin she holding drop from her mouth. 'Stop! Is how yu looking so blooming today me dear?'

'Aie, a not feeling so well all the same yu know but I cant complain,' Miss Rilla say and she fanning and wiping her face for the day really hot.

I a-listen from round the side of the house and I know them two set of eye make one and then the two of them look way quick-quick and is only silence I hear.

Then Miss Rilla say slow-like, 'Well, a jus run a Mass Curly shop to get me a little oil before dark for Poppa D never remember bring me a drop from town.'

'Eh-eh, then no so life stay me dear. Anyway some of we not even so lucky to have people bring we things from town ha-ha,' MeMa say. 'But walk good me dear.'

All this time she talking in her sweet-sweet voice and she watch Miss Rilla walk slow-like up the road because Miss Rilla carry plenty weight on her body and the rockstone them really hard.

As soon as Miss Rilla outa earshot and MeMa take her in she run inside quick time and bawl out for my big sister

Dulcie and Estrella that does wash for us sometime. 'Ai
Dulcie, Estrella, come look at this pappyshow no mi chile.'
And the whole lot of them run outside to crane them neck
up the road.

'Eh-eh, Mother-young-gal brucking style today papa,'
say the Dulcie she.

'She really looking blooming me dear I tell her though I
would look blooming too if I was brazen enough so put all
that rouge thing on my face,' MeMa say.

'An her earring look just like cartwheel. Is who she
trying fool say is gold?'

'An is poor Poppa D good boot she a-wear out,' Estrella
say as if is her boot. 'Lord, Jackass say worl no level an is
true because look how that man work him finger to the
bone an all the woman do is wear out him good boot on the
rockstone jus because she wan bus style.'

And then they say plenty more thing and they go on like
that every time Miss Rilla even step out of her yard.

O Lord. No more laughing. No more big gold earring.
No more Miss Rilla gizada to cool down me temper when
MeMa beat me. All the sweetness done.

2

'Hi yu little crying chile with the red head. Come here,'
Miss Rilla call out the day I pass her house just after she
move down from Red Ground. 'Come here, you is a Gayle
without a doubt. What yu crying for?'

O Lord Miss Rilla larger than my whole life sitting on a
rocking chair Poppa D make for her but it splintering now
and I learn when she ask question she dont want answer
for she using her apron to wipe my eye and when she done I
get a good look at her. I did think Miss Rilla was a gypsy
woman though I never in my life see no gypsy but that is
how she look. To Gawd! And me eye water done quick
quick for she gone inside the house and I studying how a big

woman can move so light and she come back out with a plateful of gizada that big and juicy and hot, and quick, I forget bout beating and eye water.

'Little sweetness always cure bad temper. Never mind though chile yu forget the hurt by the time yu marry. But take care yu dont marry already for when eveningtime come I see you with that boy that play the music so sweet the two of you nice-up past here eveningtime yu think I dont see you.'

By this time Miss Rilla laughing and laughing the way she laugh when she teasing people and she didnt have in her false teeth the first time I see her and her mouth wide open in a O in her big big laugh.

Before Miss Rilla laughing I never hear woman really laugh before, think only man know how to give deep belly laugh.

Miss Rilla used to bake things and keep in a glass case and sell them to schoolchildren and big people that pass. But most of the time she take her sweet things to Kingston to sell on sidewalk. She would travel up to Kingston with the rest of the higgler on Mass Curly truck that Poppa D use to drive. People did say that is not that she really need the money but that she dont trust Poppa D out of her sight and some people say that is the other way round but I dont business with that.

Anyway is same truck that Miss Rilla die on. Her heart just give way 'cording to Big Mout Doris. Is Big Mout Doris did tell the whole story to MeMa and MeMa just interrupting all the time and is bout Miss Rilla I want to hear.

'We jus have to wait in the middle of the sunhot you know Miss Grett, yes maam,' Big Mout Doris say. 'Cephas had was to get ride to May Pen to get Strongman and Strongman get ride to where we all was and drive we to town. Poppa D did want the truck was to turn back and go straight home but by this time all we food spoiling in the sunhot and is not the people hard you understand but is we livelihood that and pickney still a yard fe keep alive so we had was to reach town.

'So when Poppa D introduce this argument tho we all grieve we couldnt do nutten bout it. Him there a cry and a say how police a town going to take him wife body weh and not give him back and how him did promise bury her under jacaranda tree in garden so when she dead she can still hear tree branch a su-su. Some people extra yu know maam . . .

'To tell yu truth we nevva like the dead body on the truck but she didnt look so bad you know she just look like seh she sleeping and how we did fine out that is dead she dead is that she did lean over on Jennie on the bench and Jennie say "Hi Miss Rilla allow me to breathe no man you heavy to support yu know and we all want catch we little sleep before we reach town."

'Then Jennie did try ease her back on her side of the bench and all the try she try she couldnt budge her for she like dead weight and then Jennie touch her and notice that she cold cold so she try wake her and she callin and shoutin so hard she wake up everybody else in the truck but not Miss Rilla and then Jennie give out "Lord Jesus I think is dead Miss Rilla dead on me" and everybody start bawl out fe Jesus and we finally come to a real understand-ing that is dead she dead in truth so we knock on the window to get Poppa D to stop the truck and at last he must study that something wrong for he stop the truck and he come round the back and he shout out: "Is what hap-pen to the whole lot of you eh?"

'An we didnt have the heart to tell him that Miss Rilla dead so we say: "We dont think Miss Rilla feelin so well Poppa D" and he say "eh-eh" and climb in the truck and start feel her hand and her face and then he feel her heart and he saying "Miss Rill Miss Rill" quiet-like and when he feel her heart he find out that it not beating at all so now he turn round and look at all of we standing outside round the back of the truck a look up at him and we all quiet and when he look at we all he did say was "Why you all didnt tell me she dead eh" and none of we did know what to say to that.

'So he just sit there a hold her hand and everything quiet like it quiet onto death and we never even notice that day breaking round we and everybody coughing and slapping the mosquito them and not saying nothing and we shifting we foot because we dont know what to do till finally Cephas clear him throat and Cephas say, "Poppa D we know is hard and we is all grieving with you but we cant stay here all day and sunhot coming up."

'This was to get Poppa D to do something but he never say nothin and by this time we all by the roadside and a start argue so finally – you know how Cephas have a word for every occasion – finally Cephas say "Listen now Poppa D is in no fit state to drive we and since none of we can drive this truck we have to find somebody else to drive. Is not that I cant drive you know I can drive good good but like how that tiefing bwoy up May Pen fail me when I go take Test because I never give him more than four shilling the ol dawg I dont want get in no trouble with police."

'So we there arguing again and this time Poppa D crying and say how we have to go back to Springville and we say we cant do that for our livelihood on that truck so Cephas go get Strongman and Strongman come back and drive we. And we telling Poppa D he better off siddown in front with Strongman because he would have to direct him when he reach town seeing as how Strongman dont know town so good. So we manage to get him to the truck front because all the time he like a man in a dream and Miss Rilla look like she still asleep though nobody sitting beside her now. And Cephas say "Look here this is a time of sadness and the Bible say that we must respect the dead, amen. But I think we doing the right thing and God will smile on we because he understand we is all poor people and we must look after we living and if we dont sell we things we living dont eat. But I dont think that we should tell anybody in town there is a dead on this truck with this food for them Kingston people is very foolish and suspicious and they would never buy food from Springville people again. So we better take the food off quick as we reach and leave Miss Rilla with Poppa D and Strongman to look after."

'So Strongman tell we afterward that Poppa D still confuse up when we reach and he didnt know what to do but Strongman see a Special that he did know from long time – is Jane Southwell from Red Groun pickney that she did have with the Adams bwoy from Montego Bay and him turn out good-good and get job with Police – so Strongman call him one side and tell him that we have a dead body on the truck and the Special dont believe but he look inside and he see the body in truth so him study for a while and then him say as cording to how things stay Strongman better take the body to morgue for if police find out is plenty trouble. So after one piece of argument with Poppa D that is what they do.

'Anyway I hear that they still have plenty confusion with police and Poppa D did have to pay plenty money to have the body embalm and they bring it back down in a special big black car pretty cant done. I didnt see it but Jennie tell me that them embalmer man from Kingston did fix her up real nice and she did have a lovely funeral but I couldnt go because the youngest Eda sick bad again and coughing the whole night . . . I tell you one thing though Miss Grett, that Poppa D not himself at all from it happen. I never see a man take death so hard in all me born days and when you consider what she is . . . Anyway, they say you mustnt say bad bout the dead and I dont have a thing personal against her you understand because plenty time she really kind to the pickney them. But since the funeral Poppa D just sit on the same rocking chair she herself use to siddown on and is like him dont see nothing that a go on in front of him eye.

Is like he looking down inside himself all the time. But maam, if I was him I wouldnt look down inside my soul at all for I would fraid what I see. They say what is past is past and is water under bridge nuh, but the Lord say that retribution for your sin will catch up with you. Is not everybody die on truck that going to town Miss Grett, is not a Christian death that at all at all . . . While I never say nutten bad bout the dead and nothing personal bout Miss Rilla none of the two of them can really expect to have a good death after all they have on their conscience and I would not surprise if she not resting easy herself. In fact I hope they planning a good burydown with plenty rum and praying for if her duppy come back is sure to turn rolling calf because she did even look like coolie sometime and everybody know how coolie duppy bad.

'Anyway I cant linger with you at all today for the baby still have the grippe bad but I hear say Mass Curly having a hard time getting somebody to drive that truck and if another truck did pass by I would prefer to take it. Poppa D burn out just good fe nutten me dear maam . . . Anyway I sorry I cant stay for a good labrish but is gone me gone now and as they say cockroach no business inna fowl roost but is really a hard thing that happen to Poppa D.'

Ai, no more laughing. No more Miss Rilla come back from market bringing me a pocket comb or a hair ribbon. Only Poppa D and I hurry pass the house and dont say a word. It dont matter. Poppa D dont see nobody dont see me.

3

Now it look like I gone and spoil this ballad story for this is not the way I want to tell it at all. The part about Miss Rilla dying is the end part and it really should start at the beginning. Only to tell you the truth I dont know the beginning or end of anything right now for I still grieve

over my lovely friend Miss Rilla that gone and die on me.
And I suppose to sit exam this year for scholarship to high
school but Teacher go and tell MeMa I not learning at all
and he say is a sin because I am a bright girl especially at
the english language he say and could become teacher or
nurse or something like that. So MeMa beat me for I not
learning and she say she dont understand how I turn
worthless in school nowadays considering that my two
distraction Miss Rilla and Blue Boy not here anymore to
turn me fool.

To tell you truth I dont think MeMa mind if I dont pass
exam because I dont think she like how I come bright in
school and Teacher always praising me and none of her
own children so bright. And I think she vex because I am
me father outside child and I come bright. And although
she listen to Teacher and beat me when I dont study hard
and tell Teacher she want to do her best for me even
though I not her child, at the yard she say when she vex:

'Dont bother get no idea into your head bout pass exam
and go high school and that sort of impertinence for none
of my rightful children them reach high school yet and I
dont know what make you think you better than them and
I know is that teacher there putting idea into your head
that you so bright that make you carrying on this
extraness. But teacher only like you because you darker
than my children and is only that you red and not so black
like him and everybody saying how black man time come
now and they all sticking together and my children come
out too good colour to suit him. Thats why he never
encouragement them and make them fail they exam all the
time because they come out with good colour and straight
hair better than Chiney hair and everybody know this
country going to the dog these days for is pure black
people children they pushing to send high school. Anybody ever hear you can educate monkey? Well in that case
I dont care if my children dont go because nobody of

consequence going to them old high school anymore. Anyway that teacher man forming fool though. Dont bother make him put no more idea into your head for I take you from you was a baby and raise you up in good Christian home and spend money clothe and feed you and give you book and slate and pencil for school just like I give my own children and I never once treat you different from them in any way at all and I do this from the bottom of my heart because the Bible say "Suffer little children to come onto me" so dont bother make teacher turn you fool . . .'

Is so she go on and she slap the iron on the coal pot and grab a new one and when she wipe it done on the banana trash she slamming it down on the clothes the same way. Some time for so long she wouldnt say a word that I try walk way slow-like but she would see me and start up again.

'Where you think you going when I talking to you yu unmannersable little wretch you? Wait! You think say is yu friend them you with?'

And then she slam down the iron again and make up her face over the ironing and every move she make jerky and fast like she vex. Not like Miss Rilla who do everything slow-like, the same way she walk. But as MeMa talking she slamming down the iron like comma.

'I cant afford to send my own children to high school so I dont know who you think have money to send you and you should be thinking now that your place is here in this yard to care for your father and me in our old age because my rightful children not staying round here forever. No sir. They all going to town to get good job in store because their coloration is good and everybody know that them big office and store in Kingston dont want no natty head pickney work with them. So my advice to you is learn some sewing and things like that so you can stay right here and take care of we and help pay for you keep and is a pity your head so natty and red for your coloration not so bad but you wont find no nice man married to you for they dont want no natty head pickney. They looking for wife with good coloration so they can raise the colour so just learn sewing and forget the books them.'

But MeMa wasnt so bad even when she say words that really hot me is like she not talking to me at all is like she talking to the clothes she ironing or the pot she stirring or whatever she doing at the time. And even though she not me own ma she did take me in from I small and raise me up and I am grateful only she make me feel very small sometime when she start talking bout me and now between she and Teacher she really have me confuse because Teacher and Teacher Wife say:

'Lenora you are a good girl and if you only put your head to the books you can get a scholarship and go to high school and even teacher college and be a credit to all of us but this last year you havent even tried ... Lenora dont you want to be a teacher dont you want to be a nurse?'

And I confuse confuse because one mind in me say that I should study and pass exam so that I can go to high school and speak good and wear pretty dress and high heel shoes like Miss Martin the other teacher and Teacher Wife who is also a teacher and I think it would really grieve Dulcie to see me succeed like that because she always fas'ing with me head and I have to wear her old dress and she tell everybody is ol bruck I wear but is only because she stupid and cant pass anything at all and even though she older than me Teacher put us in the same class and if I turn Teacher I could get me hair straighten just like Teacher Wife. And I confuse because another voice say that MeMa will vex and she wont give me any encouragement even if I pass scholarship and Pa say he dont business. And she might send me back to my mother who I dont even know and who I hear have more children since she have me and she never once send me a Paradise Plum or come to see how I grow. So maybe I should learn sewing or how to be

postmistress and stay round here so I can take care of Pa and
MeMa in their old age because even if I go high school and
study all the people at the bank still have fair skin with good
hair and suppose I dont want teach I dont know if I could get
work anywhere else.

O Lord I confuse confuse. No Miss Rilla to tell me what to
do. No Blue Boy playing music. No nobody to tell me
nothing.

4

Like the time when I was little and I ask MeMa where baby
come from and MeMa lick on me head same time with the
coconut brush she cleaning floor with and me on my knees
beside her polishing and she lick me such a blow I drop and
she say:

'But what in Jesus name is the matter with this pickney
eh? Is force-ripe woman this? What you want to fass in big
people business for? Baby is big people business chile so
dont form fool of yourself and ask impertinent question. Is
who put idea into your head eh? Well, Jehosiphat! I never
see or hear such a thing. I have big daughter and them never
have the face so come and ask me bout them things so you
just wait your turn pickney for if you so force-ripe to be
asking them things at your age next thing I know you go try
out what you learn and praps we have another bastard in
this house.'

But I did know a girl who wasnt much older than me and
she did start to make baby even though it die and a girl at
school tell me things that I dont believe and I dont know
why MeMa so confuse when I ask her a little thing like that.
So I decide to go ask Miss Rilla but I dont know if she know
anything because she dont have no children and Poppa D
dont have none neither and I dont know if you have to have
children first before you know anything bout them.

So I ask Miss Rilla because I know she wont vex and lick me but bredda! She sat there in her rocking chair shelling peas and I helping her and her eyes look far far away like she considering and she consider a long time till her hands stop shell the peas and she sort of give a little sigh and she say:

'Well Lenora child I cant tell you in nice word because I dont know none but I not sure that you not too young to know bout them things but since you ask is man put seed in the woman belly and it ripen and nine month afterward you conceive and have baby.

'But listen child this is all I going to tell you because I dont want give you any idea bout baby now, you is to go and do your studies and train and turn teacher and when you grow up big you will meet a nice teacher man or a agriculture man with good government job and you will marry and he can do it to you so you can make baby. But dont worry about them things finish you education and dont bother interest yourself in man at all they is pure trouble . . .'

She continue to shell peas and when she didnt laugh her eyes big and shiny like ackee seed only them sad sad like picture I see all the time of Mary Jesus Mother. Her face strong, stronger than any face I ever see and we shell peas till it quiet like death.

'Miss Rilla then how come you and Poppa D living together all this while and you dont have children?'

More silence and I watch her hand stop.

'Ai child, some things you just cant explain . . . God decide that some people not to have children because there is too much suffering children in the world already and they dont have enough food to feed them but is not you decide though is God decide and you just have to accept what he say . . .'

I want to ask her more but I fraid for Miss Rilla looking sad on me and I never see her look so sad before.

But I hear them talking, I hear the women talking when they over at MeMa house or down by river washing, talking say she is mule because she barren and that God ordain all women to have children and if woman dont have children she no better than mule because God curse is on her and then they talk about the wicked thing that Miss Rilla do and how she is harlot.

So when Miss Rilla tell me why she dont have children I still confuse but I believe is God say that she not to have children for too many sad children in world already and I know my rightful mother did have a whole heap of children before she have me and she didnt have enough food to feed them so she give them away and maybe God say that she should have me so that I can be a blessing to MeMa and Pa in their old age but I dont know.

But I know this wicked thing they talking about that Miss Rilla do, I listen bout the yard and I been hearing it from I was a child. Not until about two years ago when I really old that I get to know Miss Rilla for she living in another district all this time with Poppa D until Poppa D decide to build the house near we so we turn neighbours. But this thing that happen did happen long before I ever born and I hear so much about it that even now I dont believe that it happen around here and is like the Miss Rilla they all talking about is another Miss Rilla and is not the lady I really know because I never see Miss Rilla do anything bad and everybody say that the other Miss Rilla do a wicked wicked thing and the Bible say anybody who do a thing like that will perish in everlasting hell fire. So they say.

But even though she dead I cant believe Miss Rilla in any hell fire. I know she is in Heaven though MeMa say she is the main sinner in Jamaica and look how she dont even go to church. But if you ask me Miss Rilla fly straight up to Heaven and she up there with Saint Peter and living in a little house with a rocking chair on the veranda just like her house on earth because it was so pretty and she did love it so. And she still making gizada and grater cake, wangla and drops, and all the little children in Heaven round her and she teasing them and telling them stories and they laughing all the time. Up there even the big people are her friends because nobody talk nasty bout nobody in Heaven. So Miss Rilla just keeping everybody up in Heaven laughing and she look so pretty and like Missis Queen when she dress up they ask her to wear her red dress to brighten up Heaven even though everybody suppose to wear white. And when Saint Peter see Miss Rilla in her red dress and her glass case full of bake things he say this is just what Heaven need and he get the mason up there to build her a brick oven just like the one Poppa D did make for her and she there baking gizada and grater cake, wangla and drops and all sort of sweet thing in Heaven.

So I dont see why they did have to go on bout keep up no big Nine Night for her when she die and everybody drinking up the rum and them all talking bout planting her down real deep or else her duppy come back like rolling calf which is bad duppy to haunt you. Cho! Miss Rilla have better things to do with her time in Heaven than think about this district where all they do is backbite her and they not even worth haunting anyhow.

This is how I think sometime but to tell you the truth I not sure because I feel kind of jealous now that Miss Rilla have a whole lot of other children to joke with and sometime I want to die too so that I can be with her. And sometime I not so sure that she really gone to Heaven at all since from the time I know her she never even go to church. I only know no more bake things, no more Miss Rilla, all the laughing done.

5

Is the same way she disappear the day after the murder and nobody can find her, nobody at all, and everybody looking all over the place. And the police all round a-take statement and a-measure and a-write things down in book and they couldnt find her neither and they did want to ask her all sort of question and everybody round the place a excite up themself because nothing like this ever happen before and everybody saying that it give the district a bad name and even people in Kingston get to hear bout it for it Gleaner, and they say round here that from she born she causing trouble.

And everybody arguing say what they would do if it was them and some people saying that they cant blame her if she run away for they would shame and run way too if it was them and some people say that the best thing that she could ever do is hang herself or drop into sinkhole. And they say that if she ever show herself in the district again they would stone her to death because that is what they do in the Bible to people like that. And MeMa say that no matter where Miss Rilla flee whether to hills or valleys Gods justice will find her and punish her because God is a just God and he is everywhere and he find all sinners and punish them no matter where they hide even if they quick or dead, fast or slow. And they search and search and no Miss Rilla until the excitement almost die down. Pa say that after a time Springville people never care if they find Miss Rilla because people use to drive down there in motorcar to see the place where all the excitement was happening and such a thing never happen before and they never see so much motorcar in their life and all the boy them half the time so busy looking at motorcar they forget about Miss Rilla. And that Agnes Dawson who was a child that time did run away with one of the men that did drive down in motorcar but after the motorcar did gone just a mile it start to heat up and plenty steam coming out of the engine and she so frighten that she jump out and run back home for she never go inside motorcar before in her whole life and she think it was going to explode. And Pa say that especially the shopkeeper them was glad because all like Mass Curly him never sell so much rum in him life and the whole heap of them get rich out of Miss Rilla misfortune.

Anyway after two weeks done Miss Rilla just appear sudden one day and give herself up to to Corpie down the square. And Corpie was a Special and the most case he ever handle before is when people tief goat and is only one person, Big Head Jim, that ever tief people goat. So anytime anybody ever miss goat all Corpie do is wait till Big Head come down to Springville square and he hold him and lead him off.

So when Miss Rilla give herself up to him him never know what to do. Then him suddenly remember who she is so him rush her inside the house and shut the door and he say have some lemonade Miss Rilla and treating her like Royalty.

Then he confuse some more so he rush into the bedroom and put on him Sam Browne belt that hang on the bed post. Then he fraid she leave so he rush into the hall and when he see her sitting there so quiet he rush back inside and take off the belt and put on his blue serge pants with the blue seam at the side. Then he rush back outside to check that she still there then he run inside and put on his belt and black boots. Then he take the boots off and polish and shine them. All this time he studying that plenty trouble will cause if people find her there so he decide to hire vehicle quick and take her out of the district. So he tiptoe past Miss Rilla and put his finger to him mouth to tell her to keep quiet then he creep down to Mass Curly shop to hire car and tell Mass Curly that his wife sick and he taking her to doctor. All this time the wife over at her ground big and hearty same way but Mass Curly dont know that. So he get the car and as he drive up to the house he run inside and hustle Miss Rilla into the back seat and they take off. And when he take her to the police station they take statement from her and warn her not to run away again for she important witness in the case.

By this time news spread quick quick in Springville that she give herself up and Corpie take her gone to big police station. And every jack man woman and pickney for miles round gather in the square and they jeering and shouting and calling out and waiting for Miss Rilla to come back. And Pa who I hear all these things from say that the funny thing is that when the car finally draw up and the door open, not a living soul in the crowd move or say a word for she have a look on her face that frighten every one of them and as she get out the car they all just craning them neck and looking and holding up baby and mashing one another toe but not one make a move. Is like they all behind a invisible line and Corpie take her and lead her into his house without even thinking what he doing and he shut the door and not a soul move or say a word for about five minute afterward and everyone just move off quiet-like as if they were never there. Pa say he was there and he feel that she did get a Scienceman work a set for her so nobody could touch her and nobody dare lift a finger against her.

And she stay in her house quiet from the day she come back till the trial and Bigger gone to Penitentiary for life and he didnt hang because it was a crime of passion Pa say and nobody ever see her come out of the house during that time though everybody watching all the time. And only Poppa D did visit her and carry food which really surprise everybody and cause plenty talking and upset because Poppa D was a big man and a decent man in the district and nobody even know that he know Miss Rilla much less and everybody say that Poppa D dont have no right mixing himself up with a scarlet woman like that even though other people say that is all the travel in foreign part make him head not so righted. But like how Poppa D did have money and was a very independent soul and people used to whisper how him connect up with the strongest Scienceman in Jamaica everybody carry on treat him with

respect same way when they see him and never say a word
about him or Miss Rilla to him face.

Poor poor Miss Rilla. Ai my child, poor Poppa D. I dont
need all them pot with flowers at all at all. Love bloom on
my doorstep, Miss Rilla used to tell me.

6

And it was true because I never in my life see a thing like
how Miss Rilla and Poppa D live nice to one another. No
sir. MeMa and Pa wasnt like that at all at all. I never once
see Pa bring MeMa any little sweet thing from town no
matter how much goat he sell and I never see MeMa laugh
the way Miss Rilla laugh soft sometime when Poppa D
tease her. Sometime MeMa and Pa used to frighten me till
my heart drop clear to my footbottom because, although I
shouldnt be talking these things, the two of them could
bruck some big fight and lick one another no fool.

Pa wasnt afraid of MeMa and she wasnt afraid of him
neither because she was a big strapping woman compare
to him and one time Pa did throw a vase her niece did send
Ma from America and break a glass window and if you
look you can see is still cardboard in the window because
MeMa say she not fixing it and we all can drown when rain
come and the cardboard soak and any time she mention
the window and Pa is there he get mad and is another fight
start again.

And another time Pa did sell some goat at May Pen and
when he coming back home and reach Mass Curly shop he
stop and take up a few waters and next thing we know he
staggering up the road and we could hear him clear down
Mister Ramsay corner the way he shouting. And from
MeMa hear him she start to carry on and pray and quarrel
at the same time and make plenty noise too. And what
MeMa didn't know was that Pa did have him shotgun that

he did leave down at Mass Curly and he just pick up the shotgun and Mass curly sell him cheap cheap a whole heap of cartridge he did buy off a Special.

And I dont know what did vex Pa from the beginning but so he near the house so he start load the gun and so he reach up to the house so he start firing. Eh-eh! Dulcie so frighten she drop the whole pan of white clothes she was hanging out right on the ground and run a-bawl inside the house. This time MeMa so confuse she dont even notice the clothes for she calling out to the two of we to come inside and she run and shut the door and put the sofa and all the chair behind it like barricade and it was just the three of us inside the house and I frighten so till! And I did know that MeMa frighten too for I could see her face red and she sweating like mule and her tie head dropping off and she dont even notice and while she piling up the chair she saying, 'Holy Father look down on your innocent little children Dulcie and Lenora your precious little lambs that dont old enough yet to bring any sin into your world and I thy servant who always serve you well and pay her tithe and see how this drunken son of a bitch is about to kill all of we and please God dont let him shoot we for I am your good and faithful servant Gretta Gayle amen.'

And then she gather up the two of we and drag us into the back room and Dulcie and me so frighten we hugging one another and crying and burying our head in MeMa skirt and MeMa not paying us no mind for she too busy praying and bawling out. I tell you I never so frighten in my life for all this time Pa shooting at the house for we hear when he clip a shingle now and then but mostly he just hitting banana leaf round the house and it sounding like old cloth tearing and another time he hit the zinc roof over the tank. But I dont really think that Pa mean to shoot us for when he go bird shooting he bring home more bird than anybody else and everybody know he is the greatest bird shooter in the whole parish.

So MeMa still down on her knees praying for God to come down and rescue his poor innocent children and make tribulation and pestilence strike the drunken outside for the Lord hateth drunkenness which is a vile sin and he is an abomination in his sight (that is Pa she talking about). And is a lucky thing Pa so drunk he cant shoot straight or else I wouldnt be living to tell you this now. All this time Pa cursing like mad and making a whole heap of noise and saying how he going to kill off the whole lot of we for we is a millstone round his neck and a bunch of parasite and a lot of other things.

This time Dulcie and me still hugging one another and holding on to MeMa and she still praying loud as if she want drown out Pa and him cursing and shooting. And this go on for a long time and every time Pa get quiet we know he setting up for another shot and this take a long time and then we hear 'BLAM' and bullet tear into banana leaf and this cause MeMa to pray louder as if God couldnt hear her unless she shout.

By this time we hear other people shouting at Pa but we know how these people round here stay and it sound like they all staying far away but we hear Cousin Dolphie there trying to get Pa stop shooting and go with him for another drink and Pa still cursing and shooting at the house.

Then all of a sudden it just get quiet outside and even MeMa shut up and then we hear a whole heap of people outside beating on the door and calling we come out for Pa gone and leave the gun. So MeMa move the barricade and we go outside and we see the crowd of people and no Pa and they say he gone with Cousin Dolphie who promise him a drink. So MeMa get vex again and start curse Cousin Dolphie say is people like him leading her husband astray and causing him to spend money on rum while his children starving and cause him to do wicked deeds and make his wife a nervous wreck and a laughing stock in the district. But by this time everybody round here use to how

MeMa can carry on so they dont pay her no mind and finally she quiet down and start hang out the clothes again.

Pa didnt come home till late late and he so drunk they had to carry him home and MeMa wouldnt let him in the house so they just leave him under the big mango tree with crocus bag under him head like pillow and dew fall on him and he get a bad head cold and MeMa never speak to him for one whole month and every time she hear him coughing she start sing one of her church hymn and smile a little smile and she didnt pay him no mind at all for a long time till they start talk again and quarrel again like usual.

But it wasnt only MeMa and Pa who live like that but everybody for plenty time one of MeMa church sister would come to the house with her clothes and everything and cry and say how her husband beat her and she not going to live with him again and she and MeMa lock up in the room and pray and read Bible and by the next day she would start look out of place and then she would go back to her own yard or else her husband would come and get her but you could see they not living in peace.

And is so everybody I know in the world stay, quarrel all the time. Or else two girl catch fight over man and they tear off one another clothes what a disgrace or the boys at school catch fight over marble or the big men would catch fight over woman. Lord but that is a wicked thing though . . .

Only Teacher and Teacher Wife of all the people I know did live good and never fight so I could see but they kind of starchy and not nice to one another like Miss Rilla and Poppa D.

Lord, Miss Rilla did love to tease Poppa D so! Like when Poppa D not working he there in the hall sitting in him underpants and merino reading Gleaner and Miss Rilla cleaning house.

She would say, 'Cho Poppa D come out of my nice clean hall in yu dirty old clothes yu black and ugly sinting yu.'

The first time I hear her talk like that to Poppa D my heart drop clear to my footbottom because everybody know that Poppa D quiet but not an easy man and I expect war to bruck out right away but is only talking Miss Rilla talking for she quick and flick him with her duster cloth and he raise his head from the paper and grab her but she jump way quick time and laugh and he grab a gerbera from the vase beside him and throw at her and it dont catch her for she dance to the other side of the room and quick before she grab anything else to throw Poppa D run into the room and shut the door. And Miss Rilla knocking on the door with her two fists and laughing till she see me and she say quick time, 'Hey Lenora run down to Mass Curly and get some oil for me no man.'

And I take the money and I go outside but I know she dont need none for she have two big lamp full and she always doing that to me when she and Poppa D start romping as if she dont want me around and I only like to watch them for they look so happy and they make me feel happy. And sometime I stay away for days because I feel when Poppa D around Miss Rilla dont want me.

But when she see me passing she will call out 'Hey little redhead gal what wrong with mi gizada eh? Cockroach inna it or you find another Miss Rilla?' and I know I happy again for I cant stay vex with Miss Rilla.

I have to tell you that Miss Rilla was like a slave driver to Poppa D sometime, the same Poppa D that so frighten everybody else. She would sit there on her rocking chair rocking and laughing and she have Poppa D out in the sunhot planting flowers for her or laying out rockstone to make flower bed. Eh-eh. And all this time she cracking joke and all the people passing hurrying by because they dont want Poppa D to see that they see him doing woman work. And Poppa D is a quiet man hardly say more than two word at a time but you can see that he dont mind at all for so he working he humming and so he work done so he come inside the house and Miss Rilla have a big pitcher of lemonade a wait for him and a big slice of pone and when he eat and drink done he put his head in her lap and she there rubbing his head and singing 'Kitch' and teasing him and laughing some more. Bwoy, go see MeMa do that to Pa. Eh-eh you want fight bruck! And beside MeMa there telling us how Kitch is a dirty song and we not to sing it and she dont even like it when we hum it though how she learn that song I dont know.

And I really love to see Miss Rilla and Poppa D together for the two of them so happy and everything is nice at their house and Poppa D buy Miss Rilla plenty crockery and glasses and a pretty bedspread that she say cost whole heap of money and he also buy her a stove and a sewing machine though she cant sew and a radio just like Mass Curly own but it old now and only work sometime.

And Miss Rilla house was the prettiest house in the district though MeMa use to say how the floor never shine good. But that is not true for I use to help Miss Rilla shine her house plenty time because she have a bad heart and doctor say she not to do heavy work.

And plenty people in the district vex how Miss Rilla have all these nice things and one time she did wash her bedspread and hang it out on the front line and everybody that go past slow down to look and some even bold enough to come in and fingle the bedspread and say they admiring it and then as soon as they leave they go pass remark about how Miss Rilla extra and show-off.

And about the same time MeMa was trying to convert Big Mout Doris and was telling her how the Lord provide only for his children and make the wicked to suffer and Big Mout Doris say, 'Eh, then Miss Rilla no mus be the Lawd biggest child in this district for look how she a prosper.'

And MeMa did get so vex that she just shut her Bible and tell Big Mout Doris how she just say a wicked thing and was just a tough head naygah and would never find redemption she so blasphemous and fill up with evil thought.

And Big Mout Doris say, 'Cho is because I talk truth and you dont like it,' and MeMa say that is that she would not try with this sinner again as God is her judge. And Big Mout Doris say that alright for she never hold with no religion that say that you cant press your hair and you must wear long frock because all that happen is that them Kingston girl that does wear short frock just come down to Springville and take way all the man them. Anyway to cut long story short MeMa get vex and stop talk to Doris and the two of them keep up malice long time and is all because of Miss Rilla things.

I used to wonder if Poppa D and Miss Rilla so happy because Poppa D buy plenty pretty things for her. And I dont really know because plenty time MeMa and Pa quarrel because MeMa want Pa to buy something pretty for the house and Pa say he dont have that class of money and if she want him make blood out of stone. And MeMa vex all the time because she dont have sewing machine and radio and all them thing. And sometime again I wonder if Poppa D only buy those things for Miss Rilla because he love her and want to give her nice things.

But Miss Rilla did tell me that she only encourage Poppa D at first because he did promise to build her a pretty concrete house for the house she was living in at the time leaking bad and practically falling down over her head. She say that when he start to court her at first if he was not a man of substance in the district she wouldnt bother with him because God know Poppa D black and ugly as sin. But anyway she say that he wasnt no hothead little fly-be-night bwoy, he was an establish man and he travel to foreign and he know how to talk good and treat woman nice and bring her a whole heap of little things from town. So though at first she didnt encourage him she didnt turn him away because even though he wasnt pretty he wasnt no little nobody and he did know how to dress nice.

And he did say to her at one time: 'Miss Rilla I travel all over the seven seas and is time I settle down because I want to die where I born and I want to have a son to carry on my name. But these little girls round here too flighty. I want a real woman in my yard that does know how to take care of a man. Miss Rilla I know that you are no angel but I am a man of the world for I travel and see plenty things and the foolishness that frighten the idlers round here dont frighten me. And even though you dont have the experience that travel can give a man you still understand the ways of the world Miss Rilla and the two of us have the same kind of free spirit and it don't break easy.'

And Miss Rilla say that at first she did just like to hear him talk for he could talk real nice when he ready even though he wasnt a schoolmaster or parson who is the only people she ever hear talk nice so. And he did give her a pretty gold earring he bring from Panama and she still use to wear it sometime.

She say that at the time Poppa D did start courting her she was very tired of man because all they ever do is cause worries. She say that at that time in her life it was like the world of worries was down on her head.

'Lenora,' she tell me, 'the Lord did cast me down bad bad. O God is when yu in trouble that you really know who your friend is. Because at that time every jack man that I did think was my friend desert me not a soul to call on, not a one to talk to, them same people in the district that nowadays come fingle up my bedspread on the line. And the only friend I have in the world at the time was Poppa D. The same Poppa D you see here now. He did look after me like I was his own child and he did give me words of comfort when my heart was fit to burst from sorrow and from this heartache I did have I learn that this man is the only true friend I have in this world. And is so love bloom for me Lenora, love bloom on my doorstep just like so. Poppa D ugly like sin eh? – but he have a heart of gold and he so brave! He brave just like Daniel in the lion den for he never care at all how them ignorant people badmouthing him. No sah. Poppa D would just use them up like blotting paper if they bother him. He dont fraid of no man. So chile is fifteen year now I living with Poppa D and that man never lift a hand or give me a harsh word. A tell you child, that day Poppa D come to me in my sorrow I feel just like love light up the whole world.'

7

All the same people did have some terrible thing to say about Miss Rilla and even how when she living with Poppa D and he make her a nice house and buy her a whole set of false teeth and spend money on plenty doctor bill for her she was still a carry on her slack ways. Well I dont know because I never see it. I believe that is just because sometime Miss Rilla free and easy and happy and like to laugh and tease people plenty and everybody else round here hard and miserable and thats why they hate her so.

Take Miss Rilla and Blue Boy who used to be my friend when he was still living around here, people did even spread talk in the district about the two of them which was a scandalous lie. That Blue Boy! He was my friend because he never tease me about my red head and he used to play music so sweet that I would follow him anywhere. Blue Boy never talk much at all at all and he is the only person I know that you could walk from Springville to Charlestown with, five mile, and he wouldnt say a word for the whole time. Sometime I think he just fall dumb. Blue Boy so tall and quiet-like I love him like he was my very brother.

Miss Rilla did get to know Blue Boy through me because from I small I used to follow Blue Boy all over the place when he play the fife. And when Miss Rilla move down to Springville and I used to run down to her house and visit her if Blue Boy was passing he would stop too and sit in the shade of the jacaranda tree and play his music.

The first time he stop she run inside quick quick and put in her top plate which she didnt wear all the time because she say it burn her. And every time Blue Boy come by after that she put on pretty dress. And one time she tell Blue Boy that doctor say that she have bad heart and dont have long to live but her heart still going boops-a-boops at the same old rate and she tell Blue Boy to feel her heart how it beating strong though doctor say it bad and Blue Boy look like he confuse and like he never want to feel her heart and Miss Rilla just grab him hand and place it on her heart so he could feel it and then she pop her big laugh to let him know is only joke she running with him and so Blue Boy stop looking so serious and we all laugh.

And she would do plenty things like that and at first Blue Boy didn't understand that Miss Rilla is a jokify lady so he use to confuse but after a while he understand her better and he would start teasing her first and say, 'Hi Miss Rilla how yu heart today mek me feel it going boops-a-boops,' and she would make him feel her heart and the three of us would laugh.

And another time Poppa D was away drawing cane at sugar estate down in Westmoreland and Miss Rilla tell Blue Boy that she have a shelf in her bedroom that break down and she want him to fix it as Poppa D dont have time and she tell him to come inside.

And I start to follow the two of them and Miss Rilla say, 'Lenora sweetheart see I put my cassava out to dry and I dont want fowl come and root it out and I also expect Mr Basil to pass today and I want to give him a message to take to town so stay there please darling and watch my cassava and flag down Mr Basil if he pass. And Lenora, if you see anybody look as if they coming in here run come and shout me first for I dont want anybody come inside the house it too untidy but with my bad heart I just cant fix it up today.'

224

And even though I dont like stay alone I will do anything for Miss Rilla so I sit under the tree and run fowl from the cassava all day. But Mr Basil never pass in his truck and nobody pass except some little children and I tired because I dont have nobody to talk to and I dont know what taking Miss Rilla and Blue Boy in there so long and I wonder how he can fix shelf and I dont hear no hammer going.

Anyway it getting dark and MeMa will bus mi head if I stay out after dark and I cant stand it no longer so I go up to the veranda post and I call out to Miss Rilla and the house dark and I cant see a thing and Miss Rilla call out from the bedroom 'I am coming darling.'

She come out after a while and I notice that she not wearing her head tie which is very strange for I never see her without her head tie yet and right away I wonder if Miss Rilla and Blue Boy deceive me and in there doing it. But then I think no because it still broad daylight and everybody wait until dark to go with man except for Dorinda that go with man in canepiece in broad daylight but she dont count.

So I there feeling kind of wicked because I shouldnt be thinking them things and then Miss Rilla say, 'Come Lenora and see how Blue Boy fix up the shelf nice.' And I go in the room and look and the shelf look the same to me though I never did see it when it mash down but all her little nick-nacks off the shelf and on the bed and I say yes, Blue Boy fix it nice. And then I say, 'Where Blue Boy?' and she say, 'Soon come,' and I dont know what to say for when I go outside I see Blue Boy sitting on the back step and something tell me not to ask question and not say a word so I take the big ripe mango that Miss Rilla give me and I walk home eating the mango and trying to understand it all.

But after that day I never see Blue Boy for about a week until one evening I sitting with Miss Rilla and she very quiet and I hear Blue Boy fife coming down the hill and I think Miss Rilla hear it too for she rush inside and put in her teeth and she come back out and go on like she just hearing Blue Boy and I notice that she looking please.

But all this wasnt so long before Miss Rilla die on truck, is her bad heart kill her and so she was telling truth and that is why I take it so hard because things between us wasnt so free and easy like of old and even Blue Boy seem as if he was growing away from me.

One time I did find out that when Poppa D not there plenty time people see Blue Boy going there without me and when I ask Blue Boy about it he say, 'Lenora, you just too fas' for a child your age yu know, you just love interfere in big people business.'

I ask Blue Boy since when he is big people and he tell me to hush up so I cry because Blue Boy never speak to me that way before. Then he say that I not to mind is only that Miss Rilla like him to come and play some special kind of music that only she would like and when he go down there he get plenty food to eat so I not to mind. And he tell me how Miss Rilla encourage him with his music for she say he should be on Talent Show on radio he better than anybody she ever hear and she say she will lend him the money to get to Kingston.

But I still vex and say, 'You was my friend first before you meet Miss Rilla and now you love she more than me.'

And he say, 'But Miss Rilla is your friend too.'

And I say, 'Yes and now the two of you is better friend to one another than you are to me.'

He get vex again and start to play his fife and dont pay me no mind. And is little after that Miss Rilla die and from that night she die I dont see Blue Boy again.

8

Teacher used to tell me, 'Lenora you interfere in people business too much and that is why you cant pay attention to your books. Why you have to know everything and ask question about people business so? After you not Gleaner reporter.'

But big people have a habit of not telling children anything and if they su-suing together as soon as you get near they stop and change the subject or else they send you down to spring for water or to shop to get something they dont need and all of it is to get rid of you. But I learn from long time that what big people talking is sweeter than any other talking and though I never used to understand plenty of what they say I learn plenty so what I do now is I dont let them see me when they talking so they cant send me away and I hide under house and listen. And that is how I come to learn so much about Miss Rilla though nobody know I know.

So this is how I come to the real sad part of the story and what happen is this.

One time Miss Rilla was living with a fellow they call Jiveman and is so they call him for he did love to do plenty jive. He did go America one time as farm worker and he come back with whole heap of dance move and clothes and bop talk and he jiving all the time.

This Jiveman did go away but he didnt like farm working so he come back and plenty people say that he dont like any kind of working at all and he only used to catch a little work round Christmas time when he want plenty money.

So Jiveman take up to live with Miss Rilla and this was after her previous fellow Chin who was a chiney-royal did go back to him wife and children after one time Miss Rilla did burn him with a fire stick and he lick her and she get so vex she grab an axe and was going to chop him up but he run faster than she because him smaller and he also know that Miss Rilla not so easy when she vex.

Chin so frighten that he run back to his wife who was a weak little woman that would never dare raise her voice to him much less a finger. So as soon as Chin leave Jiveman go live with Miss Rilla in the house that her mother did leave her at Red Ground and people say that she did start carry on with Jiveman long before Chin did even leave but I dont know if is true for I dont born those days.

And everybody vex how Miss Rilla take up with this Jiveman because they say how he was young and all this time Miss Rilla was a hardback woman and she didnt have a good reputation for from she small she always flirting with married men. I dont know if is true but I hear Big Mout Doris say that plenty of the girls in the district did vex because Jiveman was so handsome and did dress so well and could dance so good and the whole lot of them was after him when he take up with Miss Rilla.

Jiveman was a real sweetman because he didnt work and all the time he down Mass Curly shop playing domino and dancing and giving out him jive talk. Some people say when he drunk he have a mean temper and other people say that he didnt have to have even one drink to mean. And he quick quick to pull knife on anybody who bother him. One time after he drink plenty whites he get rough and nearly mash up the whole of Mass Curly shop and is only because Miss Rilla offer to pay for damages that they dont prison him. And everybody say how Miss Rilla just forming fool of herself over young boy.

This Jiveman live with Miss Rilla for about two year and Miss Rilla is the one who have to sell coffee and chocolate to make money to buy things for them. But all the while he there wearing pretty ganzie and serge pants and shiny shiny boot and him just walking the road all day rolling dice in him pocket or waiting for evening come to lick domino.

So now there was another man living in the district name Bigger. Bigger used to help Pa in him ground and MeMa always did say that Bigger did help Pa build the very house we living in with his own two hand and how

Bigger was a good Christian boy and couldnt hurt cock-roach and didnt drink and play domino like that other worthless lot that hang out at Mass Curly shop piazza and is only because he get into the clutches of that Jezebel that he come down and fall into the Pit of Sin.

MeMa always say, 'The laws of man is a one eye law for the innocent is made to punish while the wicked go scot free as God is me judge that woman walking about on government good road breathing God free air without shame is the biggest criminal in the whole wide world and she should be behind bars instead of Bigger and Bigger should be out here free as a bird.'

'God is a just God,' MeMa always saying, 'and what man foul up on this earth God will set right when the Great Revival come again or if not when God himself come back down to the wicked earth to judge both the quick and the dead, the fast and the slow. And when the trumpet sound Bigger poor boy who has suffered all these years will be redeemed and asked to take his rightful place in the Heavenly Host after God has purified him of his sins and that Rilla and Jiveman will burn in God fire everlasting.'

This was MeMa favourite saying and everytime the sub-ject come up she let forth with these words.

But the thing is that until this thing happen that day not a soul did even know that Bigger was fooling round Miss Rilla though how it is possible in this district for people even to cough without the whole world hear I don't know.

The thing was that everybody did have Bigger like little boy round the place and not paying him no serious mind for they all believe that he such a quiet decent fellow that he could never get into no trouble.

He used to live near Miss Rilla and sometimes he would stop to chop wood for her and run to shop and so forth and nobody ever suspect anything at all between them so nobody know how long anything going on. All the same everybody did know that Jiveman didnt like Bigger and

Bigger take care to stay away from Jiveman but they all say that Jiveman have red eye and worthless and that is why he dont like Bigger who is a clean living Christian boy.

So that year everybody did get a little Christmas work from Government to widen the road. To tell you the truth if is like Christmas work these days is more joking and laughing than working for they used to sing some song as they go along and the woman would cook some big pot of food under the nearest tree and when sun get too hot everybody break for more eating and joking.

Bigger and Jiveman was both working on the road gang and everytime Bigger come near Jiveman would get mean though Bigger never say anything. And every day Jiveman would pass word for Bigger and every day Bigger would just cut him eye and say nothing. So everything go on like that until one day when Jiveman and Miss Rilla must be have quarrel for Jiveman come to work and he not jiving at all he there looking meaner than ever.

Next thing everybody know Miss Rilla coming fast down the road and her face look like hell to pay and she cursing Jiveman all the way. So right away everybody stop work to watch the spree. And Miss Rilla cursing Jiveman how he worthless for he take some money that she did hide under her mattress and Jiveman cursing her all kind of name and big kas-kas going on between them. In the middle of the argument, Jiveman must be say something bout how it better him take the money than she give it to her sweetman Bigger.

Bigger? See here, everybody nearly drop dead.

So everybody turn to look at Bigger and he standing there not saying one word so nobody know if they should believe it or not till Miss Rilla say, 'Yes, better give it to Bigger for he better man than you.'

See here Lord! Jiveman turn wild same time and jump on Bigger and start wave him finger in Bigger face. Next thing everybody know Bigger no turn bad and start trace

Jiveman good as he getting. By this time everybody start get frighten and dont know what to do and Jiveman suddenly push Bigger.

Well, nobody who was there that day can give a full account of what happen next for all they see is Bigger come up fast with a machete flashing in his hand, flashing and flashing at Jiveman. The women start scream and the men they try to get at Bigger but is like the boy gone mad for he slashing away at Jiveman even after he drop to the ground and the blood just flowing away from him into the sunhot. O God. Never before such a thing happen in this district.

Everybody fall into confusion and one of the boys run to call Corpie. By the time Corpie run up there they finally cool down Bigger and someone tie him up with a rope and when they examine Jiveman he dead in truth.

And Pa say that Bigger just stand there with the rope round him not moving or saying no word like he struck dumb and so he stay till they finally get one Black Maria come from May Pen and the police take him away. And that is when everybody get over the shock and they move Jiveman and throw water over the road to wash away the blood and nobody can find Miss Rilla all somebody remember is that as Bigger kill Jiveman she running and running up the road by herself, all alone.

Well, that was a time of great sadness and confusion for everybody did like Bigger and while the trial last practically everybody from Red Ground and Springville travel to courthouse to watch the whole thing or give evidence. And they didnt send Bigger to hang but they give him life and hard labour. And when they hear the sentence the women bawl out in courthouse and they had was to carry Miss Rilla away under police escort for they ready to tear her limb from limb. And that is why MeMa hate Miss Rilla so and never cry at her funeral. Poor Miss Rilla.

I dont understand about murder and things like that and when they talk is so long ago that is not like the Miss Rilla I really know. And I dont see why people have to suffer for sin all their life but is so MeMa say. There is no forgiveness without repentance and Miss Rilla die so quick on truck I sure she never have time to talk to no God. And if there is no forgiveness it mean that Miss Rilla is down there burning in hell fire. But I tell you already that I don't believe that at all, I believe that Miss Rilla laughing so much that Saint Peter take her in just to brighten up Heaven.

And I tell you sometime when MeMa go on so and Teacher there nagging me and all the verb and things mix up in my head I feel I cant go through with it. I dont care if I dont turn teacher with press hair and new dress. I believe it better to be someone that can laugh and make other people laugh and be happy too. And sometime I get down on my knee and pray for the Lord to come and take me so I can see for myself where Miss Rilla gone to.

Early Morning

JOHN STEWART

About five miles east of San Fernando on the way to Princes Town lies a village where a red-topped church sits before the cemetery that slopes humpily down to the railway tracks. Next to the church stands the school, and after that come little painted houses crowded so closely along both sides of the road that no more than a quick glimpse of the canefields which roll away from their backyards to the rim of the sky is permitted between them. At the centre of the village there is the square, an oval of pasture land where football and cricket are played, and where the men not on shift at the factory gather in the shade of scattered mangoes and almonds to talk and cut each others' hair. The square is bordered by the post office, police station, and two rum shops, and behind these stand small clusters of tin-roofed cottages where most of the villagers live. Eastwards the village elongates again, finally ending about half a mile from the factory.

At this point the road forks. Black and narrow, the asphalt main road rises through Jaipaul, the abandoned Indian settlement where overgrown posts, decayed outhouses, and many gnarled mangoes remain the only signs that people once lived there. The main road goes past the dairy where Satan's bull Thunder once roamed, then curves between the fields away to Princes Town. The other arm of the fork is a gravel road stretching down between tall palms to the sugar factory which is surrounded on three sides by upward folds in the land. This factory with smokestacks taller than any tree in the countryside rumbles day and night from January through June each year, and between six and seven every morning during crop-time the workers walk, trot, or ride their bicycles in a thick safari down the palm-lined road – some to relieve those coming off the graveyard shift, others to disperse into the fields.

Descendants of slaves and indentured labourers, the dark, gaunt crowd of undernourished men and women make their way down the straight gravel road, with much cajolery and laughter. Their clothes are little better than rags; yet they appear hardy, long-suffering, capable of enduring extreme hardships down to the very day when their flesh will dry up, and their bones collapse. But on occasion, when some father can no longer face the stares of his hungry children, or some young man's love elopes to the town to become a maid or streetwalker, the despondent father or heartbroken lover slips off from his house in the dead of night armed with his rope and grease, and the following morning he is discovered hanging from a tall mango in Jaipaul, dead, released from the despair he could no longer stand.

So it is some mornings as the village prepares to meet the seven o'clock whistle, the milkboy comes in from the dairy raising a great cry, 'Dead man in Jaipaul.' The villagers hasten their dressing and rush to the scene. Beyond the junction they converge upon the tree where the corpse hangs. If it is raining they cover their heads with sheets of old newspapers, but if it is a clear morning with the sun still pink as a baby's palm, they stand or squat in clusters along the roadway staring at the tree. Rain or sun, and whether it be neighbour, father, or brother hanging dead, no villager approaches closer than six feet from the dead man's tree.

He must come down, but the villagers know that anyone crossing the six-foot boundary takes a step into the kingdom of darkness, a step few are given to withdraw. They know that the dead man's spirit is condemned to Satan's kingdom, for the zone of darkness lies just on the other side of life, a desolate realm of perpetual anguish into which all suicides inevitably pass. A cacophony of screams and lamentations, an eternity of stumbling from one agony to another await all who enter there, and no captive may pass out of the kingdom without first bringing the master another to take his place. In its first twelve hours only the suicide's spirit is free to find itself a substitute, and the villagers know that during that time they are safer beyond the six-foot boundary.

The suicide's body must come down, but immunity against its frantic spirit is given only to one of them, and the villagers send for Samuel. As the sun gets brighter more and more men set their bicycles aside to stand in close knots about the tree; women and children hurry up from the village; the gathering grows and the constable has a hard time keeping a path clear for the buses that pass through on their way to the oilfields. The suicide's relatives stand apart, his son or youngest brother in the night-shirt there was no time to change, his mother or wife weeping, but even they stand six feet from the tree and no one moves an inch nearer before Samuel comes.

It is a nervous wait, but talk though not solemn is low. A few young men who rail against waiting for Samuel because they are brave and ready to take his job are restrained by the old ones who remember Ramjohn. He was a very brave man, a husky Indian with a fierce moustache who feared neither man nor spirit. At one time it was his job to get down the suicides, and it was worth an hour's pay just to wait and see him lift his heavy body smoothly, swiftly up between the branches like a big monkey, swing deftly to the dead man's branch, and bring him down under one arm. It was worth losing an hour's pay anytime to see Ramjohn scoff at the kingdom of darkness, walk in, walk out, as though none of the archdemon's wiles could trap him. Then one day Ramjohn slipped. For no reason too, because he was not a drinking man who might have been awakened from a drunken sleep, and there had been no rain to make the tree slippery; but midway through the performance he had carried out so well many times before Ramjohn slipped. No sooner had he gathered the dead man in his arm than he came down crashing through the leaves in front of everybody and broke his neck. It is given one man among them to walk in and out of the kingdom of darkness, but nobody knows when he too might be taken right before their eyes, so the villagers wait for Samuel.

At a quarter of seven when the siren sounds its preliminary call the workers grow restive. The sun is already drawing the day's first sweat, and the timekeeper with his pencil and pad is waiting to score the late. As the blast dies out above the treetops the workers no longer contain themselves; they begin cursing Samuel for taking his time, and fresh messengers are sent to make him hasten. Some slow children are chased off to start getting ready for school, and a few men pull their bicycles from the grass. The curses grow louder, more offensive, but no one crosses that six-foot mark and the hung man dangles there temporarily neglected; for the workers gather not so much to see the victim of last night's despair, not to feast their eyes on death, but to witness a man among them face the demon as no other dares.

When the first ones see Samuel approaching the junction they pass the word, and steadily a hush returns to the crowd as the unhurrying man in khakis shuffles on beneath a flop-brimmed hat. His clothes hang carelessly with the belt buckled like a vagabond's at the side. His skin is black and coarse; a crooked nose and split lip tell he has seen much violence. Samuel's bare feet are thick with the toes spread wide, and his eyes gleam small and red in the folds of his dark face. Those villagers who call him crazy watch with mixed faces as he enters the crowd; they do not know whether to admire or fear him. Samuel takes his time, he speaks to no one. With an ease belied by his clumsy appearance he climbs the tree and does a skilful job. After he is done the villagers hurry away to their jobs and homes chattering contentedly, all except the old ones who take their time to the shady almond trees in the square to lounge and take measure of Samuel's courage over again, from the time he was still a boy at the village school.

There are not many people in the village who have seen the devil face to face although there was a time when the demon visited nightly, inhabiting his favourite bull Thunder. In those days Samuel was just a lad of fourteen in his last year of school, and like everyone else he shivered each dawn when Thunder's shrieking roar split the quiet in which the village rested. For powerful as he might be, Satan falters in the face of pure light, and that trumpeting bellow of Thunder's signalled the moment when the devil had to begin his retreat before the coming day.

The boy and his father lived alone. The old man, who had accidentally lost a leg at the sugar mill, was sexton at the red-topped church, and he took great pride in his office. He kept the church clean, and tended the flower garden before it, but above all he was punctual about ringing the bell each day at six in the morning, twelve noon, and six in the evening. Many villagers who had no clocks depended upon his bell to get to work on time, and mornings when the sexton got up too late to strap on his wooden limb, dress, and get to the belfry on time, he roused his son and sent young Sam, who could run very fast in those days.

At six some mornings it was still dark, at six Thunder had already torn the air with Satan's voice, and at first Samuel was afraid whenever he had to run from his house to the belfry. Women on their early way to market had so often been scared back home by the marauding demon that at that hour Samuel had the road all to himself, and mostly he ran straight as an arrow, never daring to look around for fear the devil might be grinning over his shoulder.

However, as the run was completed many times over without any interference from the devil, Samuel's fear grew less. Eventually he even began to grow brave, and when the old father's chest could no longer take the morning air, Samuel, with only the slightest qualms, took full responsibility for ringing the first bell. As the months passed the boy's courage grew until the day came when he ceased running to his job. No longer holding his eyes straight ahead in fear, Samuel awoke to the sights and sounds of the late dawn. He heard the owl's last hoots mingling with chirps from freshly awakened finches and keskidees; he noted the sky, the stars that shone more cheerfully than they did at night. He looked deliberately at the shadows along the road, considering which would more likely be the one behind which the devil lay, and Sam felt sure he would be brave enough to face the demon if ever the moment came. No longer whistling or singing tremulously, in his thoughts Sam often mocked and dared old Satan to show his face.

As an altar boy Sam never missed a Sunday in church, and at communion services he looked like a black angel in his red cassock and white surplice, swinging the incense, snuffing candles, carrying out all the duties altar boys perform. He was Reverend Todd's favourite and had free run of the parson's library. He could read better than some of the first-year teachers at school, and practically every day after classes he lodged himself in the reverend's house reading books that were seen nowhere else in the village. Sam was not a stupid boy; thus when he found himself thinking 'I'm brave enough for Satan – so brave he's scared to come at me,' the boy knew he should have some corroboration for such untested boldness and decided to talk to his father about his thoughts.

That evening as the old man lay trying to hold back his coughs Samuel asked, 'Pa, isn't it true that Satan's afraid of some people?'

The old man looked at his son. 'Satan's not afraid of anybody, but lots of people are scared of him.'

'Were you ever scared when you walked the road every morning to ring the bell?'

'Lots of times when I first started, but after that not so much.'

'Suppose Satan had ever come for you, what would you have done? You can't run fast like me.'

'Boy, the devil is a powerful, he won't waste time after a one-legged old man like me. I found that out one morning couple of years back and I never told anybody because I felt ashamed of myself.'

'What happened?'

'Well, I was going through the churchyard to the belfry when all of a sudden I saw a light coming down into the cemetery. It didn't come fast or slow, just floating down businesslike as though it knew where it was going. The first thing I did was turn to run. I wheeled around and took two steps, but before I ever got started I knew it was no use if that really was the devil after me. The best thing I could do was start to pray, so I stopped, leaning on my crutch with my heart leaping like a frightened frog and started the best prayer I know. I didn't stay like that a minute, I turned around to face whatever that demon was going to do, but when I looked, the light wasn't there. I stopped praying and looked up at the sky and down in the cemetery, but there was no light nowhere. I didn't know what to believe, until it struck me I'd let my imagination see that light. I knew right then my imagination had caused me to see and hear all the scary things that had kept my heart in my mouth, and that was the last time I felt scared.'

'How come you never told that to anybody before?' the

boy asked, for whenever villagers gathered in the square, or rum shop, or their homes, they spent a good deal of time comparing stories of their encounters or near encounters with the devil. Everybody heard Mary Lou the fisherwoman scream that morning the devil barred her on her way to market, and she too had seen a light, a green light; only it was like a flash of sulphurous fire that had blinded her and melted the road where she stood. Samuel himself had seen where the road had been melted and put back together again just as if nothing had happened. 'How come?' he asked his father.

The old man lay back and stifling a cough said, 'Shame son, shame. I'd spent too many years talking about Satan, being frightened at every strange sight and sound, when there was no need to be.'

His father's words did much to strengthen Samuel's thoughts about himself and the devil, but he said nothing more to the old man. The following evening he approached the priest in whom he had great trust. He entered the study where Reverend Todd was working on a sermon, and after the parson set his work aside the boy asked, 'Reverend, how come Satan scares some people and not others?'

The reverend laughed and said, 'For the very reason God blesses some people and destroys others.'

'But God blesses those that love him. Nobody in the village likes Satan, yet he scares a lot of people.'

'That's not what I mean,' the priest said, and he lowered his head in thought. He was a foreigner who did not believe much in what the villagers knew, and he always talked in roundabout words. Soon he raised his head saying, 'God and the devil dwell in every man. He who nourishes the devil experiences the fear and distress which mark the devil's works.'

The reverend's words were still not clear to Samuel, and the boy asked, 'Doesn't Satan live in the kingdom of darkness? He's not really inside everybody, is he?'

At this the priest became impatient and asked abruptly, 'Have you ever seen Satan or any spirits at all?'

'No,' Samuel replied, 'but I can feel them – especially when I go into a dark room.'

'But if you had to find your shoes in a dark room you'd enter with a light, wouldn't you?'

'Yes . . .'

'Exactly. Light nourishes, brings to life the good things in the room and chases away the dark. So is it within our hearts. The kingdom of darkness is not a country somewhere on the other side of the world, it is a small place in our hearts. We each carry our private kingdoms wherever we go – in our hearts.'

'With Satan and everybody in it?' Samuel asked.

'Satan and everybody else whom you place there. But the kingdom of darkness can be wiped away through faith in the truth, belief in God's word.'

The priest continued with another long explanation to which Samuel listened with only half an ear, and when the man paused Samuel asked the question that was really on his mind. 'Would a brave man die if he saw the devil face to face?'

The priest, who had subsided somewhat, answered, 'Not unless he weakens son, only if he weakens . . .'

'And if he didn't weaken?'

Reverend Todd smiled. 'That's a charge we should all carry, day after day,' he said. 'To see Satan face to face and not weaken.'

After Samuel rang the bell that evening he started home through the dusk firmly convinced he was brave enough to hold the devil at bay, and Satan knowing this had avoided a confrontation. Sure, if ever they met face to face he, Samuel, would have no fear. Like a warrior intoxicated with his sense of fearlessness, Samuel longed to put himself to the test. Nor would he await the devil's approach on some morning run to the bell; he would meet the demon face to face like Ramjohn, who in those days hugged the dead men on Jaipaul's mangoes like a bold giant.

Samuel went to bed early that night, and before Thunder's frightening roar stirred the following dawn he was up. He dressed and slipped out without awaking the old man. There was no late moon, but the usual morning stars glinted low in the sky as Samuel struck out through the village for the dairy. At the junction he took the asphalt road which curved through the abandoned settlement, beneath the mangoes that stood like ponderous shadows. On his way to find Thunder, to catch the devil leaving his bull, Samuel marched like a David already assured of overcoming Goliath. He would look the master demon dead in the eye and stare him down.

At the dairy he left the main road and swung into a rutted trace that took him across an open pasture towards the field where Thunder roamed. The morning breeze was cool, and the dewy grass wet Samuel's legs as he trotted on. He followed the trace down to a gully where tall canes reared all around, and with total disregard for the scorpions and snakes that breed profusely between the thick stalks Samuel crashed through the canes in a direct strike for Thunder's pasture. At last he emerged next to the wire fence which surrounded the bull's field. It was still too dark for Sam to make out anything but shadows in the field, and he paused waiting for some sign that would tell him which of the humped indistinct shapes was the devil's bull.

As Samuel stood peering beyond the fence his blood cooled rapidly. And despite the occasional fireflies that lit up for brief seconds in the distance, the fields and sky seemed gathered and silent. Samuel lifted a strand of the fence and stepped through. There were no early birds; the shadows, unlike those along the road to the bell, were formless and dense. They seemed alive enough to touch the sky, sometimes bunched in low menacing waves. They changed shapes constantly: his eyes could master nothing. And in all the coiling darkness around him and above, Samuel was alone. The realization struck home – alone. Somewhere in the shifting shadows was Thunder, perhaps nearer than he thought, and Samuel's courage began to fade. The determination and fearlessness with which he had left home were gradually displaced by a fascination that held him fixed, despite the shivery warnings he sensed each time the darkness billowed or sank. The cool breeze played upon his exposed neck and slid beneath his shirt. Suddenly Thunder roared.

Samuel felt the gushing breath of the beast slap his face, and with a cry he jumped back through the fence and bounded for shelter between the canes. Frightened, feeling very much alone, he began to cry. He was a long ways from everyone he knew, and the whole darkness seemed surcharged with an evil power that sought him out. Sobs came, then Samuel wailed, raising his voice louder and louder, wishing someone, anyone, would come to his rescue. When there were no more tears Samuel moaned drily, still crouched in the canes.

Thunder roared, his voice coming from across the fenced field, and Samuel moaned less loudly. He could hear his own whine, and suddenly he realized how unheroic it was to cower among the canes when the bull was nowhere near him. Again Thunder's roar came, from far in the distance, and Samuel felt ashamed. Quickly straightening up, he walked back to the fence and looked out across the dark field, but he could see nothing. He stood for several minutes while the dark morning became edged with grey, and still he did not see the bull. Finally turning about, he started for the church and his daily duty at the bell.

It was more than five years later when Samuel related his adventure, and then only after Ramjohn had made his fatal slip. The morning was dry and sunny when the

243

Indian fell, and as he lay twitching on the ground with the dead man in his arm, the villagers gasped, yet none went forward to his aid but the young Samuel. As though this were a moment he had long awaited, Samuel was out of the crowd in a flash, straightening the Indian's neck, prying the dead burden from his arm, but it was too late. Ramjohn kicked his last and died before the crowd, even as Samuel was wrestling with his arm. When the youth looked up, the villagers were staring at him, waiting to see the kingdom of darkness receive its third victim for that day, and when Samuel walked away alive, they gave him a wide berth. Fully twelve hours went by before anyone approached to congratulate him for his dashing defiance of Satan and the kingdom of darkness. He was immediately regarded as having filled Ramjohn's place, and when some villagers asked how could he be so brave, Samuel puzzled them with 'I know the devil, he knows me.' Later on that night when he was drinking with some older men, he told them what the words meant.

Samuel's father died soon after the son started getting down the dead men from Jaipaul's mangoes, and the boy gave up ringing the bell the very day his father passed. He had already stopped attending church and, in spite of all the reading he could do, apprenticed himself to the village shoemaker. In time, that shoemaker passed, and Samuel now fills his office too. Never a talkative person Samuel has grown more taciturn with each passing year, and nowadays he seldom speaks to anyone. About his contest with the devil he never speaks, but he gets drunk often and whenever he does there is sure to be a fight with the man nearest him. Many of the villagers say Samuel is waiting for the devil to face him again, and this time it would really be a tussle to the finish because Samuel would be ready.

So on a morning before the sun comes up, when the milkboy enters the village screaming, 'Dead man in

Jaipaul', the villagers run out to see the corpse and messages are sent to Samuel that he has a job to do. As the sun
rises, the waiting workers curse because Samuel hurries
for no one. They curse until Sam's floppy felt hat is spied
coming at the junction, and then a hush settles upon the
crowd. They give him lots of room as he shuffles through,
for no one wants to be brushed by any part of him, and
without glancing left or right he goes directly to the tree
with the shoemaker's knife stuck in his belt. He climbs,
and holding the dead man close against his breast he cuts
the rope and lowers the corpse to the ground. By then it is
almost time for the seven o'clock whistle, and before Samuel regains the ground the workers are already in flight
down the palm-lined road to the factory, some cursing
still, for Samuel has both served and disappointed them.
Yet even in their haste they are careful to make room for
Samuel as he climbs down, sticks the blade once more in
his belt, and shuffles off towards his cottage wordlessly.
They all make room for him, and the ones too feeble to
work follow at a distance in his wake to lounge beneath the
almonds and recount his tale with a mixture of derision
and respect.

The Fellow Travellers

JOHN WICKHAM

The three men, laden with baggage, came through the
door from the customs hall and went, purposefully, up to
the airline counter. The girl behind the counter, bright and
brittle, face glistening, lips phosphorescent with paint,
was only perfunctorily polite. It was almost midnight, said
the clock on the far wall.

The foyer, empty, was vaster than a football field.
Around its edges, almost like spectators bored by the dull-
ness of the game, the overnighting, waiting, in-transit
passengers were asleep, huddled in all contortions on the
benches, warming themselves cosy in the folds of thick
winter coats and blankets destined for use in quite other
climates. One blonde girl slept with her knees doubled to
her chin; looked at askew from another angle, she had
achieved the long jumper's perfect attitude; her thumb was
in her mouth and the expression on her face was blissful as
if she had already arrived in the land of her dreams. One
man, bearded and bald, slept bolt upright, the paperback
still clutched resolutely in his hands, the air around him
disturbed by only the gentlest of snores. A red-capped
porter made the journey across the vast football field saun-
tering leisurely, arrival at a destination being of no importance whatever. A benighted traveller made a vain effort to
use the public telephone, a taxi-driver poked his head
through the door to see what was going on.

Yet nothing happened. That is, until the three men
made their entrance.

The men, three very different specimens, all black, as

black as the girl behind the counter, shared the same harassed look. Their clothes were less, much less, than smart, all their faces bore the same greasy stains of travel and the same looks of frustration and disappointment at not having, even at this late hour, yet arrived at their destination. They were all angry and as they approached the girl the strident disharmony of their raised voices announced their common Trinidadianness. They all began to speak at once and the girl, confronted by the babel of tongues, put on a look of resignation. She could wait, her face said, until they realized for themselves that she could not deal with all of them at once. Her face was as blank as the unadorned wall opposite the counter.

But much as they shared disappointment and anger, the same degree of dishevelment and a common accent, it was clear from the way they held themselves – together but apart – that they were not friends. Fellow travellers forced into a temporary alliance by the common factor of their plight, but 'friends' would hardly have described their relationship.

The one who would most certainly be taken to be the leader, the dominant personality of the three, was of medium height, thickset. His face attracted attention by virtue of the very nearly total absence of any chin and of the presence of a little tuft of beard sprouting ridiculously from where one would have expected a chin to be. He had black, curly hair and a gold filling in his teeth that flashed when he spoke. He spoke too with his hands as fluently as with his tongue and what eloquence he achieved was due as much, one guessed, to his gesturing fingers and arms as to the validity of the particular case he was presenting to the girl behind the counter. He pulled out his travel documents from the back pocket of his trousers – his jacket lay in a heap on top of his bags – found his airline ticket and, with a jabbing index finger, drew the girl's attention to the details.

'Look,' he said, 'it's right here: St Croix to Antigua,
Antigua to Barbados, Barbados to Trinidad – clear, clear.
Now I get to Barbados, no plane for Trinidad. They sell me
the ticket and they say that if I take these flights I can get to
Trinidad tonight. You mean to say they sell me the ticket
under false pretences? You mean to say that?'

The girl for a moment seemed moved by the strength of
the argument. Her expression registered a concession that
the man might, after all, have a point.

'Let me see the ticket,' she said.

The chinless man recognized that he had caught the
girl's interest. He handed her the ticket but he did not stop
talking.

'Look,' he said, 'I getting real mad. I have a car, cars,
waiting for me in Piarco and I buried here like a fool in this
place, can't get to where I belong. I tell anybody I want to
spend a night in Barbados?'

His anger mounted and he turned away from the girl.
He walked a few frustrated steps and then turned back to
the others grouped like a chorus in the pool of light by the
counter.

'Look,' he said, 'I going to get something to drink. Keep
an eye on these things here.' He pointed to the three
suitcases and a cardboard box over which lay his discarded
jacket. With a slow shake of his head and shoulders to
express the disgust he felt at the whole monstrous mis-
management of his travel, he went away up the stairs to
the bar. The girl continued to examine the ticket in silence
but not with interest or as if she could or would do anything to relieve the distress of its owner. The telephone in
front of her shrilled. She picked it up and directly entered
another world.

A little man in a hat moved from his position on the edge
of the circle of baggage lying on the floor and slunk fur-
tively up to the counter. He gave the impression of having
two left hands, a double gaucherie so to speak, and his

movements were awkward in the extreme. His new clothes – canary yellow sweater, brown sports jacket of a check so blatant that one wondered what horse had been left shivering in the cold, a grey felt hat, crown uncreased, resting on his ears – made him self-conscious. Under the fluorescent light and against the sleek lines of the counter the little man cut a figure of rustic incongruity. He eyed the girl at the telephone stealthily, marvelling, one could see, at the slickness and sophistication of her brightly coloured fingernails and the casual yet artificial elegance of her coiffure. Shuffling embarrassedly, he reminded one of Charlie Chaplin of the early films, the very early films. Not that they resembled each other but they both had the same air of bewilderment, the same gawping, dumb look of wonder at smoothness and self-confidence. The girl ignored the little man and went on mouthing into the telephone. He waited, afraid to interrupt the flow of her conversation, shifting from one leg to the other.

Eventually, very eventually, the girl put down the telephone. She spoke to the little man abruptly, masking her rudeness in the jargon of her trade.

'And what can I do for you, sir?' The sarcasm in her voice was as heavy as the mascara on her eyelashes, the 'sir' came spitting out like the insult it was intended to be.

The little man's plight was the same as the one she had heard before. St Croix to Antigua, Antigua to Barbados, Barbados to Trinidad but no connection to Trinidad. It was now a trite story, not calculated to hold her interest.

'Ticket?' She put out an elegant hand, long willowy fingers full of grace.

The little man opened the leather wallet he was carrying and searched among his papers, inspecting each document in turn – immigration form, yellow vaccination certificate, passport, exit ticket, baggage claim, airline brochure, traveller's cheques. But no ticket revealed itself.

The little man was overcome by confusion. 'But I had it

just now on the plane, I see it with these two eyes.' He tried desperately to convince the girl that he was telling the truth. He went through the papers in his wallet once more, through the same pantomime of inspection, minute inspection of the collected trivia of his journey.

'But I had it, Miss.' He was becoming desperate.

The girl was unbelieving. 'But where is it now?' she asked. She sounded glad that the little man could not find, had lost his airline ticket. She sounded too as if she did not believe that he ever had a ticket.

'Miss,' the little man said, 'it look like if I lost the ticket, Miss, but I had it, I tell you, I had it. Just before the plane touch down, I was looking at it, Miss. Miss, you think I lying?'

The girl was unmoved by the little man's plaintiveness. She took a pad from a pile on the counter and began to question.

'Where was the ticket written?' she asked.

'I don't understand, Miss?' The little man's bewilderment was patent.

'Where was the ticket written?' The question was repeated, a trifle more slowly, with exaggerated, insulting patience. She was talking to a child, an idiot and therefore ought not to expect too much. Words of one syllable were required. She rephrased her question.

'Who write the ticket?' The green vernacular verb, she hoped, would convey her meaning. She was wrong.

'I don't know the gentleman name, Miss.'

The girl was rapidly reaching a point of exasperation. She racked her brain for the best arrangement of words to meet the situation.

'Where,' she asked, 'did you buy the ticket you can't find?'

That was simply answered.

'In St Croix, Miss. I tell you I fly from St Croix to Antigua.'

'Yes, I understand. Now where in St Croix did you buy the ticket you can't find?'

'I can't remember the name of the place, Miss.'

The girl let the pencil she was holding poised over the pad fall to the counter. It rolled slowly, slowly to the edge of the counter, fell and hit the floor with a sound like an explosion. She bent and picked it up.

The girl must have counted ten because when she rose and faced the little man again, she was smiling sweetly, a picture of the helpful, efficient ground hostess, the pride of her airline. No one could fault her now. She had regained her cool. It was after midnight and the little man before her had lost his ticket which he had bought from some place in St Croix he couldn't remember and expected her to find it for him, but no one could say she wasn't trying. She would try again.

'You see, sir,' she said, like a teacher, 'I will have to send a message to St Croix to check the sale of the ticket. I have to know the ticket number or where you bought it so that I can tell the agents in St Croix so that they can trace the sale. You understand, sir?'

'Yes, Miss.' The little man was eager now. 'But I can remember the number, Miss.'

The girl smiled and allowed the merest suspicion of incredulity to cross the smoothness of her face. Really, the unlikelihood of it all! The little man was speaking again. He had seen that she didn't believe.

'Yes, Miss, it started with 5-5-1 and then it had 6-3-1, 2-2-2, 1-1-8. That was the number, Miss, I can remember it as if I was seeing it now.' He was proud that he could be helpful.

'Forget it,' the girl said, 'sending a wrong number would only make more confusion.'

The little man retreated from the counter outside the pool of light, his short-lived balloon of pride punctured. He took up his position beyond the edge of the circle of baggage. He did not know what to do. He had tried. Now he was lost in Barbados and would never, so far as he knew, ever see Trinidad again.

In the little lull of silence the girl wrote, her head bent in concentration, her hair catching the light from the lamps above her head.

Suddenly, the chinless man was on the scene again. He announced his presence in his confident, no-nonsense-from-anybody voice. He was sipping beer from a glass.

'What happen now?' He demanded an up-to-date report on the situation.

'What you think could happen?' The reply came from the third member of the party. He had been silent until now. He was a soldier. He wore huge black boots with metal reinforced tips, bulbous like a clown's nose, a khaki jacket with his name in black stencilled letters on one pocket and 'US Army' on the other. His face was young, but he was cool, refusing to fuss, taking things as they came.

'I tell you all long time, we going have to sleep in Barbados. The best thing to do is to leave the baggage here and let us go into town and drink some rum.'

The proposal seemed to have its attraction now.

The little man asked, 'The baggage safe here?'

'Don't make sport,' the soldier said, 'we ain't in Trinidad, you know, we in Barbados. They don't thief in Barbados.'

'What? Now you joking.' The chinless man could not believe his ears. 'They don't do what in Barbados?'

The soldier did not feel disposed to argue the point in the face of such overwhelming vehemence.

'Barbados must be changed,' he said and left it at that.

The chinless man drank his beer, drained the glass and put it down empty on the floor next to his suitcases.

He turned his attention to the girl behind the counter.

'Miss,' he addressed her,' you decide what to do?'

The girl looked up from her writing. 'There is nothing for me to do. There is no plane going to Trinidad tonight.' Her voice now took on the bluntness of finality.

'This can't end so,' the chinless man answered. 'I have people waiting for me at the airport in Trinidad, cars waiting for me, this can't end so. You people break your contract and you will have to pay me. I know my rights, you can't fool me.'

The girl looked at the clock on the wall. It was now going on to one o'clock.

A boy in a bright red sweat shirt with 'Love and Peace' in black letters on the front came bounding up to the counter. He waved an airline ticket in front of the girl's face.

'This was on the immigration counter,' he said.

The girl took the ticket from the boy in the bright red shirt and read the name written on it. She read the name aloud and the little man moved back into the centre of the pool of light.

'That is mine,' he shouted. He grabbed the ticket from the girl's hand in an uncharacteristic burst of aggression.

'I am very glad it turned up,' the girl said. She tore a sheet from the pad, made a little ball of it and dropped it in the waste bin at her feet.

'I am very glad you found it,' she repeated, 'that saves us all a lot of trouble.'

The little man was scrutinizing the ticket.

'You see,' he said, 'you see I don't tell lies, look at the number.' He read the number out aloud, very aloud.

'5-5-1 6-3-1 2-2-2 1-1-8.'

He pointed to the number, trying to draw attention to the accuracy of his memory, to his own veracity which had, he thought, been in doubt. But no one paid any notice.

'Let us forget all this business and go into town. I tell you that is the most sensible thing to do.' The soldier was at it again.

253

The little man was so relieved that he thought a celebration was in order. The chinless man, now a minority of one, yielded, but not with too good a grace.

'OK', he said, 'but we must put away these things.'

He kicked his suitcase, and then turned to check the pieces of his baggage.

'Oh God!' he cried, 'where my TV set?'

'You had a TV set?' the soldier asked as if the chinless man's possession of a TV set were a wonder of the world, unimaginable.

'Don't tell me that they left my TV on the plane!' The possibility, unthinkable as it was, existed. He counted the number of his pieces of baggage. One. Two. Three. Four. Not one of them a TV set.

'A colour TV set,' the chinless man explained to whoever was listening. 'With a 23-inch screen. It can't hide. It ain't here. Somebody have to pay for this. Ah, ha!' There was a note of triumph in his voice. He turned to the girl.

'Miss you going have to find my TV set, you know.' His voice was ominously calm and reasonable.

The girl picked up the telephone, spoke a few words and put it down again.

'That's not my department,' she said; she was pleased, that was obvious.

She continued: 'Someone will come to see about that.'

The chinless man turned to the soldier. 'This trip have a curse on it,' he said.

The soldier picked up his single piece of baggage, his duffle bag, untied the drawstring and rummaged in the recesses. He pulled out a carton of cigarettes, tore off the cellophane wrapper and dropped it on the floor. He opened the carton and took out two packets of cigarettes. He opened one of the packets and took out a cigarette which he put in his mouth. Then he began searching his pockets, all of them, feverishly, angrily but he had to leave the cigarette unlighted in his mouth.

The chinless man was silent, staring at his bags, counting them over and over but never making them more than four. As he moved between the pieces of baggage, single-minded in his search for his missing TV set, his foot struck the empty glass he had set down on the floor. There was a tinkling, splintering sound.

The airline man arrived with a pad and asked who it was had lost a TV set. The soldier pointed to the chinless man, wordlessly.

'Let me see your baggage tags,' the airline man said, turning to the chinless man who was staring mesmerized at the splinters of broken glass.

'Your baggage tags,' the airline man asked again, sternly this time and the chinless man handed him some tags, five of them.

The airline man began comparing the numbers on the stubs with those on the bags, muttering them to himself and noting them on his pad.

A red-capped porter approached the group and the soldier tossed the unopened packet of cigarettes he was holding in his left hand over to him and pointed to the unlighted cigarette in his own mouth. The porter handed him a lighter and the soldier lit his cigarette at last.

The little man said, puzzled, 'I thought we was going down town to drink some rum.'

The girl at the counter turned away, pushed the door into the inner office and left behind only the scent of her perfume.

The soldier gestured impatiently at the chinless man staring at the broken glass on the floor and nodded to the little man. The two of them put their bags in a corner of the vast football field and went through the wide door out into the dark.

The chinless man, forsaken, stared at the broken glass on the floor and began to weep. The airline man put an arm around his shoulder and said, 'We will find your TV set. No big thing.'

But the chinless man could not stop weeping.

Legacy

NOEL CARLYLE WOODROFF

I was twenty-eight when I returned to the village and stood on the concrete wall holding back the steeply sloping hill from the pounding sea. Away to my left the shape of the coast had changed. The sea had finally got its teeth into the land and had gouged out chunks of the island. The edge was jagged and the shore was littered with rocks. From where I stood they looked slimy and green, and the water rushed into the pockets between rock and sand with a loud sucking noise.

I had lived here in this village in my youth when days were charged with a strange excitement and inactivity was a curse. I had raced my bicycle around the sea-road and had practised skidding into the turn and had made my first real friend who died before he was fourteen. The coast was different in those days. There were no rocks on the shore, only a carpet of rough, coarse sand that rested on a smooth, clay bed. Sometimes we dug for clay and modelled figures that we baked in the sun on the beach. We left the figures in rows on the beach in the night, and by next morning they had disappeared, sucked away and swallowed by the sea and the sand would be washed smooth as the high tide receded in the early dawn.

Even the pasture was not the same. Now it was covered by waist-high razor grass; the drilling rigs had been uprooted and the sites abandoned, and at one end excavation work had been carried out for earth-fill. The pasture used to be filled with cows munching grass all day long and sleeping standing up all night. Our house was on the edge of the pasture within full view of the sea. To my young mind the pasture meant safety, especially on windy nights when the sea roared and rushed up the sloping beach on to the land. In the morning the sand would be chopped and scarred but the sea was contained.

One year there was a hurricane, and the sea poured over the lip of the coast, drowned the grass and left salt within the earth. The cows were removed and the pasture was abandoned until the sun bleached the salt out of the green grass. That was the way it was in those days. The sea was always there. It drew us from morning until night, even when it turned grey and cruel and spat sand into our ears; even when it tugged at our cold arms and legs and rumbled in hunger in its great bowels. It was always there, biting at the land and spitting at the coast, roaring defiance at the little village poised precariously at the end of our small island.

Syo was my only friend. I rescued him one evening on the beach when a bigger boy was pounding him on the head with an empty kerosene can. I threw sand in his attacker's eyes and saved Syo from a severe beating. As soon as he could talk he said to me, 'Let's be friends and we'll raid the golf course tomorrow.' He never asked my name. He called me Daley because he had just read of a comic book gunfighter called Daley. I never heard Syo call me by my real name.

Syo had strange feet. His ankles were high off the ground and his arches were impossibly curved. We used to compare footprints in the smooth sand on the beach. Because of his strange ankles and because he was so short, the boys on the beach called him Anklehigh. When this nickname became popular, I used to rescue Syo from at least three fights a week. When I was not there he was always beaten because he was so small but aggressive. When he was beaten on the beach he would refuse to go home but would spend the night at my house. We shared a small bed and I soon discovered that when Syo was beaten, he woke up in the middle of the night and wept, his small body shaken by quiet sobs. Once I put my arm around him and he pulled away and spent the rest of the night, without a pillow, on the cold floor.

It was Syo who introduced me to Ben, the fisherman. We went down the beach to the fish-market to pick herrings out of the nets as the catch was brought off the boats. There was something strange that morning. There seemed to be no catch and there were groups of people standing on the sand. Syo approached a tall and muscular man with a grey-streaked beard standing on the side of a beached boat, staring out to sea. I heard Syo say to him, 'How's your mother?'

'She's dressed in grey with white lace,' said the fisherman, 'she is a bastard, a slut and a whore, she's a rotten, stinking murderess, she's a curse, a death curse.' I was shocked and I froze as I realized that the man was drunk and his eyes were wild and yellow foam from his chewing tobacco flecked his lips as he cursed his mother. Later Syo told me that Ben called the sea his mother.

The sea had been wild that night, and a fishing boat capsized just as the nets were cast. The other boats searched for survivors by the light of the boat-lanterns, circling and circling and calling and calling almost all the night. Two of the men could not be found. The sea had swallowed them and had hidden them in the deep. The boats had returned, filled with raving, drunken men, and Ben was overcome by the loss.

I got to know Ben well after that. He was an old man but he was strange and deep. He and Syo understood each other well. Their conversations were weird as if each could read the other's mind. I sat on the sand a little way off and listened to their talk as Ben filled Syo's mind with the mysteries of the sea.

'On wild nights on the black sea we see strange boats

NOEL CARLYLE WOODROFF

with green lights and a woman's voice tells us to cast our
nets. We cut our engines and drift and give no answer.
Then they go away. And they sing in the distance and their
laughter sounds like silver bells floating back to us in the
night.' Ben muses, his eyes black with memory.

'Take me with you,' pleads Syo. 'I know their song.
They want an answer. Take me with you.'

But Ben says, 'You don't know the answer. There is no
answer for the sea-ladies. The only answer is silence. And
maybe we will get a good catch and all return home.' Ben
told us how close the coast of Venezuela was and of the
villages and the señoritas of the Main. He told us how
grizzled sea-men cried and begged the sea when the waves
swamped their laden boats and the flambeaus went out.
Syo drank in all Ben's talk with an unearthly glow in his
eyes, and he would talk to the sea the way Ben did and call
the sea his mother. And he begged and begged Ben to take
him out on the night fleet, if perhaps the sea-ladies might
come calling.

One night Ben took Syo out with him. From my bedroom window I heard the drone of the boat engines as the
fishing boats crossed the bay and swept out to deep water.
The lanterns were lit and Syo's dream came true. Ben later
told the tale. Sometime during the night the sea-ladies
came, he said, and no one knew when Syo slipped into the
water and swam towards their boat. That is what Ben said,
but I never knew what to believe. Probably crazy Syo just
jumped in to take a swim or something. But Syo quietly
disappeared, and the boats came home. No one searched
for Syo because a thunderstorm swamped the village after
the boats returned. Syo was missing for two days before
the news was brought that his body was washed up on to
the beach.

Syo's body lay cast up on the beach, bloated and grey-
white. I watched and tried to recognize my friend, but the
living thing inside the flesh was gone and that swollen

wounded thing was not the body I had held and fought with and touched and loved like a brother. I knew if I touched it, it would be cold, clammy and soft. A horrible feeling took hold of me that if I touched Syo my fingers would stick to the dead flesh and would never be torn off. That night I dreamt I touched Syo, lying cold and swollen on the surf's edge, and then ran through the village like a mad man at new moon, dragging Syo, stuck to the ends of my fingers. Every time I looked back as I ran, he seemed to swell a little more. I sprang out of bed, still asleep and screaming, until my mother, trembling with fright, calmed me down.

On the beach the crowd of villagers stood, struck dumb by the tragedy. No one seemed to know what to do. We stood until Syo's mother burst through the crowd and mewed at the sky's face. Yes, she mewed. Her face was twisted with grief, her nostrils dilated and her eyes filled with despair as she struggled to give vent to her grief. But no sound came but a high-pitched mew, like the sound of a small, lost kitten. Her whole face was a mass of swollen veins as she struggled to speak.

Then she burst out, 'Why me Lord, why me Lord, why me Lord?' and she fell upon her son's body. Under her weight, clear fluid mixed with sand flowed from his nose. My skin felt loose upon my flesh and I swear it moved and crawled over my body. I was only fourteen and sick with fear and grief; no one thought of taking me away as I stood in the sand and felt the wound open in my mind. In the sky above the white clouds floated, and the quiet, blue sea gurgled round my ankles.

Ben never went to sea again. I think the sight of Syo's body drove him slightly mad. He was very old anyway and now, cut off from the sea, his age descended on him like a blanket. He dried up before the eyes of the village and his eyes grew red with rum. He smiled fatuously at all during the day and at sunset he went down to the beach and cursed the sea. I saw him often cursing the sea and the waves roared back at him and swept the sand at his feet, inviting him in. One evening I heard him cry: 'Mother, mother, mother!' But the bosom of the sea was lost to him, a demented man fastened to the land while his soul ranged madly over the deep. One day Ben just collapsed and died, in the middle of the fish-market over an open basket of fish. He just fell and was dead. That night the sea was quiet, its voice muted to a whisper. The moon shone on the water and lovers strolled on the beach. Old fishermen said that Ben's soul fled away and plunged into the arms of the deep. No one fished for over a week. It was then my family moved to Port of Spain.

In the city school I had trouble, of course. I was the country boy, unused to the ways of the city. I didn't know the taxi fares or the names of the streets. I was lost among the lights and on the playing fields racked by the noise of tin-drums and wildly cheering schoolgirls. The glory of winning at football was lost on me. But I was lonely. I never made a friend. I walked alone until the open wound had healed and the scars in my mind throbbed only a little. It was that, that shaped me, that legacy of my youth. It burned and burned within and made me strong. It spoke to me in the quiet morning hours until I found a kind of joy in the pain of memory. And when grief passed, the unfinished life of Syo touched me with a sweet sadness and made me tender.

I was twenty-eight when I returned to the village and stood on the concrete wall holding back the steeply sloping hill from the pounding sea. Away to my left the coast had changed, and the little village still teetered on the edge of the island. My old acquaintances had left, and as I drove through the streets I recognized no one. I couldn't tell if the rhythms of the village had changed or if they remained the same. But the fishing trade had died; the sea had spawned a line of derricks, their hollow tentacles reaching into the depths for oil. There were one or two decayed and rusted carcasses of boats along the shore. But as I stood, the song of the sea went on and on, and deep within I understood and responded to the song of an old friend. The sun's glare upon the water stabbed daggers into my eyes as I turned and said to the sea, 'It is finished', and walked back to my car.

Glossary

baakoo   a spirit in the form of a little man kept in a bottle, who can use his powers in the service of his captor. A *baakoo* that escapes from the bottle can be disruptive, often like a poltergeist.

baasskap   white paramountcy in South Africa.

Babylon   wickedly oppressive. *Babylon* (in Rastafarian usage) is symbolic of oppressive authority.

batchy   bachelor flat.

bolom   aborted first-born foetus which has become a supernatural servant.

bragadap   big and sudden.

brucking style   dressing up, trying to look fashionable.

buffootoo   big and clumsy.

chantwelle   lead singer in St Lucian folk ritual; singer or teller of tales.

chibat   god.

chiney-royal   offspring of Chinese and Negro (or Chinese and Indian, or Chinese and European).

coolie   East Indian (often pejorative).

crapaud   toad.

crapaud smoke your pipe   things are very bad for you.

cunny   cunning, intelligence.

cut-capoose   confident (like an expert rider on a horse), arrogant.

day cleaned   day broke (*day clean* means daybreak, dawn).

dharu   rum.

Diwali   Hindu festival of lights.

diya   small earthen lamp.

douglah   person of mixed Indian and Negro descent.

drops   a sweet with small chunks of coconut.

dunza   money.

duppy   ghost.

dutty   dirty; the ground.

facety   impudent, rude.

fas'ing   interfering.

fet   good luck magic.

gayelle   stickfighting ring.

gizada   an open tart filled with grated, sweetened and spiced coconut.

Gleaner   was published in the *Gleaner* (the Jamaican newspaper).

grabbaliciousness   greed, greediness.

grater cake   a sweet made with grated coconut.

haffe   have to.

high cunny   great cunning.

hogplum   a plum-like fruit and the tree that produces it.

inity   Rastafarian for 'unity'. (Rastafarian practice often transforms a word by replacing one of the syllables with 'I'.)

iree   a St Lucian pronunciation of *irey*.

irey   happy, at peace.

ital   healthy, pure; Rastafarian food uncontaminated by salt or any other forbidden ingredient.

Jack Mandora   phrase which introduces the traditional ending of the Jamaican Anancy story: 'Jack Mandora, mi no choose none!' The formula is usually taken to mean: 'Don't blame me, the story-teller; I am not directing the story at anyone in particular.'

jumbie   ghost.

kas-kas   quarrel, dispute.

labrish   gossip.

leggo beast   (like) an animal or person running wild.

macca   prickle, prickles; prickly.

Middle P   Middle Passage.

naygah   Negro (but pejorative).

obeah   'black magic', 'sorcery'; human manipulation of spirit-force, usually perceived as negative.

oonu   you (plural).

Paradise Plum   a sweet (red and orange in colour).

Poco   Pocomania (Pukkumina), a branch of revivalism which combines African and European religious practices.

poui stick   stick cut from a *poui* tree (which is hard and strong).

pragging   depending on hand-outs.

prags   hand-outs, odds and ends.

quailed   wilted, shrivelled.

rahtid   extremely angry or annoyed; an exclamation indicating annoyance, anger or amazement, etc.

rass   a swear word, often used for emphasis or in an exclamatory way to show anger, disapproval, excitement, etc.

rawtid   alternative spelling and pronunciation of *rahtid* (see above).

red eye   a mean, envious disposition.

redibo   fair-skinned Negro.

rolling calf   folklore monster taking the form of a calf with fiery eyes.

semp   a bird.

shac-shac   a percussion instrument; maraca.

Shango   an Afro-Caribbean religion, of Yoruba origin.

shitstem   a Rastafarian pun on system.

simitu   a fruit.

soucouyant   an old woman who at night turns into a ball of fire and sucks the blood of humans.

stocious   stylish, high-class.

su-suing   gossiping.

toute-bagai   everything.

travaseau   a person of mixed racial ancestry; a sexually exciting woman of mixed racial ancestry.

vaps   whim.

voops   unexpected, sudden. (A sound suggesting sudden-
ness, or imitating sudden movement.)

wagga-wagga   plentiful.

wangla   a sugar cake with nuts.

Zion   (like Pocomania with important differences) a
branch or revivalism which combines African and European religious practices.

Notes on Authors

Neil Bissoondath

Born in 1955 in Trinidad. He read French at York University, Canada, and now lives and works in Toronto. His publications include a collection of short stories, *Digging Up the Mountains* (Toronto: Macmillan, 1985; Penguin, 1987) and a novel, *A Casual Brutality* (Toronto: Macmillan, 1988).

Erna Brodber

Born in 1940 in Woodside, St Mary, Jamaica. She read History at the University of the West Indies and did graduate work in Sociology in the USA, Canada and Jamaica. She is a freelance sociologist. She has a VWI Ph.D. in History. She lives and works in Jamaica. Her publications include two novels, *June and Louisa Will Soon Come Home* (London: New Beacon, 1980) and *Myal* (London: New Beacon, 1989).

Timothy Callender

Born in 1946 in Bridgetown, Barbados. He read English at the University of the West Indies in Jamaica. His publications include a collection of short stories, *It So Happen* (Belfast: Christian Journals Ltd, 1975) and a novel, *How Music Came to the Ainchan People* (Barbados, 1979). He was also a painter and an art teacher. He died in October 1989.

Hazel D. Campbell

Born in 1940. She studied at the University of the West Indies in Jamaica. She has been employed at the Jamaica Information Service and has done freelance work in the media. She has published two short-story collections, *The Rag Doll and Other Stories* (Kingston: Savacou, 1978) and *Woman's Tongue* (Kingston: Savacou, 1985).

Jan Carew

Born in 1925 in Agricola, British Guiana. He has studied in Europe and the USA and is a university professor in the USA. Among his publications are novels, including *Black Midas* (London: Secker & Warburg, 1958), *The Wild Coast* (London: Secker & Warburg, 1958) and *The Last Barbarian* (London: Secker & Warburg, 1961), a book of poems, *Sea Drums in My Blood* (Trinidad: New Voices, 1981), and a collection of short stories, *Save the Last Dance for Me* (Harlow: Longman, 1976).

Austin Clarke

Born in 1934 in Barbados. He studied Economics at the University of Toronto, and has taught in various universities in the USA. He has worked as a broadcaster, and has lived in Toronto since 1955. He is the author of six novels, including *The Meeting Point* (London: Heinemann, 1967), *Storm of Fortune* (Boston: Little, Brown, 1973) and *The Bigger Light* (Boston: Little, Brown, 1977), and an autobiographical memoir, *Growing Up Stupid Under the Union Jack* (Toronto: McClelland & Stewart, 1980). He has had three collections of short stories published, *When He Was Free and Young and He Used to Wear Silks* (Toronto: Anansi, 1971), *When Women Rule* (Toronto: McClelland & Stewart, 1985) and *Nine Men Who Laughed* (Markham: Penguin Books Canada, 1986).

Merle Hodge

Born in 1944 in Curepe, Trinidad. She read French at the University of London, and went on to do an M.Phil. She has been a lecturer in French at the University of the West Indies in Jamaica, and has worked in adult education and people's education programmes in Grenada. Now employed in Women and Development Studies at the University of the West Indies in Trinidad. Her publications include a novel, *Crick Crack, Monkey* (London: André Deutsch, 1970; Heinemann, 1981).

Abdur-Rahman Slade Hopkinson

Guyanese, born in 1934. He studied at the University of the West Indies in Jamaica and has been a teacher, journalist and an information officer. He has lived in Guyana, Barbados, Trinidad and Jamaica, and is now based in Toronto. His publications include a play, *The Onliest Fisherman* (Trinidad: UWI Extra-Mural, 1957), and books of poetry, *The Four and Other Poems* (1954), *The Madwoman of Papine* (Guyana, 1976) and *The Friend* (Guyana, 1976).

Clyde Hosein

Born in 1940 in Trinidad. He has been employed in advertising, print journalism and the electronic media. He lived in London for a while, then returned to Trinidad, and now lives and works in Toronto. His publications include a collection of short stories, *The Killing of Nelson John* (London: London Magazine Editions, 1980).

Jamaica Kincaid

Born in 1949 in St John's, Antigua. Her publications include a collection of short stories, *At the Bottom of the*

River (New York: Farrar, Straus and Giroux, 1983); a novel, *Annie John* (New York: Farrar, Straus and Giroux, 1985); and a non-fiction book about Antigua, *A Small Place* (Farrar, Straus and Giroux, 1988). She lives in the USA, and is a staff writer for the *New Yorker*.

John Robert Lee

Born in 1948 in Castries, St Lucia. He graduated in Library Studies from the University of the West Indies. He has published several books of poetry, including *Vocation* (Castries: 1975), *Dread Season* (Castries: 1978) and *Saint Lucian: Selected Poems 1967–1987* (Castries: 1988).

Earl Lovelace

Born in 1935 in Toco, Trinidad, and grew up in Tobago and Port of Spain. He has studied and taught in the USA, and now teaches at the University of the West Indies in Trinidad. His publications include *Jestina's Calypso and Other Plays* (London: Heinemann, 1984), a collection of short stories entitled *A Brief Conversion* (London: Heinemann, 1988) and four novels, *While Gods Are Falling* (London: Collins, 1965; Longman, 1984), *The Schoolmaster* (London: Collins, 1968; Heinemann, 1979), *The Dragon Can't Dance* (London: André Deutsch, 1979; Longman, 1981) and *The Wine of Astonishment* (London: André Deutsch, 1982; Heinemann, 1984).

E. A. Markham

Archie Markham was born in 1939 in Montserrat. Since the mid fifties he has lived mainly in Britain and Europe. He read English and Philosophy at university. He has published several books of poetry, including *Human Rites* (London: Anvil Press, 1984) and *Living in Disguise*

(London: Anvil Press, 1986), and a collection of short stories, *Something Unusual* (London: Ambit Books, 1986).

Ian McDonald

Born in 1933 in St Augustine, Trinidad. He read History at Cambridge. Since 1955 he has lived in Guyana, where he is now Administrative Director in the Guyana Sugar Corporation. He is also joint editor of the literary journal *Kykoveral*. His publications include a novel, *The Humming-Bird Tree* (London: Heinemann, 1969) and a collection of poems, *Mercy Ward* (Calstock: Peterloo Poets, 1988).

Earl McKenzie

Jamaican, born in 1943. He studied in the USA and Canada and has a Ph.D. in Philosophy from the University of British Columbia. He has been teaching in Jamaica at Church Teachers' College and at the University of the West Indies.

Roger McTair

Born in 1943 in Trinidad. He studied in Canada, and lives in Toronto, where he is a freelance writer and film-maker.

V. S. Naipaul

Vidia Naipaul was born in 1932 in Chaguanas, Trinidad. He read English at Oxford and is the author of nine non-fiction books and eleven books of fiction, among them *Miguel Street* (London: André Deutsch, 1959), *A Flag on the Island* (London: André Deutsch, 1967) and *In A Free State* (London: André Deutsch, 1971) which include short stories. He lives in the United Kingdom.

Michael Reckord

Born in 1943 in Clarendon, Jamaica. He studied English and Journalism at Carleton University, Ottawa and has worked in journalism, public relations and education in Jamaica. He writes theatre reviews for a Jamaican newspaper, the *Gleaner*. He is also a playwright.

Andrew Salkey

Born in 1928 of Jamaican parents in Colon, Panama, he went to Jamaica at the age of two. Read English at the University of London. Broadcaster. He is the author of five novels – including *A Quality of Violence* (London: Hutchinson, 1959) and *The Late Emancipation of Jerry Stover* (London: Hutchinson, 1968) – at least nine books for children, three books of poetry and a collection of short stories, *Anancy's Score* (London: Bogle L'Ouverture, 1973). He has edited many anthologies of Caribbean writing. He lived in London from the early 1950s until 1976. He is now a professor at Hampshire College in Massachusetts, USA.

Samuel Selvon

Born in 1923 in South Trinidad. He is author of a short-story collection, *Ways of Sunlight* (London: MacGibbon & Kee, 1957; Longman, 1973), and ten novels, including *A Brighter Sun* (London: Wingate, 1952; Longman, 1971), *The Lonely Londoners* (London: Wingate, 1956; Longman, 1972) and *Moses Ascending* (London: Davis Poynter, 1975; Heinemann, 1984). He was based in London from 1950 until 1978, and now resides in Canada.

Olive Senior

Born in 1941 in Jamaica. She studied Journalism at Carleton University, Ottawa, and in the United Kingdom. Until recently she was editor of *Jamaica Journal* and managing director of Institute of Jamaica Publications Ltd. Her books include *A–Z of Jamaican Heritage* (Kingston: Heinemann Caribbean & the Gleaner Company, 1983), *Talking of Trees* (Kingston: Calabash, 1985, poems), *Summer Lightning and Other Stories* (Harlow: Longman, 1986) and *Arrival of the Snake Woman and Other Stories* (Harlow: Longman, 1989).

John Stewart

Born in 1933 in St Madeleine, Trinidad. He went to study in the United States in 1955 and studied English, Creative Writing and Anthropology. He has a Ph.D. in Anthropology from UCLA. He is now a professor in the English department at Ohio State University. His publications include a novel, *Last Cool Days* (London: André Deutsch, 1971) and a collection of short stories, *Curving Road* (Urbana: University of Illinois Press, 1975) and *Drinkers, Drummers and Decent Folk: Ethnographic Narratives of Village Trinidad* (Albany: State University of New York Press, 1989).

John Wickham

Born in 1923 in Barbados. He is a meteorologist, journalist, senator and editor of the literary journal *Bim*. His publications include a short-story collection, *Casuarina Row* (Belfast: Christian Journals, 1974) and *World Without End* (London: New Beacon, 1982), a series of short memoirs.

Noel Woodroffe

Born in Mt Pleasant, Tobago in 1952. He grew up in Trinidad and has a Ph.D. in English from the University of the West Indies. He has been teaching in Trinidad.